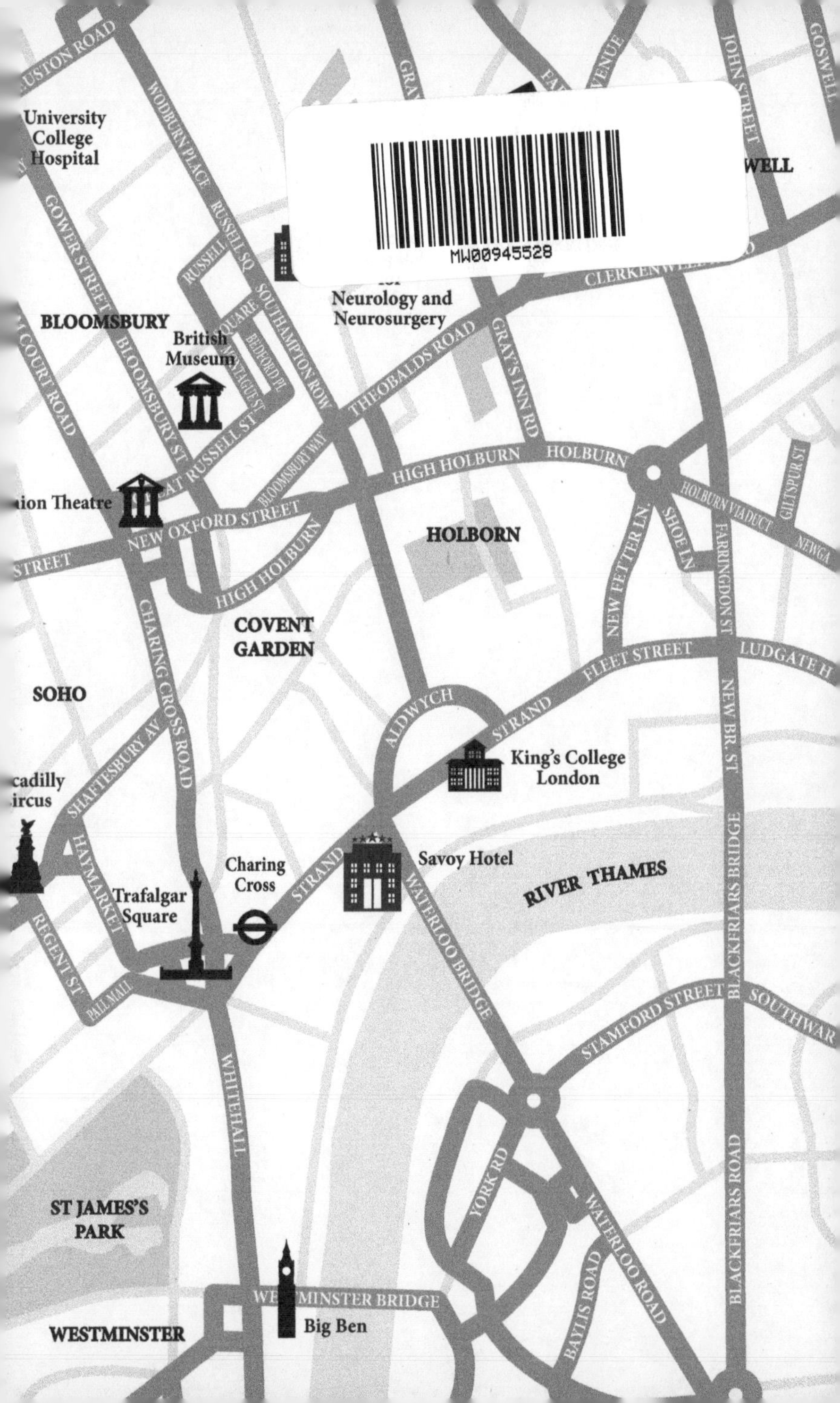

EUSTON ROAD
University College Hospital
WODBURN PLACE
GOWER STREET
RUSSELL SQ
SOUTHAMPTON ROW
BLOOMSBURY
British Museum
BLOOMSBURY ST
BEDFORD PL
MONTAGUE ST
Neurology and Neurosurgery
THEOBALDS ROAD
GRAY'S INN RD
CLERKENWELL
JOHN STREET
GOSWELL
BLOOMSBURY WAY
HIGH HOLBURN
HOLBURN
HOLBURN VIADUCT
GILTSPUR ST
NEW OXFORD STREET
HIGH HOLBURN
HOLBORN
NEW FETTER LN.
SHOE LN
FARRINGDON ST
COVENT GARDEN
FLEET STREET
LUDGATE H
SOHO
CHARING CROSS ROAD
SHAFTESBURY AV
ALDWYCH
STRAND
King's College London
NEW BR. ST
Savoy Hotel
RIVER THAMES
Charing Cross
HAYMARKET
Trafalgar Square
REGENT ST
PALL MALL
WATERLOO BRIDGE
BLACKFRIARS BRIDGE
STAMFORD STREET
WHITEHALL
YORK RD
ST JAMES'S PARK
WATERLOO ROAD
BAYLIS ROAD
BLACKFRIARS ROAD
WESTMINSTER BRIDGE
Big Ben
WESTMINSTER
MW00945528

The Five Clues, book 1 in the Don't Doubt the Rainbow series, has been shortlisted for the following awards:

Dudley Children's Book Award 2021
People's Book Prize 2022
Hampshire Book Awards 2022
CrimeFest Best Crime Fiction Novel for Children Award 2022

Praise for *The Five Clues*:

A compelling, page-turning mystery. Written with professional insight into well-being and the mental health impacts of grief, this is a murder mystery to open hearts and minds. Edie Marble is the lie-busting heroine we need now more than ever!

Sita Brahmachari, author of _Kite Spirit_ and _When Shadows Fall_

A race-against-time adventure, but also a story of a young person learning to cope with stressful situations and the loss of a parent.

Bridget Galton, _Ham & High_

Dotted with North London landmarks, this page-turning thriller incorporates puzzles that enlist the reader as co-detective. To stretch the brain further, Kessel offers an extra psychological/spiritual dimension.

Angela Kiverstein, _The Jewish Chronicle_

Edie is still grieving for her mother, killed a year earlier in a horrible accident, when she discovers a secret note … Kessel handles plot and character well and this DIY detective story will appeal to fans of Holly Jackson and Sophie McKenzie.

LoveReading4Kids

A tense murder mystery. The story is a thrilling 'David versus Goliath' battle, threatening to engulf Edie and her family.

Simon Barrett, _Armadillo_ magazine

Brilliantly written and unputdownable, *The Five Clues* is a great read which illustrates the virtue of resilience.

Sammy Margo, chartered physiotherapist and author of _The Good Sleep Guide_ and _The Good Sleep Guide for Kids_

A rich and meaty book, it is also pacey and engaging – and can be enjoyed as an adult too. A great read at any time.
Hugh Montgomery, author of *The Voyage of the Arctic Tern*

A page-turning mystery that just might change your own life!
Michael Neill, international bestselling author of *The Inside-Out Revolution* and *Super Coach*

[Edie's] capacity to self-reflect will no doubt serve as a rich source of inspiration, curiosity and learning for countless young people.
Brian Rubenstein, CEO of iheart and author of *Escaping the Illusion*

Enjoy the rapid action of Edie Marble's journey as a new fictional detective is born!
Bob Cox, education consultant and author of the award-winning Opening Doors series

The story is fast-paced and dramatic, with constant twists and turns as Edie attempts to solve each clue and complete the investigation her mother started, drawing the reader in and capturing their attention for all seventeen chapters.
Eve Foley, Children's Books Ireland

It's not often that a book well and truly stops me in my tracks – in a good way – and then I end up thinking about it at night, in the morning and when I'm supposed to be cooking dinner. Mesmerising from start to finish and a pacey page-turner.
Helen Heaton, reviewer for Mendip Children's Book Group

This teen mystery is full of adventure and action. The story keeps you guessing and I couldn't put it down at all.
Sissi Reads, book reviewer @sissireads

The Five Clues is cool in many ways. It has an Alex Rider approach to crime-fighting in that it is non-stop action.
Mandy Southgate, book reviewer at Addicted to Media

The Five Clues is a timely and welcome addition to school and public library YA mystery/suspense collections, highly recommended.
Midwest Book Review

Here's what other readers have been saying about *The Five Clues* ...

A brilliant book which covers topics such as truth, integrity, commercial greed and exploitation in an easy-to-understand way for young people.
Wendy Flood, primary school teacher

The cover of the book is reminiscent of blackout poetry; I was 'hooked' from that alone. A non-stop page-turner of the best kind. I'm looking forward to the next adventure with Edie!
Shirley Munn, school librarian, via ReadingZone

A page-turning mystery which immerses the reader in the world of ethics and science. I highly recommend it to secondary school students who enjoy a book combining courage and conspiracy!
Ruth Cornish, school librarian, via ReadingZone

Relatable characters and relatable moments that deal with very raw emotions in a beautiful way. I could not put the book down.
Kirsty Lock, NetGalley reviewer

This is my new favourite book and I will be recommending it to all my friends. It is an exciting read and kept me gripped throughout, trying to work out the clues as I went along. I can't wait for the next one.
GirlsRule, age 13, for Toppsta.com

Incredibly exciting, and I just couldn't put it down.
Marcus Hoang, via LoveReading4Kids

This is a great book full of adventure and friendship and puzzles to solve. I loved it! I love the character of Edie. It's great to see a crime-fighting girl. I can't wait for the new *Outside Chance* book.
Lily O'Dwyer, via LoveReading4Kids

I loved reading this book. It is a thrilling read, learning what happened to Edie's mother and trying to solve the clues by myself.
Ravenpuff, age 13, for Toppsta.com

This is such a gripping story – filled with adventure but also the reality of grief and loss.
MrsD271015, for Toppsta.com

ANTHONY KESSEL

DON'T DOUBT THE RAINBOW

August 2022

Dear Hugh,
Hoping you enjoy
Edie's latest
adventure!
With love
Anthony.

OUTSIDE CHANCE

Crown House Publishing Limited
www.crownhouse.co.uk

First published by
Crown House Publishing Limited
Crown Buildings, Bancyfelin, Carmarthen, Wales, SA33 5ND, UK
www.crownhouse.co.uk
and
Crown House Publishing Company LLC
PO Box 2223, Williston, VT 05495, USA
www.crownhousepublishing.com

First published 2022.

British Library Cataloguing-in-Publication Data

A catalogue entry for this book is available from the British Library.

Print ISBN 978-178583588-9
Mobi ISBN 978-178583652-7
ePub ISBN 978-178583653-4
ePDF ISBN 978-178583654-1

LCCN 2022936751

Printed in the UK by
CPi, Antony Rowe, Chippenham, Wiltshire

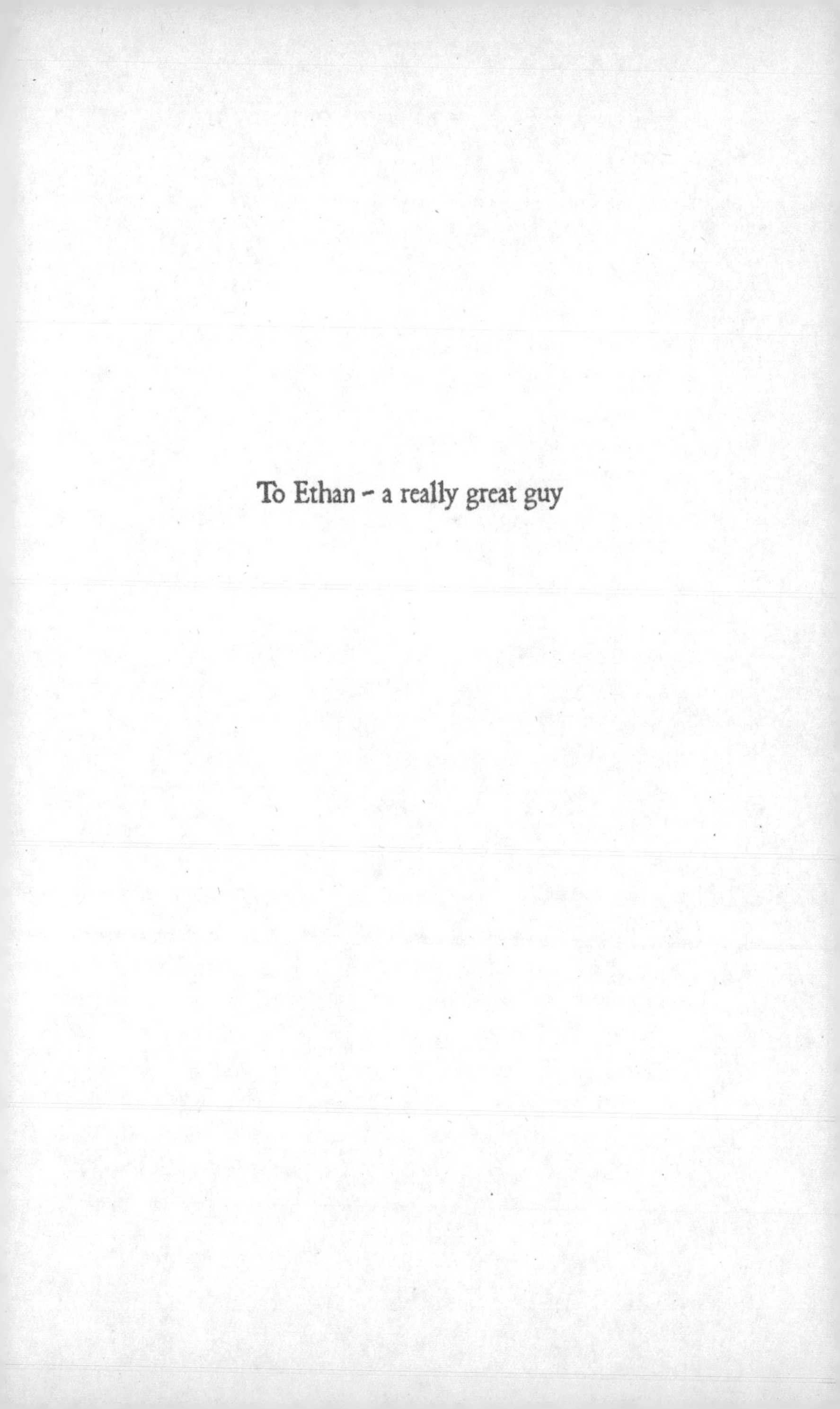

To Ethan – a really great guy

CONTENTS

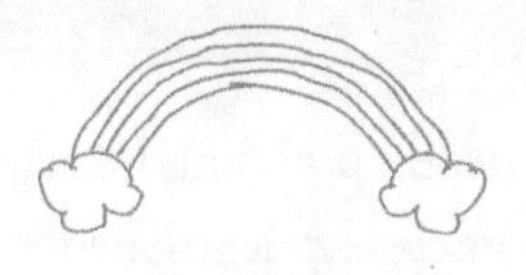

PROLOGUE: THINGS CHANGE

It was a strange and discomforting feeling, not knowing how you'd arrived at the place that you found yourself in. But thinking about that was a luxury Edie couldn't afford right now. She came quickly to her senses and knew she was in big trouble.

First, Edie had to get out of the space in which she was trapped – the cupboard that contained all the overalls for art class. She pushed the ones on hangers aside and used her feet to shift them onto the floor out of the way. Luckily, there was a little light coming through the cracks around the cupboard doors, but it flickered annoyingly, interrupting Edie's ability to see what she was doing.

Was that a paint pot next to her feet? Edie leant down and grabbed the object. It was, and she used it to bang as hard as she could on the inside of the cupboard doors. She had tried with her fists briefly already, and had hollered as loud as she could, but nobody had come to her rescue. Maybe the clanging of ceramic on wood would help. It didn't, and Edie was starting to get worried. And hot, very hot. She took off her sheepskin coat, way too thick for indoors, and let it drop to the floor. Next came the school blazer. In a moment of brief illumination, Edie was reminded of the T-shirt she was wearing underneath: pink letters on the front read 'Catch Me If You Can'. Somebody clearly had.

Frustrated, Edie whacked the paint pot on the back of the lock. The pot shattered into pieces, one cutting deep into her right hand. A glimmer of light showed blood streaking down her palm towards her wrist. Edie yelled out, a guttural shriek of anger and desperation. All that was left now, she thought, was brute force, so she took a step back and a breath in. Pursing her lips and pulling her arms together to strengthen her upper body, Edie's shoulder barged the door.

There was an encouraging creak but it didn't budge. Edie stepped back again, gathered her energy and slammed herself against the door. The wood around the hinges cracked, the right-hand door gave way and Edie tumbled out. Winded from the fall, Edie started to pull herself upright off the floor, but immediately realised that her problems had only just begun.

As she stood, it was the temperature that struck her first, like a blanket of thick, unwanted heat. Edie looked around her classroom and quickly saw what the trouble was. Flames were licking at the wooden blinds on the far external wall – the wall with a door and windows to the outside playground. It looked as if the fire might have started in a rubbish bin in the corner, which was already charred, but Edie couldn't be sure. And it didn't really matter at this stage.

Then the smoke hit her. The first wave made her gasp, and Edie's hand moved instinctively to her throat. She remembered school fire safety training: the firefighter had told them that it's often the smoke that kills people rather than the flames. He had conveyed something else that was important, really important. Now, what was it? Edie closed her eyes tight and tried to recall. 'Come on!' she screamed to herself. 'You're a detective, work it out!' Oh yes, if you're ever in a fire stick close to the floor, where there is less smoke, and try to crawl to safety. Choking, Edie got down on her knees.

Steadily, she made her way over to the back wall, away from the flames, where she knew the main door to the internal corridor was located. So far, so good, Edie thought, as the heat seemed less intense further from the windows. Her heart sank, however, as she pulled down on the door handle. It wouldn't move. She tried to turn the lock underneath, but that wouldn't shift either. Edie cursed: who would want to do this to her – trap her in a cupboard and then in a blazing classroom? The doors on the new Highgate Hill school building were so solid that there was no chance of getting out that way.

Although her mind told her not to get close to the fire, Edie realised that her options were limited. She looked around – the flames were beginning to encircle her, spreading along both side walls. The whiteboard had darkened and coloured pen marks were dripping down the surface. On the opposite wall, Edie saw her friends' contributions to the term's India project gradually turning to ash. First, Allegra's poster of the Taj Mahal, then Yasmina's 3D wall hanging of the Himalayas and, finally, Edie's favourite: the gorgeous tiger mosaic by Lizzie. It was strange, though, as the creations reminded Edie of primary rather than secondary school. Regardless, they were all gone in seconds.

Edie crawled slowly towards the far wall with the windows. Every breath burned her throat now and thick smoke raked at her lungs. Yet, despite the developing furnace she spluttered on, the temperature almost unbearable. As she reached the wall, Edie leaned upwards to grab the handle of the door to the playground. She grimaced as it scalded her already bloodied palm, and instinctively recoiled. On the floor was a rag, which Edie wrapped around her sorry hand, and then yanked down hard on the handle. Like the other door, this was locked too.

Edie wasn't going to give up quite yet, though. One thing that her mum had taught her was to be a fighter. She stood up tentatively, aware of how dizzy she was beginning to feel, and used both hands to raise the classroom chair next to her above her head. With all the power she could muster, Edie smashed the chair against the window. In a form of defiance, the window bounced the chair straight back at her. Edie tried once more, but again it was in vain.

Tears welled in Edie's eyes and she collapsed helplessly back to the ground. What was there left to do? Still on her knees she peered upwards, as if searching for assistance from the Almighty, but no hand of God came down to help her. Instead, Edie saw thick smoke gathering. Embedded in the ceiling were the smoke alarms and sprinklers, oblivious to the deathly situation. What on earth was going on? Why hadn't they been activated by the fire? The world was still against Edie, it seemed, and she was desperate.

With no idea what to do next, Edie staggered towards the desks in the corner. She knew she was close to passing out and could barely breathe. She crawled underneath one of the desks and just sat there. Was this it – the end of her short life? The end of her detective hopes and dreams? She wondered if her brother, Eli, would miss her or even care. Everything seemed so unfair, so terribly unfair, and Edie just couldn't understand why this was happening to her.

The sobbing intensified as Edie's mind drifted in and out of thoughts and consciousness. This was it, and what an awful way to go; in a place where her happiness had been shattered at some point back in time that she couldn't quite grasp. And alone, all alone. Edie was crying uncontrollably now, and everything around her was turning to black. She reached her arms out in front of her.

'Mum … I want you, Mum,' she wailed.

Leaning forwards, a little quieter now: 'Where are you, Mum …?'

Blubbering, losing a sense of her surroundings: 'Mum, where are you?'

And then Edie felt arms around her shoulders, pulling her forwards and embracing her. Confused, she opened her eyes into the darkness.

'It's okay, sweetie – you're safe,' came a voice.

And she knew she was, as Edie became aware of the familiarity of her bedroom.

'You're alright,' the deep voice comforted her. 'You're alright.'

'I want Mum,' Edie bawled into her father's neck.

There was a moment's silence as Dad held Edie tight. 'I know, sweetie,' he said softly. 'I miss Mum too.'

CHAPTER 1

THE BABYSITTER

When Edie finally re-awoke in the morning, the first thing she noticed was the broken blind on her window overlooking the back garden. She didn't bother using the curtains, thick hand-me-downs from the au pair's room of a few years back, and relied on the black-out roller blind to keep the room dark. Or dark-ish. The blind was at a slight angle, so didn't quite reach the bottom. The mechanism was broken: Dad hadn't fixed it for weeks, despite the promises. Not that Edie really cared, especially at weekends when she enjoyed watching dust motes floating in the sunbeams streaming through the gap in the blind, comforted by the knowledge that there was no need to get up for school.

A glance at the clock on her bedside table showed it was 11:37. No point in breakfast now, Edie thought. It was almost lunchtime; might as well stay in bed a little longer. A thin, sad smile spread across Edie's face as she remembered that Dad had stayed with her for quite some time in the night after her troubling dream. An hour, maybe two? Edie couldn't be sure, which meant she'd fallen asleep with him stroking her head – that always worked. Over the past three months, Edie had got closer and closer to Dad, which was heartening. She shared more and he listened more. And he accepted Edie more: an acceptance, or appreciation, based on a deeper understanding of who Edie really was. The bond was stronger and Dad was more available if Edie needed him – and not just for car rides to the station. He was a good dad; she'd forgive him the broken blind.

Edie reached over and grabbed her iPhone from next to the clock. House rules meant it should be turned off at night, so she pressed the power button and within moments she was reconnected to the world. First up, all the overnight WhatsApp messages: there were a bunch from two different school chat groups, but Edie immediately went to her private chat with Lizzie. Accompanied by an angled shot of her best friend's head on a pillow was one message, sent an hour earlier:

What's up, Sherlock? Lunch in Crouch End? XX

After a quick response, Edie threw back the duvet and sat upright. She contemplated what the weekend promised: detective work for sure, with a couple of cases that she needed to progress; time with Lizzie, keen to be her Dr Watson; perhaps a little shopping in Camden Town; babysitting for a neighbour; and, easy to forget, bat mitzvah class at the synagogue on Sunday. On her fingers, Edie counted down, slightly nervously, from June: one, two, three, four ... just over six-and-a-half months before the big event. No complaining, she was the one who'd insisted on having the coming-of-age Jewish celebration, delayed from her thirteenth birthday because of Mum's death.

Stretching, Edie stood up and took a few paces over to her desk. She'd created a good working space, modelled on her mum's highly organised office area. As she looked at the tidy surface, Edie remembered one of Mum's mottos: an ordered desk means an ordered mind. And you needed that to solve crimes.

Edie inspected the in tray she'd marked 'Current Cases'. At this stage, each ongoing numbered investigation had its own see-through plastic wallet and sticky label. Top of the pile was the case she'd provisionally named 'Ethan Stephenson', which had come to her attention just a few days earlier. Edie felt that Ethan was a kindred spirit as they'd both lost a parent, and she was happy to spend more time with him. Ethan's case file was blank at the moment, but she would find out more this weekend.

Next up, 'Missing Dogs'. This was an odd one. Edie had been contacted by a Mrs Solomon whose dog had disappeared on Hampstead Heath. Having failed to get any support from the police, the woman had reached out to Edie after reading about the schoolgirl's heroic exploits in the *Ham and High*. At first, the case reminded Edie of other banal ones she'd been approached about, given her rising profile and popularity. Most of these were from kids at school: lost mobile phones, hacked computer accounts, social media problems. Others were from random adults, such as letters that had never arrived or stolen tyres. All of these uninteresting cases were sitting unsolved in plastic folders at the bottom of the pile – not exactly material for a supersleuth. However, on hearing of two other dogs that had disappeared in the vicinity over the previous month, Edie's interest had been piqued. This missing dogs case needed looking into further, which she planned to do later in the day.

After throwing on a pair of leggings, white T-shirt and navy hoodie borrowed from Dad, Edie caught sight of the grey cardboard box file marked 'Completed Cases', sitting above the desk at one end of a white shelf. Edie didn't need to open it to know how little lay inside – and nothing that came anywhere close to the magnitude of Creation.

Edie needed her fortunes to change.

Downstairs in the playroom, Eli grunted in response to Edie's greeting. Glued to his FIFA video game, her brother was playing against a friend whilst simultaneously FaceTiming the same opponent. Each player could therefore hear what was going on in the other's home, which meant self-conscious Eli didn't want anyone around, and made his feelings clear to his loitering sister.

'In the middle of a game!' he stated forcibly.

Ejected from the children's space, Edie climbed the few steps to the main hallway and skulked into the lounge, where Dad was sitting comfortably in his favourite armchair in the far corner by the window, newspaper in hand.

'Anything interesting happening in the world today?' Edie asked as she made her way across the room.

'Oh,' Dad replied. 'Not really. Just doing the crossword. Want to help?' Before Edie could respond, he added with a smile, 'After all, you never know where solving a crossword clue might lead ...'

Edie grinned and sat on the large sofa.

'Thanks, but I think I might go and meet Lizzie in Crouch End for a bit, if that's okay?'

'Sounds alright,' Dad replied. 'Thanks for checking. Any other plans for today?'

Edie told Dad about going to see the woman about the lost dog, then babysitting later.

'Well, take your keys with you as I'll be out with Eli at football training this afternoon.' Dad paused before adding: 'And, just so you know, Miss Watson will be coming over this evening for dinner, and we'll probably watch a movie.'

Edie bristled. Somehow it just didn't feel right, Dad with another woman. That person being the school art teacher just made matters worse – although, secretly, Edie quite liked her.

'You can call her Emmeline,' Edie responded tetchily, 'not "Miss Watson" all the time.' She stood up: 'Anyway, I'm going out now, so I'll see you later.' As Dad refused to be provoked, Edie stopped at the lounge door, turned and threw a softer remark over her shoulder: 'Love you, Dad!'

'Love you too, sweetheart. Be careful. And stay in touch ... text me.'

'I will!' the young detective promised, although often she didn't.

The afternoon proved to be a strange one. When Edie arrived at Costa Coffee in Crouch End, Lizzie wasn't there. She waited fifteen minutes before Lizzie eventually arrived, unapologetic and without much of an explanation. They chatted for a while and had a hot chocolate, but Lizzie wasn't her normal bubbly self. Edie checked if everything was alright, which revealed nothing, then suggested that Lizzie join her on the visit to Hampstead Garden Suburb.

Her offer was declined, so Edie took the 210 bus alone. She arrived at number 62 bang on three o'clock, rang the bell and waited. Nobody answered and no dog barked, so she rang again. A minute later, Edie knocked on the door with her knuckles, painfully, but still the front door failed to open, so she called Mrs Solomon on the mobile number she'd provided. The call went through to answerphone, so she left a message.

Over the next half an hour, Edie repeated the whole cycle twice more, but to no avail. There was no car in the driveway and no signs of life. Through the windows, she observed a very neat home; from the decor it was probably lived in by an older person, which fitted with Edie's sense of Mrs Solomon's age, based on the emails and one short telephone conversation. Something didn't seem right, though: Mrs Solomon had sounded serious about her missing dog and very keen on meeting Edie, so where was she?

Eventually, Edie returned home. Back in her room, she spent a few hours doing not very much, before preparing to head out again. Putting on her coat and shoes in the hallway, she heard a voice.

'Hello, Edie,' announced Miss Watson, who'd appeared without a sound from the kitchen. With her wavy auburn hair straightened, the school teacher looked even prettier than normal.

'Oh, hello Miss Watson.' Edie had been hoping to avoid such an encounter.

'How's your weekend going? Doing anything interesting?'

Dad appeared behind the school teacher, providing Edie with the opening she needed. She grabbed her keys and half-turned at the front door.

'No, nothing interesting, just babysitting. I've got to go now, Dad … I'm late for Max's mum!'

Edie closed the front door behind her and started walking the ten houses to the right on Cecile Park to begin her babysitting duties.

'Hello, Edie,' greeted the neighbour.

'Hi, Mrs Redmond,' replied Edie with a charming smile. 'Sorry I'm a bit late.'

'You're not late,' added the well-groomed woman in her late thirties, glancing at the wall clock. 'Well, maybe a couple of minutes. But it really doesn't matter. We're in good time. Come inside,' she beckoned. 'And please don't call me Mrs Redmond. It's Donna.'

Edie followed the woman into the hallway which, with its brown-and-white original Edwardian floor tiles, looked remarkably similar to Edie's own home. But the ground floor layout was different, completely open plan, and Edie was led to the kitchen area at the far end, where Donna pointed to a bar stool at the counter.

'Have a seat. Do you want anything to drink?'

'Oh, I'm fine, thank you.'

'Are you sure? Maybe a Coke, orange juice … or some water?'

'Okay then. A Coke, please.'

Donna took a large bottle of Diet Coke from the fridge, decanted some into a glass and added ice. As she placed it in front of Edie, a quiet voice sounded from the living room, near the bottom of the stairs.

'I can't sleep,' announced four-year-old Max, causing both Donna and Edie to turn round together.

'What are you doing up, Max?' asked the boy's mum. 'You're supposed to be in bed.'

'I told you. I can't sleep.'

Donna looked at her watch as she walked over: 'It's well past your bedtime, my friend.' She leant down to pick up her son, dressed in his favourite Spiderman pyjamas, but he wriggled assertively out of her arms. 'Come on, Max, please,' Donna insisted. 'Daddy and I are going out for dinner.'

'I want Edie to read me a story,' Max declared forcibly.

'But she's just arrived,' replied his mum. 'And I've got to finish getting ready.'

'I don't mind reading him a story,' Edie intervened.

Donna peered over her shoulder at Edie: 'Are you sure?'

'Really,' Edie insisted. 'I don't mind at all.' Edie looked over at Max's beaming smile, then added, 'It'll be fun.'

'Well, thank you, Edie. That's very nice.' Donna focused back on her son: 'Just ten minutes, Max. Do you understand? Ten minutes.'

He nodded, prompting Edie to make her way across the room towards him. Halfway there, however, Donna surprised her babysitter.

'Edie, once you've finished with Max, there's something I'd like to talk to you about before Scott and I go out for dinner.' Edie looked over uncertainly. 'It's personal,' she added, 'but it won't take long. It's to do with your ...' Donna pursed her lips as if unsure how to express herself. 'It's to do with your detective stuff.'

Fifteen minutes later, Edie and Donna were sitting on the sofa in the lounge. Despite his initial enthusiasm, Max hadn't stayed awake beyond the fox meeting the mouse in *The Gruffalo*, after which Edie had checked in on his two-and-a-half-year-old sister, Olivia, fast asleep in her cot in the room next door. As Donna applied her make-up, her husband, Scott, had explained to Edie what to do should either child wake up, including showing her how to warm some milk. Although Edie was on the young side for babysitting toddlers, the neighbours trusted her intelligence and common sense. Scott had then gone back upstairs to get ready, leaving his wife and Edie alone.

'Right,' started Donna, her tone hushed and hesitant. 'Right ...' she repeated, staring past the girl, her eyes darting upwards.

'What's the matter, Mrs Red … I mean, Donna?' Edie asked gently.

Donna smiled. 'It's a little hard to explain … and a little, well … peculiar … but let me start at the beginning.'

'Okay.'

Donna exhaled. 'When I was at university – Cambridge University – I had a close friend … a best friend, actually. Her name was Rachel Summers. We met on the first day … queuing up for freshers' ID.'

'What are freshers?' Edie asked.

'Oh, sorry. Freshers are freshmen – meaning it's your first year at university.'

'Just a sec,' interrupted Edie. 'I'd like to take some notes, if that's okay?'

'Sure,' Donna agreed. Edie reached into her school bag and pulled out her maths notebook, which she opened at the inside back page. Not imagining babysitting duties taking this turn, Edie hadn't brought her Supersleuth stationery with her, so she had to make do.

'You said you met on the first day,' Edie prompted.

'Yes, we were waiting for our ID passes and started chatting and … well … we got on brilliantly from the moment we met. Although we were studying different subjects, we were both at the same college – Queens' College – and at Cambridge it's the main place to socialise, for friends … sports … and it's where you sleep … in one of their halls of residence.'

'Okay,' Edie said. 'So you became good friends?'

'Much more than that, Edie. We became incredibly close … and were virtually inseparable. Yes, there were boys and parties – and our studies – but Rachel and I were like soulmates. We spent almost all our spare time together.'

'Can I ask a question?'

'Yes, of course.'

'You said you were studying different subjects. What were they?'

'Right,' said Donna. 'Rachel was studying medicine, initially, then switched to psychology after the first year. I was studying engineering.'

'Engineering?'

'Yes.' Donna was accustomed to people's surprise at her subject choice. 'I loved sciences at school, especially physics, so engineering was a natural path.'

After jotting down a few points, Edie probed: 'And what do you do now, if you don't mind me asking? For a job?'

'I don't mind you asking at all, Edie.' Donna smiled. 'After my course finished, I stayed in Cambridge and did a PhD, and after that I got a job working for the government – over ten years ago – and I've been there ever since.'

'For government?' Edie queried. 'Like, in politics?'

'No, definitely not politics for me!' Donna clarified with another grin. 'Security services.'

'Do you mean you're, like, a spy?' Edie's mind whirred. 'Did you hear about my mum's case?'

Donna frowned but otherwise remained impassive. 'I did indeed hear about your mum's case – she was a very courageous woman … Now, don't you want to know the rest of my story?'

'Absolutely,' assured Edie, her intrigue rising.

'Well, as I said, Rachel and I were best friends until halfway through our final year at Cambridge. Then, all of a sudden, we had a big falling out.' Donna paused, as if troubled by the memory.

'What happened?' Edie asked.

Donna looked past Edie towards the stairs that led up to their bedroom, where her husband was still getting ready. 'It was because of a boy, as you might imagine.' Donna brushed her straightened long brown hair away from her eyes. 'Rachel was absolutely besotted by this boy – who was also at Queens' – and we talked about him endlessly. He was doing a master's degree in international relations. He was handsome, funny, captain of the college football team … Rachel became infatuated, although he never showed any interest in her.'

Edie was drawn in: 'So, what happened?'

'I had an affair with him,' Donna stated abruptly. 'No, sorry, not an affair – that's the wrong word. We had a kiss at the Valentine's Day college party and then started going out. Rachel was hysterical when she found out … mad at me … inconsolable. She completely froze me out … refused to meet … to talk … and, well, that was it. We never spoke to each other again. It was incredibly sad.'

Shocked, Edie looked her neighbour straight in the eye. There had been fallings out with Lizzie from time to time, but she couldn't imagine things ever getting that extreme. Edie checked: 'You never spoke again?'

'No, we never spoke again … and even avoided places where we might see each other. We finished our degrees in the summer and went our different ways. Some years ago, I learned from another Cambridge friend that Rachel had emigrated to Canada a few months after graduation – and, as far as I'm aware, nobody has heard from her since.'

'And what about this guy … this man?' Edie asked.

'Oh,' said Donna. 'He's upstairs. It was Scott.'

As if hearing his name, Scott shouted down that they needed to leave in ten minutes, otherwise they would miss the dinner reservation. Donna was ready, smartly dressed in pristine tapered jeans and a black jacket – with her handbag sitting on a console table near the front door. She folded her hands on her lap and straightened herself, as if she meant business.

'Let me get to the point, Edie. All of that was just the background, which you needed to know, but things began to get a bit … how can I put it … weird … yes, weird … about two weeks ago.'

Her attention ratcheted up a notch, Edie noted the time period in her notebook: 'What happened?'

'Okay, so this is quite hard to explain, even for a scientist … no, especially for a scientist! About two weeks ago, I was shopping in Covent Garden and took a break to watch the street performers on the piazza.'

'Oh, yes,' Edie nodded. 'I went there with my mum a couple of times.'

'Right. Well, I was watching a mime artist, along with … I don't know … about thirty other people. As he did his Marcel Marceau act, I was looking across the semicircle of people and … there she was. Rachel, or at least I thought it was her. Rachel used to have light-brown hair. The woman in the crowd had similar hair colour but with some darker brown … probably dyed. And she had large dark sunglasses on. Besides that, I was fairly sure it was Rachel.'

'Did she see you?'

'No, she seemed transfixed by the mime performance.'

'So, what did you do?'

'Nothing. My stomach sort of heaved … the surprise of it all … but I composed myself and walked away.'

'Okay.' Edie's eyes narrowed. 'It sounds like a coincidence. If it *was* Rachel, she may have been on a visit to see family. Or maybe she's moved back to England?'

'That's what I thought,' Donna said, her voice muted, obliging Edie to lean in. 'Except that I was out for dinner with an old school friend in Camden Town a few days later in a restaurant called Gilgamesh, which is very large, and when I went to the washroom between courses I saw her again. Over the other side of the room.'

'You saw Rachel in the restaurant?'

'Yes. From a distance, I was pretty sure it was the same woman as in Covent Garden, so I weaved over between the tables, keeping plenty of space between us. Closer up, I got a good look and it *was* Rachel. No question. She was with another woman I didn't recognise.'

'That is strange,' Edie commented. 'Did you talk to her?'

'No! No way. It ended so awfully at university … and I'm not even sure if she knew that I married Scott.'

'Okay,' Edie said, puzzled. 'What did you do?'

'Nothing. I kept an eye on her, finished my meal and then came home.'

There was a short silence as Edie processed the information, before asking: 'And what is it you want me to do?'

'Wait a moment, I haven't finished yet,' replied Donna. 'You're gonna find this hard to believe. A few days later – last Monday – I was on a lunch break from work in Vauxhall and was about to go into the Pret across the street from my office, when I saw Rachel sitting in the window, reading a book.'

'What? Again?' Edie sat bolt upright on the sofa. 'Did she see you this time?'

'No, definitely not. She was lost in whatever she was reading and didn't look up, so I just walked on.'

Edie made a note of the days and locations, then posed the most obvious question: 'Do you think Rachel is following you?'

'No,' came the instant retort. 'In my work … in field training … we're taught to look out for that sort of thing, but Rachel was completely oblivious … totally unaware that I was around. But there's one more thing …'

'You haven't seen her again, have you?'

'Yes! Well, I think so … I mean … I've been getting a bit spooked, so I'm not 100 per cent sure. But yesterday – I try to work from home on Fridays – I went into the Post Office …'

'Sorry, where was this?' Edie interrupted, scribbling in her notebook.

'Here – around the corner in Crouch End!'

Edie noticed that her neighbour's hands were trembling slightly. Clearly agitated, Donna took a deep breath and continued.

'I went in to buy some stamps … just some stamps. It wasn't planned. I happened to be passing the Post Office and remembered we'd run out. I was at the back of a long queue when I saw a woman at the counter who … from behind … I mean, I couldn't see exactly … but from behind looked just like Rachel.'

'And she didn't see you, I'm guessing?' Edie added mischievously, getting used to the run of things.

'No, but this time I followed her … from quite a distance … as I didn't want her to see me. Rachel – or the person who looked like Rachel – walked towards the Clock Tower, went left up the high street, then left again onto Crouch Hill. I was quite far back, at least 100 metres, but I'm fairly sure the woman made a right – once over the brow of the hill – and into that funny place, the Alba Hotel.'

'The Alba Hotel?' repeated Edie. 'Just around the corner from here?'

'Yes. That seems to be where she's staying.' Donna paused then finished abruptly: 'And that's it. That's my whole, rather odd, story.'

From Donna's glazed eyes Edie could tell she was unsettled by what had happened, but Edie still didn't know what the point was. 'That's a really strange story, Mrs … I mean, Donna. But what is it you want my help with?'

'I'd like to hire you, Edie,' Donna proposed quickly, glancing at her watch. 'As a sort of private detective. It's just too strange that Rachel and I would be in the same place, at the same time, four times over the last two weeks. I want to know what's going on, whether Rachel *is* actually tracking me down. I want an explanation.'

Edie tried to stay composed. Somebody, and somebody serious at that, wanted Edie to do some proper investigative work – something she could get her teeth into. The prospect was exciting.

'You want to hire me,' Edie summarised, 'to find out why your old friend, Rachel, has appeared – or reappeared – in your life four times in the last two weeks. Is that correct?'

'Yes, that's essentially it.'

'But why don't you tell the police what's happened? Let them look into it?'

'I can't. There's been no crime, so there's nothing to report. And it would sound so silly because what I've just told you doesn't make any sense. And I can't do the investigation myself because … well, first, I haven't got the time and, second, if I got caught doing something like that, it wouldn't go down well at work.'

Loud footsteps indicated an adult descending the stairs. Donna concluded the conversation in a whisper: 'I'll give you £100 now for … well, expenses … if you need to buy anything, go anywhere, that sort of thing, and another £100 if you solve my problem.' Donna glanced secretively towards the hallway where her clearly oblivious husband was putting on his coat.

She held out her hand. 'Will you do it?'

Edie looked down. A small envelope was being presented furtively to her. The question, though, was hardly worth asking. She reached out and accepted the envelope, then shook her neighbour's hand and answered: 'I will.'

CHAPTER 2

BECOMING A DETECTIVE

To Edie's surprise, Max and Olivia's parents returned from dinner later than they'd indicated. Shortly after half past ten, Edie heard keys rattling in the front door, accompanied by the giggles of a couple who'd clearly enjoyed a fair few glasses of wine. Donna's tipsy state meant Edie was unable to ask her the questions she'd been pondering throughout the evening and, instead, she took her £24 babysitting payment, texted Dad and then walked the ten houses back down the road to her own home.

The next morning, Edie woke early, her mind buzzing. By half past nine, she was showered, breakfasted (her stomach full of too many Cheerios) and standing at the ready by the front door. Bearing in mind her plans for the day, Edie was dressed in joggers, T-shirt, hoodie, faded denim jacket and an old pair of Nikes. As Edie glanced approvingly in the large hallway mirror, Dad appeared from the kitchen and grabbed a set of keys from the ceramic bowl on the console table.

'Don't forget judo after Hebrew,' Dad reminded her.

Edie closed her eyes in dismay. 'Crap. I'd completely forgotten.'

'Language!'

'It's only "crap", Dad. It's not even a swear word.'

'Okay,' he relented easily.

'It's just that I had other things to do, and haven't got that much time ...'

'You need to go,' Dad insisted. 'I've paid for the term.'

'Alright, Dad! I know. I will. I just need to change a couple of things then.'

In the lounge, Edie made a phone call and sent some WhatsApp messages. The day was going to be even busier than she'd envisaged, although, deep down, Edie was excited by what lay ahead. She just had to get through the routine stuff first: Hebrew classes were boring but necessary, otherwise she wouldn't be ready for her bat mitzvah. Judo was less of a priority, but after the life-and-death experiences of her last case, she needed to be able to defend herself better.

Four hours later, Edie was sitting in Starbucks in Golders Green, a ten-minute walk up the high street from the synagogue. The Hebrew session had passed uneventfully, but judo – held in the same venue – had taken a painful turn. Twice in a ten-minute period, Edie had been floored by basic moves that she should've been ready for: first, by a two-handed shoulder throw – or 'Morote Seoi Nage' as the teacher, Dominic, preferred to call it (he also liked, somewhat irritatingly, to be referred to as 'Sensei') – and then by a scoop throw. Embarrassingly, Edie's opponent on both occasions was a Year 6 girl, Gabby, who was half Edie's size. Dominic had taken Edie aside and given her a semi-strict talk about the dangers of being distracted, after which Edie had concentrated better. Still, the experience had reminded Edie of the power of judo as a martial art, albeit at the expense of now drinking her Frappuccino with a sore left hip and painful coccyx.

'What's happening here?' asked a loud voice sharply in Edie's left ear.

Edie recoiled in surprise. 'Oh, hi Ethan,' she managed once she realised who'd snuck up on her. 'I didn't know you were already here,' she added, unhappy at being caught off guard.

'Need to keep on your toes, detective!' Ethan teased. 'I've been in the corner, watching you, but you didn't notice.' This just made Edie feel worse.

Ethan brought a second chair and his coffee over to Edie's table. 'How was judo?' he asked innocently.

'Fine,' Edie replied a fraction too quickly. It was only two o'clock on a Sunday and she'd already been found to be unprepared twice. Edie needed to be more in the moment, more alert to what was happening around her.

'And batty class?'

'Dull, but I know I have to do it. At least the rabbi's nice.'

'Yeah, boring as hell,' Ethan echoed. 'And I hated getting up early on a Sunday. But … I guess it was worth it in the end. I got a shedload of gifts – and money. Lasted me nearly three years.'

After a moment, Edie asked gently, 'How's your mum?'

Ethan's eyes wandered briefly to the street scene outside the window as he considered the question. 'The doctors say she's recovered from her pneumonia … fully … and she's been out of hospital for, like, two months now. But she doesn't seem better to me.'

'What do you mean?'

Again, Ethan hesitated before answering, his eyes now fixed on the table. 'She's thin, doesn't eat much … and doesn't really go out the house. I don't know whether that's from the illness … or from Dad's death. She says she wants to move on, but she seems … really sad … depressed.'

Ethan looked up. 'What about your Dad? How long did it take before he … well … got back to normal again?'

It was Edie's turn to reflect. 'If you mean, how long before he wasn't depressed and was able to get on more easily with work, the surgery … and stuff. Well …' She paused for a moment, as if mentally doing the sums. 'Quite a while … over a year. But I don't even know what normal is any more. Everything's changed forever. I don't think he'll ever "get over" Mum dying, but, as my grandfather once told me, in time you learn to live with the loss.'

Silence descended. Finally, Edie asked, 'So, what exactly is it you wanted to speak to me about, Ethan?' Edie glanced at her watch, conscious of her tight afternoon schedule. 'You said it was important and to do with my detective work.'

'Yes, okay.' He took a quick sip of his coffee. 'It's my brother, Martin – who you met once at our house after the whole thing was over with my dad's boss.'

'Yeah, I remember. He's at university … studying to be a doctor?'

'That's right, in London, and it's to do with that. It's a bit complicated.'

'One moment,' paused the budding detective. Edie opened her Supersleuth notebook and grabbed a pen. 'Right, I'm ready.'

'It's like this. Martin is sitting his exams at the end of his first year at med school, but he's recently failed the biochemistry exam. He'll have to retake it later in the summer, and if he fails again, he's chucked out of university.'

'Oh,' said Edie. 'That's bad.'

'I know. The thing is, though, Martin doesn't believe he actually failed the exam.'

Edie frowned. 'What do you mean?'

Ethan took a breath. 'In the exam, as well as lots of short questions, there were two main essays, and one of them was about the pancreas.'

'That's an organ in the body, isn't it?' Edie interrupted, recalling biology class. 'The bit inside the body that makes … insulin?' Her forehead creased with uncertainty: 'To control the sugar level in your blood?'

'Exactly,' Ethan replied quickly. 'And if it doesn't work properly you have diabetes. And that's apparently called the *endocrine pancreas*. It's the main bit of the pancreas that everybody knows about. But the other part, the *exocrine pancreas*, makes hormones to help you digest your food.'

'Okay,' said Edie, noting the differences in her notebook.

'In the exam,' continued Ethan, 'the essay question, according to Martin, was about the exocrine pancreas. He says he wrote a really good essay, but his tutor told him he only got 18 per cent for it.'

'Hmm,' responded Edie, wrinkling her forehead again.

'Yeah. A few other people did the same – five or six – and also failed. But everyone else in the year, maybe 200 students, apparently wrote about the endocrine pancreas – the wrong bit – and they all passed.'

'That's not fair,' Edie said.

'No! I know. And so does Martin. He complained to his tutor – Dr Bannon was his name, I think – who said Martin was wrong about the essay, about which part of the pancreas it was on, that it was just one of those things. He told Martin to put his head down, do the retake in the summer and then changed the subject.'

Edie posed the obvious question: 'Couldn't Martin just show him the exam paper?'

'No. There was no physical paper. It was all done electronically on university laptops on desks in the exam hall … and Dr Bannon refused to show Martin the original paper – or anything on a laptop – when they met.'

Edie's mind was ticking over. 'And what exactly is it that you and Martin were hoping I could do?'

'Well, we were hoping that …' But Ethan was interrupted by the Santigold 'Disparate Youth' ringtone on Edie's phone. The boy smiled as he recalled playing the same song on the crazy drive back from Cambridgeshire with Edie a few months ago.

Edie blushed. 'I need to get this,' she apologised, noticing the call was from Mrs Solomon.

Standing up and heading to the corner of the store, Edie answered and was immediately struck by the shakiness of the voice. Mrs Solomon sounded even more upset than the previous day, and Edie reassured her she'd be there soon.

'I need to go now,' Edie told Ethan after ending the call. 'I'm sorry.'

'Is everything okay?' he asked with concern.

'Yes, sort of … it's just … never mind. It's complicated. One of my other cases – an old woman I was helping has been attacked. She's in hospital.'

'Is she alright?'

'I think so. Listen, I'll message you later about your brother and his exam stuff. I'll try to help if I can.'

And with that Edie put away her notebook, packed up her bag and was off.

Halfway to the Redmonds' house yesterday, Edie's phone had rung. Apologetic about missing the meeting at her house, Mrs Solomon explained what had happened. Before she was due to meet Edie, she had gone back to Hampstead Heath to search for her lost dog. Wandering around the precise location where the dog had gone missing, Mrs Solomon had noticed two men acting suspiciously in the undergrowth. She'd entered the wooded area to take a photo, at which point one of them had shouted at her and knocked the phone aggressively from her hand, which in turn sent Mrs Solomon tumbling to the ground. Knocked unconscious, Mrs Solomon wasn't found until an hour later by children playing football. An ambulance had been called and she was now in the Royal Free Hospital with concussion and a black eye.

Edie's intention was to go to see Mrs Solomon that day, but a further call after she'd left Ethan revealed that Mrs Solomon was now too tired, so it would have to wait. Instead, something else had moved up the agenda of Edie's investigative plans.

On the back row of the top deck of the 210 bus, Edie put on her headphones. She needed a moment to pause and take stock, plus a bunch of older teenage boys were making a racket down at the other end of the bus, Stormzy blasting from their mini-speaker. Thankfully, they left as the bus approached Whitestone Pond.

Edie opened Spotify on her phone and went straight to her favourite playlist, 'Songs to Remember Mum'. First up on shuffle mode was 'Maybe' by Birdy, one of Mum's favourites. They'd had tickets to see Birdy together at the Scala in Kings Cross but Mum's death – no, not death, murder – meant the tickets had been given away. Edie closed her eyes: it all felt like an eternity ago, but also as if it were only yesterday. How was that possible?

As the acoustic guitar washed over her, Edie's eyes welled up, but no tears appeared. Instead, she sniffed a little, smiled and enjoyed the gentle watery sensation underneath her closed eyelids. In a not unpleasant way, Edie forced an image of Mum to appear in her mind. It was important for her to do this regularly because she had noticed that the mental image – which felt more real than a photo – was fading with time. Edie screwed her eyes up tighter. Hair:

light brown, wavy. Eyes: blue-green, with a little grey (Edie wished she had the same eye colour herself, instead of dark brown). Lips: what were they like again?

As Edie imagined the touch of her mum's lips on her cheek, the lyrics of Birdy's song came through strongly. Like the chorus suggested, Edie was doing something she dreamt of and believed in – investigating crimes and putting the wrongs of the world to right. The only problem was that she would have preferred to be doing it *with* her wonderful mum rather than *instead* of her.

With an effort, Edie brought herself back to the present. Concerned about her best friend, Edie texted Lizzie about talking later that evening, then messaged two other girls from school – Charlie and Yasmina – about helping out with some detective work. Since Edie had become a bit of a national celebrity, people at school had suddenly wanted to be her friend, and she'd found it increasingly difficult to tell who was genuine and who was a fake attracted by the limelight. Edie's nemesis, Rosie, for instance, had been trying hard to get close, although Edie still didn't really trust her. But Charlie and Yasmina seemed authentic, so she'd brought them into the fold. The whole friendship problem was mirrored in Edie's other, smaller circle of friends at the synagogue: knowing whom to trust was as much a challenge for teenagers as it was for adults.

At Beaumont Rise, Edie got off the 210 bus, crossed the main road and then walked all the way down Ashley Road until the junction with Crouch Hill. At the corner, she sat on a small wall, reached into her bag and, from a zipped section, pulled out the photograph from the envelope she'd been handed by Donna Redmond the previous night.

Sitting on the lawn of Queens' College, Cambridge, with the famous Mathematical Bridge in the background, Donna's long-lost friend had a kindly face, gentle eyes and a welcoming smile, framed by shoulder-length hair and a clumsy fringe. Of course, Rachel Summers probably didn't look much like the old photo now, fifteen years later, so Edie brought the image closer to inspect it more carefully. Was that a mole above Rachel's right upper lip?

Distraction was both an art and a skill, Edie remembered from reading Conan Doyle, and she was about to get some practice. She jumped off the wall and walked up the unpleasantly steep Crouch Hill away from Stroud Green. Just over the top of the hill stood the Alba Hotel – an expansive old Edwardian house converted into bed and breakfast accommodation.

In the driveway outside the hotel, Edie gathered herself. She took several deep, meditative breaths, cleared her mind and focused. Confidently, she walked up the winding concrete stairs and pushed the front door which unfortunately failed to budge. Crap, she thought, the first part of her plan had already gone awry. Another deep breath and the back-up plan was mentally activated: Edie rang the buzzer and stared directly into the CCTV camera above the doorway.

'Can I help you?' asked a woman's crackly voice.

'Oh yes. Thank you,' Edie replied in her sweetest possible voice. 'I want to make an enquiry for my grandparents who are coming over from Canada and need somewhere to stay.' The Canada bit was partly true, although everything else was a lie – Grandfather David's wife was long dead. Regardless, a buzz was followed by a click and the front door gently opened.

Inside, the spacious hallway had the same diamond-pattern floor tiles as the houses in Edie's own nearby street. Two guest rooms, with the numbers 1 and 2 on their doors, opened off the hallway, at the end of which was a large staircase. On the wall next to the stairs was a small laminated sign marked 'Reception' with an arrow underneath, from where the same crackly voice shouted: 'Come on through.'

Observation was also key to detective work, so Edie tried to take in everything she saw: an umbrella stand, a wooden table with a multitude of flyers for tourist attractions in London, an old barometer and a comments book for guests. Edie glanced at the book cursorily as she walked past, suddenly struck by what information it might hold, but the recent handwritten names were largely illegible.

As Edie reached the staircase, footsteps from the top echoed down. Edie looked up nervously, and then breathed a sigh of relief as an elderly couple descended slowly. Smiling briefly at them, Edie turned left and arrived at reception, beyond which lay the breakfast room and garden.

'So, young lady, your grandparents are visiting from Canada' to which Edie nodded. 'And when exactly might that be?'

'In the autumn,' Edie responded. 'October. The middle of October.'

'Okay,' said the middle-aged woman behind the counter in an eastern European accent. 'Any particular dates yet?'

'No. They're flexible.' Edie then switched into information-gathering mode: 'Have you been working here long?'

'Well, I'm the owner of many years – and the manager,' replied the woman, a fraction suspiciously. 'So, I guess you could say I have been working here a long time.' Lowering her gaze, she clicked her mouse and scrutinised the availability page on the desktop computer. 'October isn't so busy for us,' she stated, rolling the mouse with fingernails adorned with neon-blue nail polish. 'You're lucky – plenty of spaces.' She looked up: 'Just let us know as soon as your grandparents decide.'

'Thanks,' Edie said, but the woman hadn't finished. 'Would you like to see a room? Maybe your grandparents would prefer the ground floor to avoid the stairs?'

'That would be good,' Edie answered, before moving on to the next stage of her plan. 'But I meant to say that there's a strange man hanging around outside, pushing a shopping trolley. A homeless guy, maybe. But he seemed to go through the back door into your garden.'

'Oh no!' replied the woman, irritated. 'Not another one. We get them more and more, coming off the Parkland Walk just around the corner. Do you know it?'

'Yes, I do. I know it very ...'

'It's even worse now. Ever since the police shot dead that criminal ... or assassin ... a few months ago. And that local girl got famous.' Edie's stomach clenched with the fear of being recognised. 'Anyway, since then more and more people visit, which means more homeless people looking for scraps.' The woman lifted up the bar flap and ducked underneath. 'Excuse me, I need to check the garden.'

As soon as she was heading out of the rear garden door, Edie dipped under the counter and grabbed the computer mouse. The availability page was still open. Edie clicked the tab that switched the display to 'Today'. Twelve rooms were listed, each with a name alongside. As Edie scrolled down the list, searching for 'Summers', she heard fresh footsteps from the top of the staircase. Nobody with that surname seemed to be staying at the Alba at present, but Rachel might have changed her surname. Edie tracked the column for first names, some of which were listed in full, others just initials. And there it was, just one room – room 8, single occupancy – with 'R' in the forename column, along with a red dot that indicated the guest was currently in the hotel.

Through the breakfast room window, Edie could see the owner making her way back from the far side of the garden, whilst inside the building Edie heard the footsteps pause at the bottom of the stairs. She closed the computer page quickly, ducked back under the reception counter and pushed herself flush against the archway that led into the hallway. Out of sight, Edie closed her eyes and composed herself. Very slowly, she peered round the archway and saw a woman in a baseball cap – maybe in her early forties – examining the leaflets for London's many theatres.

It was hard to see her face clearly, but all of a sudden she straightened up and looked over in Edie's general direction. For an instant, Edie caught sight of the woman's profile, although she had to look away. Was that a mark above her lip?

With a click, the front door opened and the guest stepped outside, just as the owner was opening the rear garden door. Edie knew exactly what she had to do next.

Whereas surveillance referred to detailed observation of a given situation – for instance, watching a house or an office – what Edie was now attempting was tracking, or trailing, a suspect. Although she'd not anticipated this happening today, she felt ready as she'd been reading up about tracking techniques.

Edie waited until the last moment to leave the Alba Hotel, in order to put some distance between herself and the woman. Ensuring the front door closed quietly behind her, she quickly descended the stone steps and then looked left and right up and down the street. And there she was, just thirty metres away, walking down the hill towards the centre of Crouch End.

Pulling the grey hood over her head, Edie followed from a safe distance. Although there were several pedestrians on the pavement in-between them, the woman was easily recognisable by her stylish baseball cap.

At the traffic lights, the woman turned right towards the Clock Tower, then crossed the road again by Barclays Bank. By now, Edie had put her headphones in her ears to look even less conspicuous, but she kept the music off. Too much noise would diminish her alertness.

Suddenly, the woman stopped, half-turned and leant over something. Edie ducked into a Greggs doorway and pretended to be busy with her phone. With lots of other pedestrians now flitting by, Edie's target drifted in and out of view, but through one opening in the crowds, Edie noticed the woman reach into her handbag and give some money to a person sitting on the pavement. Next, the woman stood up briskly and entered Waitrose. Edie counted to twenty and followed her into the supermarket.

Inside, it was teeming with hordes of Sunday shoppers and, initially, Edie lost visual contact with the woman. Edie walked purposefully up the fruit and vegetable aisle then down through chilled foods. By the third aisle Edie was getting concerned that she'd lost her subject, but as she peeped round the corner of the fourth, her prey came into sight just a few metres away. Something must have caught the woman's eye, though, since she glanced away from the coffee selection and towards Edie. In reflex, the young detective pulled herself back and stood flush to the shelves of baked beans.

The woman didn't seem to be rattled, however, as half a minute later she walked innocuously towards the tills, oblivious to her follower's presence. Delicately, Edie lurked twenty metres behind, keeping other customers in-between. The woman began to use a self-service checkout. Edie was straining to see her face clearly when her own arm was suddenly tapped from behind. Adrenaline surged through Edie's body.

'Hello, Edie,' said a familiar voice. Edie spun round, surprised at whom she found herself facing. 'Fancy bumping into you here,' Donna Redmond said with a wan smile. 'What are you up to?'

Edie twisted to look back over towards the checkout area, then decided better of it. 'Just buying a few groceries … for home … for dinner,' she explained with an unnecessary level of apology.

'And what delicious dinner are you planning?' Donna asked in the manner of somebody used to questioning. The mildly unsettling half-smile stayed fixed, making Edie reluctant to engage.

As her mind raced with possible recipes, Edie was rescued by her phone ringing. 'I'm sorry, Mrs Redm … I mean Donna … but I must get this.' The unknown number suggested otherwise.

'Hello,' Edie answered hesitatingly, as she moved away from her neighbour and waved to suggest their encounter was over.

'Oh, hi' came a breathless (or maybe anxious?) male voice. 'Is that Edie … Edie Franklin … I mean Marble?'

'Yes. Who's this?'

'It's Harry. Harry Coranger from school.' Stunned, Edie's heart skipped a beat and her face reddened. She wasn't used to getting calls from the captain of her year's school football team. He was far too cool.

'Oh, hi,' she managed feebly, trying to stay calm.

'It was me who emailed you a few months ago,' Harry continued, 'saying I needed your help.'

Edie wandered nervously into a far corner of the supermarket by the frozen foods. 'But you never followed it up,' she responded.

'I know, I'm sorry. But there are reasons. I'll explain, but now I'm in terrible trouble. And … and …'

His voice was shaking so Edie held her phone closer to her ear.

'And I think something dreadful is about to happen.'

CHAPTER 3

AN INCONVENIENT TRUTH

'What was wrong with you on Saturday?' Edie whispered to Lizzie in the middle of Monday morning assembly. 'Is everything okay?' As Edie waited for a reply, the newish head teacher, Mrs Plunkett, droned on with countless announcements.

'Yeah, fine,' replied Lizzie a little too quickly. 'I was just tired.'

'Shhh,' hushed Mr Bowling, the maths teacher.

'Because of the three recent assaults,' continued Mrs Plunkett in her steely monotone, 'Waterloo Park is now completely out of bounds. The police will be doing extra rounds this week and your parents have all been informed.' Stern and brusque, Mrs Plunkett had already developed a fearsome reputation with the pupils.

Edie leaned in closer to Lizzie: 'Well, you seemed in a bad mood.'

'I wasn't in a bad mood!' Lizzie batted back. 'I told you. I was just tired.'

'Shhhhhh,' insisted Mr Bowling.

Dialling down the tone, Edie added: 'Well, I really need you this weekend. On Saturday. Remember? For the surveillance on Hampstead Heath.'

'Yes,' Lizzie said sharply, without looking at her friend. 'I remember.'

'Two more things,' added Mrs Plunkett. 'First, just a reminder that our new mental health programme is starting later this week. It's called PoWaR, which stands for the Principles of Wellbeing and Resilience, and involves eight sixty-minute sessions. The first four sessions are before the half-term break, the rest afterwards. We're piloting the programme in one class in Year 8 and one in Year 9.'

Mrs Plunkett cast her eye across the sea of faces in the vast hall, and then adopted a warmer tone: 'We all know how many mental health difficulties … challenges … there are out there nowadays, for children as well as adults, so I hope this course helps. And if the first two classes like it, and our evaluation suggests it works, then we hope to roll it out to other classes across the school.'

Ill-advisedly, Lizzie turned again to Edie: 'That's us, isn't it? We're one of the classes?' But Edie didn't have a chance to reply as Mr Bowling swivelled round, this time holding a finger up to his lips and looking severe.

'And finally,' Mrs Plunkett concluded, 'Ms Dylan wants to say something about the film this lunchtime.' The head teacher walked away from the podium, the heels of her smart black shoes clicking on the wooden floorboards.

Scruffily attired, the geography department leader shuffled across the stage to the podium.

'Good morning everyone,' Ms Dylan began, then waited, although the silence stayed unbroken. 'Right. Monday film club is at lunchtime today. We'll be showing the

Al Gore film – sorry, Al Gore, he is … I mean was, the vice president of the United States … almost became president. Anyway, we'll be screening his film *An Inconvenient Truth*, an extraordinary documentary about climate change. Important for anyone interested in this area. The screening starts at half past twelve in the auditorium, and those attending are allowed to start afternoon classes a little late. You're welcome to bring lunch with you.'

At break time, Edie bought herself a peach green tea at the Triangle Café in the inner courtyard, then sat on one of the benches shielded from the May sunshine by the large oak tree. It was the first week of the two-week rolling timetable, which meant that Monday morning started with double science, thankfully now over, and would continue with maths and then art before lunch. Those subjects were okay, except that art meant seeing Miss Watson, which was embarrassing.

Allowed to look at their phones during break, Edie checked for emails on her two accounts – ediemarble@gmail.com and ediemarblesupersleuth@gmail.com. Apart from junk, the only email of note was from Mrs Solomon, who'd tried to send a photo over but failed. Anyway, Edie was due to see her in the hospital after school, so she could check what had gone wrong then.

On this occasion, Edie wasn't caught unawares. She saw Harry Coranger emerge from the path that led to the tunnel under Southwood Lane. Despite the telephone urgency he was walking slowly, almost gingerly. Harry didn't see Edie at first, allowing her time to observe: Harry appeared drawn and tired, his clothes dishevelled. And he looked on edge.

Eventually, Harry clocked her and came over. He sat down, perched on the front few planks of the bench, leaning forwards with his arms on his thighs. Harry's eyes darted around. Was he embarrassed to be seen talking to Edie, she wondered, or was it something else?

'Were you limping?' Edie asked after a few moments.

'No ... well, maybe a little,' Harry admitted begrudgingly. 'Hurt my knee playing football.'

'Oh, when was that?' Edie questioned, evidence-gathering beginning immediately in a new case.

'I don't know! At the weekend maybe.' Harry turned half to his right to look at Edie. 'Anyway, what is this, a quiz?'

Edie recoiled at his abruptness, although she realised that she had to get used to this kind of thing. She needed to find out information, but people didn't always like being interrogated. 'No, of course not. You just looked like you were in pain.'

Harry returned to looking straight ahead, so Edie could only see his profile. 'Sorry,' he said tentatively. 'I just haven't been myself recently. And ... well ... I asked *you* to meet *me*, after all.'

A Year 9 boy grabbed a can of Fanta from another kid in the far corner of the courtyard. Shouts followed and the boys squared up to each other briefly, before a sixth form prefect came over and pulled them apart. They all ended up with orange stains on their white shirts.

Aware that there wasn't much time remaining in break, Edie pushed on: 'You sounded very worried on the phone. Can you tell me what it's about?'

Harry said nothing for a bit. His shirt was hanging out and Edie noticed that one of the lower buttons was missing. His curly, shoulder-length black hair looked unwashed, but he still looked cool. Girls said Harry was good-looking, and Edie could understand why, but she wasn't sure if he was her type. Eventually, Harry spoke.

'It's my stepfather,' he said quietly. 'There's something wrong. It started when I sent you that email three months ago … It settled for a bit … but over the past few weeks he's been acting so strangely. He's up to something … I know it. I just don't know exactly what it is.'

Edie made to get her notebook out of her bag, then thought better of it, and decided to just listen instead. Harry continued. 'I'm worried – very worried – that something bad is gonna happen.'

It wasn't much to go on, Edie thought, but at least it was a start. She'd been reading about probing witnesses, and how you need to gain their trust and develop rapport in order to get to the crucial information. 'I'm sorry to hear that. What does your mum think?'

'My mum's gone,' Harry countered quickly. 'When I was three.'

'I'm so sorry,' Edie reacted sympathetically.

'Oh, no! Not that,' Harry stated forcibly. 'She's not *dead*. Just gone. It's all quite complicated. My real dad left when my mum was pregnant with me, just disappeared one night – to the United States apparently – and I don't think my mum ever heard from him again. She met Heath – my stepdad – when she was pregnant, and he brought me up with her until … well … she was drinking a lot and then one night, when I was three, she just took off as well. I don't remember anything about it. She was from Jamaica and Dad – Heath – wondered if she'd gone back there … or even Sierra Leone, where her family came from originally. Ever since then, Heath's brought me up. He's like a dad … is my dad …' Harry's voice trailed off.

Edie thought about her situation. Through her own mum's death Edie could relate to things being tough, but she couldn't really imagine never having known her mum properly. Would that make it easier when that person disappeared from your life, or worse? She brought her attention back to the boy next to her.

'You said on the phone that you thought something worse than bad – something dreadful – was about to happen,' Edie probed. 'What do you mean?'

Harry thought carefully. 'My stepfather's been behaving really oddly for quite a few weeks. Like I said … he's just not like he usually is. And he goes to weird places – or, at least, not where he tells me he's going.'

'Can you be more precise? Where does he go?'

'I don't know, it's just *not* where he tells me he's going to be. But there's more …' Harry paused for a moment as if uncertain whether to share. 'I think my stepfather might be a terrorist,' he stated bluntly. 'Might be plotting some kind of awful terrorist thing.'

Edie baulked. 'Terrorist?!' she exclaimed, too loudly. One of the kids with a Fanta stain looked over momentarily, then seemed to lose interest. 'Sorry,' she added more quietly. 'What makes you think that? You said he was really nice.'

'I've heard him in his study ... sometimes on the phone. The door's always closed but ... I thought I heard him say the word "attack".'

Edie whitened. 'Really? That's serious. Are you sure? Have you tried ...?'

'And we get strange things delivered,' Harry interrupted. 'Things that don't really make sense.' He cupped his head in his hands, leant further forwards and shook it from side to side. 'I dunno ... maybe I'm imagining it all ... and I'm tired ... haven't been sleeping well.'

Edie glanced at her watch, conscious of the limited time. 'What about the police?'

Harry shook his head assertively. 'I can't ... I mean, the police would think I'm crazy ... and I don't want to get him into trouble. I love him ... and I'd go into care if he was arrested. No other relatives. I don't know what to do.'

Harry turned a little to face Edie. He looked incredibly sad. The moment seemed to hang awkwardly, and then the bell rang for the end of break. Pupils started making their way into various buildings for their lessons.

Edie and Harry stood up together, and he turned towards the detective: 'Can you come to my house after school today? We can have a look around.' He paused. 'I mean, I've already had a look myself ... obviously ... but together we might find something.'

Taken aback by the proposition, Edie stumbled over her words: 'Oh … yes … maybe', then remembered that she was supposed to go and see Mrs Solomon later. 'No, I'm sorry,' she corrected, without even thinking of asking where Harry lived. 'I've got to go to the hospital after school. It's a case … a different case.'

'Oh,' Harry replied, downcast.

'But maybe tomorrow? Or Wednesday, after school?'

'I've got football training tomorrow, but Wednesday's okay. See you at the gates after school.'

At the end of art class Edie couldn't get away quick enough. It wasn't Miss Watson's fault – she seemed totally cool with everything – but Edie felt strange, clumsy even. Seeing the teacher in her own house and also in class just seemed wrong. Unfortunately, Edie's eagerness to be the first to leave the art room provided Miss Watson with an opening.

'Hi, Edie,' the teacher said as Edie was exiting the door.

'Oh, hi Emme … I mean Miss Watson,' Edie remarked over her right shoulder, remembering she needed to use the right title when at school.

'How's everything?' came the next unwanted question.

'Everything's fine, Miss Watson,' Edie replied curtly. 'Sorry, but I've got to rush. I want to see the climate change film.'

'Oh, yes, *An Inconvenient Truth*. It's amazing. I hope you enjoy … well, enjoy isn't really the right word. I hope you get something from it.'

With a faint nod of acknowledgement Edie turned on her heels, walked down the flight of stairs to the ground floor of the art building, then went speedily towards the tunnel underneath Southwood Lane. She caught up with Lizzie just before the double doors that led into Dyne House.

Edie tapped her friend on the shoulder. 'Did you get a sandwich?' she asked, a little out of breath. From her school bag, Edie removed her asthma inhaler and took a couple of puffs. As she held in her breath, Lizzie's answer surprised her.

'No. Don't think I'm gonna bother with the film. I'll just go down to the canteen.'

'Oh! Are you sure everything's okay, Lizzie?'

'Yes, fine. I told you ... just don't fancy the film. The others are in there. I think it's just starting.'

Edie watched briefly as Lizzie walked off and then went into Dyne House. Inside the large theatre – used for drama performances, film screenings and various presentations – it was very dark, and Edie stumbled as she warily descended the steep aisle stairs.

'Psst' came a hiss from the right. Edie peered and made out Charlie who was beckoning to her. Tripping over feet as she made her way across the row, Edie sat down in-between the tall girl with ginger hair in ringlets and her shorter companion, Yasmina, with her straight, jet-black hair. Yasmina's parents had moved to London from India when she was just a toddler. Both bespectacled, the two girls made a slightly odd, even goofy, pair.

As Edie settled down in her seat, Ms Dylan finished her introduction about the Academy Award for Best

Documentary Feature the film had won in 2007, and how tragic it was, over a decade later, that little had changed. Ms Dylan reminded the pupils of how vital it was that they play their part in protecting the planet from climate change, in taking action. Mum had instilled the same activist mentality in Edie, and moments like these still jolted her from contentedly going about her day to suddenly having a head full of sad memories – although such moments were becoming less frequent and the painfulness was diminishing.

The documentary film was framed around a lecture that Al Gore was giving to a large audience about the history of climate change and its development into a planetary crisis. Distressing photos and videos showed melting ice caps, flooding, droughts, wildfires, hurricanes and typhoons, the destruction of beautiful coral reefs and the mass extinction of species. Planet earth systematically destroyed by humankind.

It was depressing, and the truth was very inconvenient to politicians. Like Mum, Edie was passionate about the environment and knew climate change was a big problem. At home they did various things to live sustainably – Dad had even bought an electric car – but it didn't sound like nearly enough.

'He made another film,' said Yasmina, leaning over. 'A sequel. A couple of years ago. It's even more depressing than this as nothing's really changed.'

But Edie was absorbed in watching the credits roll at the end of the film. Messages appeared, one after another, with ideas of what each person can do to make a difference. If the politicians can't save the world, perhaps people can collectively. Inspired, Edie grabbed her notebook and wrote down each one. The messages gave Edie hope. And there's nothing more precious than hope.

At the end of the school day Edie took the bus towards Hampstead, walked down the long and windy East End Road, then turned right at Southend Green into the Royal Free Hospital. Inside, doctors, nurses and patients' families tore around the lobby at breakneck speed. She took the lift to the sixth floor, where the unimaginatively named Ward 6 East was located.

At the central nurses' station, Edie asked a woman in dark-blue uniform – whose badge indicated she was the ward sister – where Mrs Solomon was located.

'Oh, yes. Mrs Solomon,' said Sister Gemma. 'Lovely lady. Horrible though … her assault. I mean … who does that kind of thing?' Edie nodded, but she was aware she had to be home for dinner. 'We put Mrs Solomon in the single room – end of the corridor on the left.' Sister Gemma pointed the way. 'Are you her granddaughter?'

'Oh, no. I'm just a friend … neighbour … I mean, a friend.'

'Well, you can be a neighbour *and* a friend. Anyway, I'm sure she'll be delighted to see you.'

Edie smiled, set off as directed and found the room easily, confirmed by the woman's name on the door: 'Violet Solomon, age 78'. Edie knocked, waited, got no reply, so rapped the door harder. This time a frail voice invited her in.

'Hello, dear' came the gentle greeting as Edie stepped inside. The private, white-walled space wasn't as depressing as Edie had imagined, although hospital room aroma hit her nose immediately, so Edie left the door open to get some ventilation.

'It's good of you to come, young lady … I've not had many visitors,' Mrs Solomon said quietly, and Edie was struck by the weakness of her voice. 'Now, take your coat off, dear, and come over here where I can see you.' She motioned to the chair on the other side of the bed.

Edie took the school bag off her shoulder, placing it on the table by the door next to what was, presumably, Mrs Solomon's mobile phone – clearly cracked and damaged from the altercation on Hampstead Heath. Edie was surprised the phone hadn't been stolen. She put her coat on the door hook and went round to the other side of the bed to sit on the wipe-clean armchair.

Mrs Solomon seemed pleased to have company. 'You are pretty,' she remarked, making Edie blush. 'Even prettier than in the photos in the paper.' Mrs Solomon reached over and took Edie's hand in hers, resting them both on the crisp white sheets.

'Look at me,' she said with a forlorn expression. 'I'm a mess.' And indeed she was. Edie was taken aback by the bruising and swelling on the left side of Mrs Solomon's face, which had forced her left eye shut with an engorged eyelid. Aside from the facial damage, the woman's left arm was in a plaster cast. Even the green hospital gown, with a splattering of dried blood, reflected the unpleasantness of the incident.

'My left wrist is broken … my head hurts … and my eye … it's so painful. I can't see anything, although the doctor says the eye's not damaged and will get better.'

'That's good,' Edie sympathised.

'That's not all of it! I've got three broken ribs, and every time I cough or spend a penny it's agony!'

Lost for words, Edie sat quietly until Mrs Solomon settled down. Self-conscious, the patient wiped away a tear with her good hand, shook herself out of her self-pity and continued.

'I read about you in the *Ham and High* … the local paper … so courageous how you took on that nasty drug company … and I'm so sorry about your mum.' Mrs Solomon squeezed with her right hand and Edie gladly squeezed back gently. 'And it said in the paper that you're getting one of those national awards … what did they call them … oh yes, the Brave People Awards, I think.'

'Yes, that's right. In a couple of weeks. At the British Museum.'

'Well, that's just wonderful, my dear.' Mrs Solomon squeezed Edie's hand once more. 'Thank you so much again, young lady, for helping me find my dear old Quincy. The dog's named after an old TV show I used to like. He's just everything to me – my best friend since my husband died four years ago. I got him free direct from a specialist because of his limp. I don't have any children … a few friends … but Quincy is everything. Keeps me company, keeps life worth living.'

'I'll do my best, Mrs Solomon,' Edie explained, with rising concern about the older woman's expectations. Pen and notebook now at the ready, Edie was keen to start: 'Mrs Solomon, please can you just tell me everything that happened – from the beginning.'

'Yes, of course ... Sorry, I know I get a bit flustered. And, please, do call me Violet.'

Over the next few minutes, Mrs Solomon shared all she knew with Edie; how she regularly took Quincy for a run on Hampstead Heath, where he liked playing with other dogs in the big space by the lake.

Then Mrs Solomon described how, nine days earlier, Quincy had ventured – unusually for him – into the wooded area behind the famous bendy tree, from where he'd simply disappeared. She'd searched for her beloved dog for hours but to no avail.

'It was like he'd been lured into that wooded area,' she asserted.

'Okay,' Edie said, on to her second page of notes. 'Now can you tell me exactly what happened last Saturday, please.'

Next, Mrs Solomon recounted how, with the police coming up with nothing, she'd decided to take things into her own hands. On the first sunny day since Quincy had vanished, she'd gone to the same area of Hampstead Heath at the same time as a week earlier. After watching from a nearby bench, she'd noticed one of the many dogs charging around suddenly veer off towards the undergrowth close to where Quincy had headed. Strangely, this dog also seemed to be hobbling a little.

'So, you followed that dog?'

'Yes, of course,' Mrs Solomon responded. It was muddy and dark and, out of nowhere, she'd seen two men, one of whom looked like he was feeding something to a dog. The other man had come closer, so she'd decided to take a photo on her phone. The man first yelled and then kicked at the phone, sending it flying and making her lose her balance. She'd fallen sideways onto a log, which the doctors said had caused the black eye and broken ribs, whilst her outstretched arm had sustained a fracture.

'As I mentioned,' Mrs Solomon added, 'I don't think they were trying to hurt me. One of the men seemed quite gentle with the dog, and the man near me looked almost apologetic. As I was lying on the ground, he came over and seemed concerned. He had a quick look around, but he didn't find my phone – a passer-by did later – and then left with his friend. After that, I fell unconscious until I was found soon after.'

'That's terrible. Do you have that picture of the man on your phone, Violet?'

'The phone's all cracked and broken … useless now, I think. The photo of the man is dark and blurred – impossible to make anything out. The police had a look. They're interested in the assault, but I don't think they care about my Quincy.' She motioned to where the phone lay on the table by the door. 'I tried to send you a photo of my dog yesterday … but it doesn't work, except for phone calls.'

'Does your phone automatically upload photos to the cloud?'

'The cloud? I don't know what that is, my dear.'

'Alright, one other question. What kind of dog is Quincy?'

'I thought you might ask as I forgot to mention before!' Violet Solomon said enthusiastically. 'I got my neighbour to go into my house yesterday – she has keys – to bring you a proper photo of Quincy. He's a gorgeous English springer spaniel, brown and white, with those big floppy ears. Here, have a look.'

From the bedside table, Mrs Solomon produced a white envelope, which she pressed into Edie's hand. 'Go on,' she insisted. 'Take a look.' But Edie's mind was elsewhere. Memories of a dream when a book, which became an envelope – containing something rather different to a photo of a dog – had been placed in her hand with a demand that she look at it.

'Go on, my dear. Open it up now. No time to lose!'

Edie felt paralysed, unable to do as instructed. Plus, she was beginning to feel anxious. A pounding in her chest was growing in intensity, her palms were sweaty and she was starting to feel light-headed. Was it the envelope that had triggered this or something else?

Edie's trance was interrupted by Mrs Solomon gasping and turning ashen. Edie glanced up at the woman, who was staring mesmerised at the door.

'What are you doing?' Mrs Solomon barked. Edie looked over towards the door, through which a man had entered. A man who didn't look like he worked at the hospital. A pulled-down baseball cap obscured the top half of his face, and a scarf wound across his chin and mouth covered the bottom half. Vitally, though, his hand was on Mrs Solomon's mobile phone on the table next to the door.

Time stopped for a few moments, all three locked in the uncertainty of what would happen next. Then, the intruder whipped the phone into the pocket of his bomber jacket, twisted round and bolted. Edie saw blue jeans and white trainers disappearing out the door.

Instinctively, the detective was up and chasing the man. Behind Edie, Mrs Solomon shouted 'Stop! Stop that man!' At first, nobody seemed to pay much attention, then two nurses came out of their office. By then, the robber was sprinting down the corridor towards the ward exit. Edie tried to follow but her legs were weak. She needed to stop him leaving the area, but he was fast and she couldn't seem to get her body moving. Instead, Edie was becoming breathless.

At the nurses' station, halfway along the corridor, Edie stopped and half-collapsed onto the counter. She was gasping frantically now and her heart was pounding uncontrollably fast. This was different to shortness of breath with her asthma, and she was feeling giddy.

Out of nowhere, a chair appeared and Sister Gemma gestured for Edie to sit down. On the verge of passing out, Edie collapsed onto the seat.

A gentle hand touched the back of Edie's neck, and the sister's calming voice advised her to sit forward with her head between her knees.

'Breathe into this,' the senior nurse added, producing a paper bag.

'You'll be fine … don't worry … everything will settle down. Just try and stay calm and breathe slowly.'

CHAPTER 4

HOW TO SAVE THE PLANET

'How is she?' Dad asked gravely when he received a call from Sister Gemma. After being reassured that his daughter was absolutely fine, Edie's dad was provided with an explanation of what had happened.

'What are you talking about?' Dad was incredulous. 'My daughter's never had a *panic attack* before!' Edie's bemused dad was given a brief account by Sister Gemma of how the nurses had helped Edie, and how the attack had settled very quickly. Half an hour later, Dad picked Edie up from the hospital. He kept her off school the next day – and obliged her to see the GP.

The surgery's youthful new doctor was called, appropriately, Dr Young. Edie immediately warmed to the fresh-faced and cool-looking arrival, with her nose and ear piercings. Edie felt she was someone she could relate to more easily.

Vicky Young spent almost forty minutes with Edie. First, she listened attentively to her story. Next, she fully examined Edie and organised some basic blood tests. Finally, the GP sat with Edie and explained her findings.

'We don't refer to panic attacks so much now. Rather, we call it "panic disorder", of which episodes – or attacks

– are a feature. Panic is an extreme form of anxiety, so the experience can be very distressing. Is that what it felt like to you in the hospital?'

Edie thought about the question. 'Not exactly. I had some of those symptoms you described – my heart racing, sweaty, body trembling – and I couldn't catch my breath. But I wasn't ... like ... worried about dying.'

'No, but you said it started when you were sitting next to the bed.' Edie nodded. 'And the envelope in your hand made you feel anxious for some reason?'

'Yes, that's right.'

'Well, I imagine that's how it was set off. There's often a trigger factor.'

'So, what can you do to treat panic attacks – I mean panic disorder?' Edie was keen to know.

Dr Young shimmied her chair over from behind the desk to be closer to Edie. 'Panic attacks are actually quite common in teenagers, especially in the context of a traumatic life event. And you've certainly had more than enough to start something like this. And, in answer to your question, there are two aspects to controlling the problem.'

'Okay.' Edie was eager to know what could help.

'The first thing is how to avoid having future attacks. Stress is often a factor that contributes to attacks, so try and keep out of tense or stressful situations as much as possible.' Edie's brow puckered; she was keenly aware that stress was part of a detective's life.

'Do plenty of exercise – it doesn't really matter what kind – eat well and make sure you get enough sleep.' Edie felt self-conscious: she did virtually no exercise (apart from judo), had been sleeping badly and adored takeaways.

'Alright, I can try that. But what if I feel one of those attacks starting again?'

'Right,' said the doctor clearly. 'This is important. Don't fight the attack, and remind yourself that it will pass ... They don't normally last more than twenty minutes maximum – often just five or ten. If you can, sit down and stay where you are. Try and focus on peaceful, relaxing things. And somebody stroking your back or comforting you can help.'

'They gave me a bag to breathe into at the hospital,' Edie mentioned.

'We don't really suggest that any more, but it can be helpful, especially if you've been breathing really fast – hyperventilating is the medical term. Paper bag, though, never a plastic one.'

Edie felt overwhelmed by all the information, and concerned that the problem might interfere with her detective work. 'I read on the internet that there are drugs you can use to treat it.'

'Yes, there are. That's the second part of what I wanted to say. If the attacks ... or disorder ... become more frequent or get worse, then we can try something like CBT – that stands for cognitive behavioural therapy. It's a course of sessions with a psychologist where they teach you specific techniques. And, yes, there are drugs that can be used if that doesn't work. But let's not think about that right now. This will all most likely settle down, so try not to worry ... stay relaxed. You can even try meditation ... or mindfulness ... recordings on the internet.'

'They've got those on Spotify,' Edie added.

'Even better. I want you to come back and see me again in two weeks. Or sooner, of course, if anything happens or you need to talk again.' The GP stood up to indicate the session was finished and leant over to shake Edie's hand. 'One last thing. Is it okay if I share our discussion with your father? You're a very mature girl and I wanted to check.'

'Yes, of course, Dr Young,' Edie responded, then turned towards the door.

On Wednesday, Edie got up early. She felt fine, and there was a lot to do.

From the shed on the garden decking, Edie grabbed some fresh hay which she sprinkled – along with chopped broccoli from the fridge – on the floor of Günther's cage. Edie found it hard not to pick up her guinea pig for a cuddle, but today he'd have to make do with a stroke instead.

Shouting goodbye at Dad and Eli, Edie left the house at a quarter to eight and turned right along Cecile Park. Normally, she took the bus to school, but today she fancied the walk and some fresh air – plus a bit of time to think about the day ahead.

At the end of the road, Edie made a left up Crouch Hill towards Hornsey Lane. Her mind was abuzz with the different cases, which she was trying to order in terms of danger and solvability. Just a week earlier, Edie had been disappointed at the speed of progress of her detective work, but now it seemed like there was too much going on. At the weekend, Edie intended to organise her thoughts and make a proper plan. Structure brings you freedom, as Papa had once advised her.

Paying no attention whatsoever to her surroundings, Edie ploughed headlong into someone coming out from the Alba Hotel. Edie's school bag fell to the ground and, unzipped at the top, half the contents spilled out. Losing her footing, Edie stumbled to the ground, her shoulder hitting the nearby wall.

'I'm so sorry!' came a woman's voice from behind Edie. 'I didn't see you coming. Are you okay?'

'I'm fine,' said Edie without looking up, focused on shovelling pens, pencils and books back into her rucksack.

'No, I've hurt you,' insisted the woman. 'Look, your blazer's all scuffed up,' she added, brushing the dust away from Edie's upper arm.

Embarrassed, Edie twisted towards the woman. First, she saw just the shoes, ankles and trousers of someone who'd crouched down low to the ground. Next, Edie looked up to see the one face she wished to avoid.

'Are you sure you're alright? You seem to have gone very pale.'

This was terrible detective work, Edie thought, bumping clumsily into a suspect in one of her very own cases. Edie was going to wreck it before she'd even got properly started.

'You look familiar ...' the woman said, as she helped Edie to her feet. Casually dressed in a yellow sweater and dark grey jacket, the woman peered more closely at Edie. 'Have we met before?'

Initially dumbfounded, something dawned on Edie as she gathered herself. Was this an opportunity, perhaps? It was important for a detective to be flexible in the moment, taking advantage when an opportunity arose.

'Maybe,' she answered. 'I was here – I mean inside the hotel – a few days ago. I think I saw you then,' Edie lied, keen that any supermarket encounter stay unconsidered.

'Well, that must've been it,' replied the unsuspicious woman. 'Are you staying here? No, that's a silly question – of course you're not, you're in school uniform.'

Edie repeated her fib: 'My grandparents … from Canada … are coming over and are thinking of staying here.'

'Oh, that's nice. It's very comfortable here,' she said, glancing over at the hotel. 'And cheap – for London, that is!'

It was all Edie needed. 'You sound English. Are you here for a holiday … or to see family?'

'Oh no!' the woman corrected. 'You're right, though, I am English, but I moved to North America after university …'

As the woman paused wistfully, Edie's detective radar started beeping, aware that she might be on to something – but also knowing that she needed to stay cool. 'North America?' Edie asked innocently. 'Whereabouts?'

The unwary woman seemed willing to engage in conversation. 'Canada first, but then I moved to California for a while – Santa Monica – and now I'm back in Toronto. For love … always moving for love.' The woman's mind seemed to be drifting, but she refocused her attention: 'Anyway, is that where your grandparents are from, Toronto?'

'Yes, Toronto, but I've never been there … hardly ever see my grandparents.' Keen to find out more, Edie tried to deflect the conversation tactfully: 'So, how come you're in London?'

'I'm researching a new book,' the woman replied gamely. 'I haven't been back in London for years, so I need to see how it's changed – make sure the book is accurate. I'm a novelist.'

'Wow!' exclaimed Edie, genuinely impressed. 'That's brilliant. What kind of books do you write?'

'Detective books, actually. Thrillers. The latest one is set in London and Cambridge. I'm actually visiting Cambridge on Saturday to do some research. There's going to be a grisly murder in the famous Fitzwilliam Museum.'

'What's the book called?'

'It's called *Serendipity*.'

'What does that mean?' Edie probed, unfamiliar with the word.

'Well, serendipity normally refers to good things happening by chance. But, in my book, I explore whether good things might happen for reasons beyond chance, beyond luck.'

Edie was about to say something else, but the woman glanced down at her watch. 'I'm sorry,' she said. 'It's quarter past eight and you'll be late for school. Look, it's been lovely to meet you and – again – sorry to have knocked you over.'

'Don't worry, I'm fine,' Edie repeated. 'And I won't be late. It was nice to meet you too.'

As Edie turned to go, however, the woman tapped her on the arm. 'You didn't tell me your name.'

'Oh, it's Edie.'

'Well, have a good day, Edie,' the woman said, as Edie waited with bated breath.

'And I'm Rochelle.'

After school, Edie made her way to the gates where she found Harry Coranger leaning against a nearby wall. Although they were in the same year, Edie and Harry were in different classes for most subjects and Edie hadn't seen him during the day. Unless, she wondered, he'd been deliberately avoiding her.

Edie greeted Harry warmly: 'Hi.'

'Hi' came a colder return.

'Do you still want to go to your house?' Edie asked, imagining he might have changed his mind.

'Yes, of course,' Harry replied grumpily, although the way he promptly set off suggested no lack of interest.

'Hey, wait!' Edie hurried to catch up with Harry at the bus stop opposite the school. 'I don't even know where you live.'

'Sorry.' Harry glanced at the bus app on his phone. 'There's a 214 coming in two minutes, then the next one's not for eighteen minutes.'

'Okay. So where do you live? I thought you cycled to school, anyway.'

'Camden, and I do cycle sometimes,' Harry responded, seeming calmer. 'But I knew you were coming back today. And we don't have much time – we need to get there before my Dad gets back from work.'

'Right,' Edie said, at which point the 214 bus appeared.

A few minutes later, they were sitting at the front of the top deck, children from different schools filling most of the seats further back. For a while, neither Highgate Hill pupil said a word. Then, as the bus descended West Hill towards Gospel Oak, Edie broke the silence.

'Harry, if you want me to help, then you're going to have to tell me more about what's going on.'

Harry sighed heavily. It was clearly an effort for him to open up, Edie observed, but it was essential if she was going to help him. 'Okay,' Harry conceded. 'Why don't you ask me questions – you're supposed to be a detective – and I'll try to answer them?'

That was all Edie needed, so she grabbed her notebook. 'First of all, how did you know my Supersleuth email address – I hadn't told anyone about it or even set up the detective agency back then?'

'That's easy,' Harry replied quickly. 'I know the guy at the printing shop where you got the Supersleuth cards made. He's my friend's brother and he told us about your plans when we were out bowling one evening.' Harry smiled – an appealing, asymmetric smile that had a natural warmth.

And so Edie proceeded with her questions. Harry's dad, Heath Coranger, worked as a landscape gardener at Regents Park. He sounded like a great father, but Edie was interested in his recent unusual absences.

'Well,' Harry sighed. 'For weeks, Dad just hasn't been around like he usually is ... No, that's not quite right ... He's been saying he would be somewhere, then he just isn't there.'

'Can you give me an example?'

'Yes. School football matches. I'm the captain of the Year 8 team and he's never missed matches … but this term he's missed three out of four – including a cup final.' Clearly troubled, Harry didn't want to look directly at Edie, so carried on staring out the window as the bus advanced through Kentish Town towards Camden Town. A siren wailed as a yellow-and-blue chequered police car raced away from the local police station.

'And what does he say when you ask him where he's been?' Edie asked once the din had abated.

'He says he's been at work … had to work another shift … one of the other gardeners was off … stuff like that. But I don't really believe him. You see, he never normally lies and his face gives him away when he does. And he loves his job – he's been there for years – but he's never had to do extra shifts before.'

'Is there anything else?' Edie probed further.

'Yes, there is … but we get off at the next stop.' Harry stood up, rang the bell and they both descended the steep stairs. Once off the bus, they started walking left up noisy Camden Road, away from Camden Town and its popular market.

Edie waited for Harry to add to his answer, which he did when there was a break in the traffic. 'He's got some strange bruises on his arm. He thinks I haven't noticed … keeps his sleeves down … but I can see them when he comes out of the shower. His legs too, I think.'

Edie made a note, but Harry clearly wasn't finished. 'And he doesn't often have dinner with me any more. We've always done that together. He's a brilliant cook … vegetarian … but now he says he's had a big lunch or will eat later.'

'Maybe that's true?' Edie enquired.

'Could be,' Harry agreed. 'But it doesn't feel right. We used to cook together, but now we never do.' Edie nodded: one thing she knew for sure was how important it was to trust your instincts.

Opposite Camden School for Girls they turned right down Murray Street. 'One more thing. Dad's got some new friends. I don't even know if they're real friends, more like new people he hangs out with. And I don't really like them.'

Before Edie could interject, Harry pointed down the street towards Camden Square and North Villas: 'That's where Amy Winehouse … the singer … died. Gets lots of tourists, it's annoying.' Instead of going in that direction, however, Harry turned sharp left into a very narrow street called Camden Mews. 'This is our road, just down the end … Oh, and I should warn you, my dad's a big environmentalist, really green, so it's an eco-house.'

Unsure exactly what to expect, Edie was surprised as she neared Harry's two-storey, cottage-like home.

Both side walls were covered in grass, or some other grass-like material, as far as Edie could tell; it was certainly odd to see grass (or whatever it was) growing vertically. The front walls had some kind of cladding, which made the house look padded. On closer inspection the padding appeared to extend to the side walls too, underneath the grass. Solar panels were attached to every free space on the roof, and the eaves guttering had cup-like contraptions to catch rainwater and channel it indoors.

Whilst the adaptations to the exterior made the building look a bit ugly, the garden was stunning. At the front, foliage of different kinds interweaved with flowers of all shapes and colours: Edie recognised an early pink fuchsia, blood-red rhododendrons, a purple lilac, tulips and end-of-season primroses (Mum's favourite flower; Dad's was snowdrops). Mixed with these were dozens of assorted potted plants, carefully placed to complement the design.

Edie followed the stepping stones over a small mound that added height to the garden, on the top of which was an elegant rockery. On the other side, the path led to an oval pond with water lilies: a frog leapt off a floating leaf as Edie approached, making a delicate plop as it hit the water. Transfixed, Edie's reverie was broken by Harry beckoning her over as he opened the front door.

Inside, the house had a modern and airy feel: an open-plan kitchen-diner, plenty of natural light and an abundance of wooden furniture. It was cosy and warm, although Edie couldn't see any radiators.

'There's underfloor heating through the whole house,' Harry explained. 'Electric, powered through the solar panels on the roof. Most of the water we use, except for drinking, is collected from the roof and gutters. We shower in rainwater …'

'Is it hot?' Edie enquired.

'Yeah. Same as normal – just rainwater instead.'

Through the kitchen window, Edie gazed out into the back garden. Completely different to the front, it looked like a giant vegetable patch. Edie could make out broad bean plants and possibly chard leaves amidst a sea of other edible greenery. Behind the vegetable patch were several trees covered in white and pink blossom – fruit trees that would likely bear apples, pears or cherries later in the year.

In contrast to all the natural wonder, attached to an outside wall on the right-hand side of the house was an electric car charging point and a narrow driveway.

'We have an electric car,' Harry volunteered from behind Edie's back. 'Dad must be out with it now. We were one of the first people to get one, years ago. I told you – he's kind of crazy green, ultra-environmentalist … wants to save the planet.'

The messages from the end of *An Inconvenient Truth* were very much on Edie's mind.

'Look, I don't know how much time we have,' Harry cautioned. 'Dad said he'd be working late today, but that doesn't explain why the car's gone – he always cycles to work – so let's start searching.'

'What are you suggesting we should be looking for?

'I don't know. As I said, I've already had a good look around, but maybe with your eyes … well, maybe you'll have better luck.'

'Look out for anything out of the ordinary,' she directed. 'Anything that seems out of place. Maybe been moved. And be sure to check the less obvious spots.'

'I'll take the loft, the only place I haven't looked properly. Maybe you should check downstairs,' Harry suggested. Edie agreed.

As she was already in the kitchen, Edie started searching the space systematically, but she soon stopped. Nothing looked suspicious and time was limited. She considered the other ground floor spaces, and the study beckoned to her.

It was unlocked, so Edie immediately got on with the task. The room was small but well organised, with only enough space for a desk and shelving. On the walls were a number of family photos: Harry had no siblings, so Edie imagined the baby and toddler images were of her new school friend (could she call Harry a friend now?), and she presumed the woman with Heath Coranger in the older photos was Harry's mother. She was beautiful and they looked happy. Edie paused momentarily, her own memories clouding her mind. She snapped out of it. Edie checked behind the photos and then turned her attention to the shelves.

Unable to find anything behind or on top of the books, Edie was drawn instead to the books themselves. Some were fiction but the majority were non-fiction. There were several books by Al Gore and many others with unusual titles, although it was easy to imagine what they were about: *Environmental Ethics*, *How Are We to Live?*, *The Energy Glut* and *The Uninhabitable Earth*.

Now the desk. Frustratingly, the four desk drawers were all locked with no sign of the key. On the desktop was a stationery tray containing a few bills and a letter from HM Revenue and Customs. Nothing of any interest, but Edie still took photos of each of them on her phone. Collect and catalogue all possible evidence, she thought.

With time now critical, Edie stopped what she was doing, took a second and then closed her eyes. She needed assistance from somewhere. She took four deep breaths, in and out, before opening her eyes and peering slowly around the room. Is there anything I've missed? she asked herself. At first, there was nothing and then, checking the floor, Edie realised she'd overlooked an obvious place: the wastepaper basket.

Several pieces of recyclable material were inside the brown bamboo bin. Kneeling down, Edie rifled through each item quickly, flattening out crumpled pieces of paper – but, once again, to no avail. At the very bottom, though, was something that didn't look like regular paper. Edie heard Harry's footsteps on the stairs as she smoothed out a scrunched-up envelope. On the front was Heath Coranger's name and address as well as 'PRIVATE AND CONFIDENTIAL'. Whatever was inside had been removed.

Edie heard Harry shout out asking where she was. 'In the study,' Edie replied as she turned the envelope over. On the back there was an official red stamp. Just before Harry entered the room, Edie screwed up the envelope again and buried it at the bottom of the bin. But she had mentally noted what the stamp said: 'University College London Hospitals (UCLH)'.

With the search of the interior of the house complete, they ventured outdoors into the back garden. May sunshine had appeared between the clouds, adding to the aura of tranquility. Close up, Edie could now see a rhubarb clump and rows of spring cabbages and baby lettuces, and between them freshly cultivated soil where other vegetables would undoubtedly appear. There was also an intricate drainage system, which ensured that all areas of the allotment received plenty of water. Edie was stunned by what was possible in terms of living with nature and self-sufficiency.

'Pooh!' she exclaimed as something acrid hit her nose. 'What's that *smell*!?'

Harry laughed and pointed to the back of the garden on the right-hand side. He had beautiful hands, and Edie noticed the paleness of his palms. 'Oh, that's the compost heap, where we put all the natural waste. It doesn't usually smell like this, but I think Dad's been neglecting it.'

'Well, it stinks.' Edie held her nose.

'Come on,' Harry encouraged, leading her round the back of the vegetable patch. 'Let's have a look at the shed. Dad spends a lot of time there. He's converted it into another office.'

Half a minute later they were outside a large-ish outhouse – more of a cabin than a garden shed – with green-painted timber cladding.

'It's locked.' Harry rattled the handle. 'There's a padlock too.'

'Is that unusual, or has your dad always done that?'

'Not sure,' Harry frowned. 'I don't remember two locks.'

'Come over here,' beckoned Edie, and Harry joined her at the window. 'What's that inside?'

They both put their faces up against the window, but the frosted glass obscured their view. 'I can't see anything properly,' Harry said. 'It's too hard to …'

He was startled by a noise from behind, which caused them both to twist round abruptly.

'I don't think you'll find much of interest in there' came a genial man's voice from ten metres away.

The man held out his arms. Instinctively, Harry went straight towards him and enjoyed a welcoming embrace. Edie was struck by how much love was embodied in that one simple gesture: a good hug. She was also surprised by the sensitivity and tenderness of the captain of the football team, with his tough exterior and cool manner. Clearly, he adored this person.

Harry smiled. 'Hi Dad. How was your day?'

Edie realised that the silent electric car had caught her unawares. The Toyota was once again parked in its spot. Two other men got out of the car as Heath Coranger replied, 'My day was fine, thank you.'

He looked over at Edie. 'And who might this be?'

'Oh, sorry,' Harry replied coyly. 'This is Edie from school. I was just showing her the house … and the garden.'

Sporting muddied jeans, dirty hiking boots and a black puffer jacket, Heath Coranger looked rough-and-ready cool. Windblown shoulder-length hair and sunglasses added to the effect. 'Well, hello Edie.' He held out a hand. 'Nice to meet you.'

As Edie accepted the handshake, the two other men came over. One was short, stocky and dark-skinned and the other tall with Scandinavian looks and long, wispy, fair hair. 'This is Sven,' said Heath Coranger, half-turning in the men's direction. 'He's from Norway. And this is Jarrah – it's an Aboriginal name. He's from Australia.' Heath's associates nodded but didn't offer their hands.

'I thought you were at work?'

'Earlier, yes. Then we had a meeting with the Confederation Against Planetary Extermination – with one of their committees.' Heath closed down that direction of discussion and looked at Edie.

'So, what do you think of the place then?'

'It's amazing!' Edie replied enthusiastically. 'Really amazing – I love it. We've been learning about the environment and climate change at school – and we've just watched that film, *An Inconvenient Truth*. Have you seen it?'

'Oh yes,' Heath answered, suddenly appearing tired. 'Many times, but it's old news now. Things have got so much worse since.'

'But if we all did what you've done ...' – Edie motioned at the garden and house – 'and did all the things they suggested at the end of the film – the messages – then we ...'

Edie was interrupted, however, by a low calm voice. 'It's too late for all that, I'm afraid,' said Jarrah, without a hint of emotion. 'There's only one thing we can do now to save the planet.'

'What's that?' asked Edie innocently.

'It's obvious,' Jarrah replied coldly. 'Kill all the humans.'

CHAPTER 5

THE POWER OF THOUGHT

Edie didn't sleep well that night. Although Harry's dad had immediately said that Jarrah was kidding, Edie wasn't so sure. She'd stayed a few more minutes at Harry's house, but Heath Coranger's accomplice had remained stony-faced throughout. And the uncertainty was disturbing. Jarrah's comments had been flitting around Edie's mind as she lay in bed. Eventually, she put her favourite Spotify playlist on in the background, and the music seemed to do the trick. She woke up with the chorus of 'Hands in the Garden' by Half Moon Run pleasantly in her head, and then got ready for a school day she was rather excited about.

Via their WhatsApp group, Edie had organised for her gang of girlfriends to meet together over lunchtime. In a vacant room in the secluded art building, the four moved aside various painting implements and huddled around a large tabletop. Edie took a swig from her Dr Pepper and breathlessly kicked off.

'Thank you for agreeing to work together to solve the case of the missing dogs.'

'Cases, isn't it?' interrupted Yasmina. 'You said it was more than one case.' Yasmina took a small mouthful from an egg mayonnaise sandwich. Edie had a strange fondness for

Yasmina that wasn't universally shared. Bright and always cheery, she was meticulous and could be a bit of a stickler.

'Yes, that's right, Yasmina. It's one case … of a number of missing dogs.'

'Well, how many dogs is it exactly?' Yasmina persisted.

Edie sighed. 'I'm not sure of the precise number, but I think it's three or four at least. Maybe more. There's Mrs Solomon's dog, of course, and another one that she told me about on the phone. Their dog apparently went missing a couple of weeks ago … same sort of location.'

'That *is* strange,' Lizzie chipped in, which pleased Edie, as her best friend had seemed less engaged than the others up until now. Then again, Edie hadn't really made the extra effort to check if everything was okay with Lizzie.

'Yes! That's why we're investigating!' Taking her positivity down a fraction, she added: 'I've been searching the local newspapers online and I've found another definite case – three weeks ago, also Hampstead Heath – and at least two possible others.'

'Did you phone up the ones from the newspaper?' Lizzie asked.

'I've been meaning to, but I haven't had a moment. In each case, it seems that the dog has gone missing in an area within about a 200 metre radius of where Mrs Solomon was assaulted.'

From her school bag Edie produced an A4 map of Hampstead Heath, printed in colour from Google Maps, which she laid out on the table. A sea of green was intermittently bisected by narrow paths, blotches of blue signified various ponds and a castle-like image indicated Kenwood House. A black cross inside a circle marked where Mrs Solomon's dog had disappeared, and another cross nearby represented where her friend's dog had last been seen. Two other crosses, in blue, were the possible locations of other missing dogs.

With all the girls leaning over the map, Edie began to share her plan. 'This is a four-man surveillance operation. I mean four-woman operation … no, that doesn't sound right.'

'Let's just call it a four-person operation,' Yasmina suggested.

'Okay,' Edie agreed. 'A four-*person* surveillance … team.' With a pencil she pointed to the various crosses: 'These are roughly where the dogs have gone missing … all around this large area of grass … close to the lake but over the other side of this small footbridge.' She tapped the map for emphasis.

'Are you sure that's a footbridge?' Yasmina questioned, rubbing the tiny black symbol as if it was a smudge.

'Yes, absolutely. I know this part of the Heath, and I've also done some reconnaissance work.'

'Reconnaissance?' wondered Charlie. 'Like what?'

'Like … I went there after school on Tuesday to check it out.'

'Okay,' Charlie said, semi-placated.

Using a red pen, Edie carried on outlining her strategy: 'I've chosen locations for each of you, so we'll have eyes on as large an area as possible.'

'Won't we be together?' asked Lizzie, concerned.

'No, that's too limiting.' Edie drew a red 'L' on the map: 'Lizzie, you'll be stationed here. There's a bench so you can sit down, but maybe bring an iPad so it looks like you're busy with something.' Lizzie nodded, with less than full interest. 'Yasmina, you're here … and Charlie, you're here … near this gate that leads to the wooded section behind the lake.'

'Can I bring a book?' Yasmina asked.

'Yes, of course, but you must make sure you keep a lookout for what's happening, especially on the edges of the grassy area, as that's where the dogs seem to disappear.'

'Is it alright if I bring my dog with me?' queried Charlie.

'No.' Although, she reconsidered immediately: 'Actually, that's not a bad idea, Charlie. What's your dog called?'

'Alan.'

The other three girls laughed. 'Your dog's called Alan?' Lizzie teased. 'That's ridiculous.'

'Yes,' insisted Edie, keen not to waste time. 'That's fine, Charlie. Bring Alan with you – it'll make you blend in with the crowd.' Taking out her phone, Edie glanced quickly at the weather app. 'It's going to be a mixture of sunny and cloudy all day on Saturday … 20 or 21 degrees … so bring water and snacks too.'

'What about a disguise?' Lizzie probed facetiously.

'Yeah! A moustache and hat!' joked Charlie.

'No disguises,' said Edie, straight-faced. 'Just dress normally. We don't want to draw any attention to ourselves. All the other dogs have gone missing around lunchtime, so we should meet at half past eleven and stay until … maybe three or four in the afternoon.'

'That's four hours!' exclaimed Yasmina. 'I didn't know it was going to take *that* long.' Charlie and Lizzie looked similarly downcast at the prospect, but Edie knew what was needed.

'It may be shorter. It depends on what happens.' Edie tried to gee them up. 'Come on guys – could be good fun!'

Whilst they all inspected the map and absorbed the plan for the day ahead, silence descended, which Yasmina eventually broke. 'Edie, what exactly are we looking for?'

This was familiar territory. 'Anything suspicious,' Edie answered. 'Anything at all that looks unusual. A person that seems out of place perhaps ... somebody loitering ... and especially keep an eye out for any dogs that stray off towards the undergrowth.'

'And what if they do?' Lizzie wondered. Charlie's and Yasmina's expressions suddenly became more serious.

'Don't follow immediately,' Edie directed. 'Call us first. Use the WhatsApp group. Once you've called, you can walk towards the area where the dog has gone and one of us will join you. Avoid direct confrontation, but ... if it looks like somebody is going to steal a dog, we need to try and follow – and get some photos. But we do it *together*, so we're safe. Understood?'

They all grunted affirmatively, with no real idea of what they were letting themselves in for.

A classroom in the maths block had been chosen for the afternoon special programme on good mental health. Dad had gladly signed the consent form for Edie's participation, in the knowledge that the course was informed by the Three Principles understanding of how the mind works – the same approach to psychological wellbeing that Edie's mum had been so passionate about. For Edie, the course was a further opportunity to connect with Mum, although her friends were attending without a clue what to expect.

On a table at the front of the classroom was an array of implements, including a snow globe, tennis balls, play dough and coloured pens. As well as the whiteboard and computer screen, there were two extra flip charts to the side. Edie glanced around the room, fascinated. Tacked to each wall were large pieces of paper filled with various images, some with cut-out sections.

'What the hell's going on here?' Lizzie whispered to Edie as they sat at a pair of desks in the second row.

'Not sure,' Edie answered cautiously.

'Is it too late to leave?'

'Yes, definitely too late. Anyway, we should give it a chance.'

After a fidgety few minutes for the class, Miss Watson counted the number of pupils in the room with the finger-in-the-air technique beloved by teachers, and then closed the door.

A smartly dressed woman in a grey suit stepped forward. 'My name's Sarah,' she said confidently. 'And this is my colleague, Toni.'

Toni had the coolest shoulder-length braided hair – which Edie thought might be extensions – and wore very large, almost circular, glasses. Toni waved sweetly at the class, allowing Sarah to continue.

'Both Toni and I are trained school teachers, but we spend most of our time now delivering the PoWaR programme. The reason why we do that is because in the last few years we've seen – over and over in different schools – how much this programme can impact on people's lives. You see, what you're going to learn in these sessions isn't like *anything* you've ever learned before … not like, geography, biology, history … No, you're going to learn something to guide you through the struggles we all experience at some point. Something that will be helpful to you for the rest of your lives.'

'What about maths?' a male voice shouted from the back of the class, semi-chuckling to his mate in the next seat. 'That's pretty important, Miss, isn't it?'

'Yes, it is,' Sarah replied, calmly and crisply. 'But it isn't as important as this. What's your name?'

'Billy Barnes,' the boy replied, grinning. Everybody twisted round to look, unsurprised as Billy had a reputation as a joker.

'Well, Billy. First thing, there's no need to call me Miss. You can call me Sarah, and you can call my colleague Toni. Second, let me ask you: has anything – anything at all – ever happened to you that you've found difficult?'

Suddenly, Billy looked embarrassed, the eyes of the class focused on him. 'No … not really …' he mumbled. He was interrupted by his friend nudging him and whispering something the others couldn't hear. Even more red-faced,

Billy continued unenthusiastically. 'Well, I suppose …' He hesitated.

'Billy,' Sarah added gently. 'It's okay for you to tell us, but it's also absolutely fine if you'd prefer not to.'

'No, it's alright Mi … I mean Sarah … I don't mind saying. Some people know anyway. A few weeks ago my cat Barney died. Run over. I found him by the side of the road. I know it's, like, only a cat, but I loved Barney. He used to sit on my lap every night when we watched TV. And nobody else's. It's been hard … upsetting. I can't get that image of him in the road out of my head.'

'Thank you, Billy,' Sarah said supportively. 'That's good of you to share. Now, just imagine – not just you but everybody in this room – that an upsetting experience like that was a little bit easier – perhaps a lot easier – to live through. That would be helpful, wouldn't it?'

The class was silent. Who could disagree with that?

'Alright,' Sarah resumed after a pause. 'This will be quite a journey over our sessions together – a journey we want you all to enjoy and learn from. But it's not normal learning, it's what we call "inner learning". So, there's no need to take any notes at all during the course. Just listen and participate.'

Edie was struck by the atmosphere in the room. Usually, when people came in from outside school to teach something, everybody treated it as a bit of a laugh. Already this seemed different.

Sarah continued: 'Along the way it will be fun, for sure, but we'll also be talking about serious stuff that happens in life. And there are two important things I want to say about that. First, if anybody gets troubled by what we're discussing, then please tell either one of us or Miss Watson.' Sarah glanced over at the Highgate Hill school teacher, who acknowledged her with a nod. 'Second, in order to be able to do what we want to do, we would like to come to a group agreement about how we will behave.'

Grabbing the remote control, Sarah projected a PowerPoint slide onto the whiteboard. The first slide was a list of statements that Sarah asked the group to agree to following. Whilst the class murmured affirmatively, Edie was particularly struck by the last one:

- Put your hand up when you want to speak.
- Listen when others are speaking.
- Don't laugh or make fun of what people are saying (respect difference).
- Keep an open mind.

'Good, thank you,' Sarah said as she concluded the group agreement. 'And now I'm going to hand over to Toni.'

Toni seemed as if she liked a bit of fun. 'I want you to all stand up please,' she instructed lightly. 'Now, I want you to sit down if your answer is "yes" to any of these statements. But, you *must* be honest – your friends will know if you're not. Okay?' Everyone agreed so she started.

'Sit down if you've been to Italy.' A third of the class did so, including Edie and Lizzie. 'Sit down if you don't like roller coasters.' Three more pupils took their seats. 'Sit down if you've eaten an orange today.' Nobody moved, to the class's general amusement. Four random-sounding questions later and Billy again found himself the focus of attention as the only remaining pupil standing. Only this time Billy looked happy, although he didn't really know what he'd done to deserve the packet of Maltesers thrown to him as a prize.

Once the class had settled down, Toni played an animated video about the PoWaR programme, which Edie remembered stood for Principles of Wellbeing and Resilience. The first four sessions of the programme would be about understanding how the mind works and the remaining sessions were about how this applied to real-life situations.

When the video had ended, Toni addressed the class meaningfully: 'There are two points from the video that I'd like you all to think about over the next few days – talk to each other and speak with your families – as they are key and we'll be coming back to them in more detail throughout the programme.'

Toni walked over to a flip chart and lifted up the front cover to reveal the first key point, which she read out aloud to the class: '*Where do you think your feelings are coming from?*'

Straight after, Toni repeated the question but emphasising the word 'think', prompting one of Edie's classmates to put his hand up energetically.

'Yes, go ahead,' Toni encouraged.

'That's easy,' Matt Howarth volunteered. 'I'm happy when Spurs win and sad when they lose!' Cheers and boos erupted in equal measure across the room.

'Well, let's see about that shall we, Matt,' Toni replied steadily. 'And, remember, keep an open mind.' Toni returned her attention to the whole class.

'The second key point in the video was this: *What if we have everything we need in life already inside us?* It's a question we'll be coming back to later, but before the break please can you …' At the word 'break', there was an instinctive shuffling of pencil cases, forcing Toni to raise a hand in the air which they'd agreed was the sign for quiet. Surprisingly quickly, the children around did the room did so and silence descended.

'Thank you,' Toni continued. 'I would like each of you to circle, on the piece of paper you have on your desk, four of the topics you'd like us to cover in the second half of the course – the topics about real-life problems. We can't possibly do all of them, but we will cover the most popular ones. Hand your paper in at the front and *don't* put your name on – it's anonymous. Please be back here in ten minutes.'

exams
concerns around money
anger
stress
addictions
social media
potential
how the mind works
depression
conflict
self-confidence
bad habits
insecurity
motivation
bullying
worry
relationships
worries about
peace of mind
food
the past
anxiety
communication
worries about the future
insomnia

____

____

____

I'd like to know more about...

Circle any topics that you would like to explore or add some of your own on the lines

Edie looked down at the topics and intuitively circled the four of most significance to her: 'anxiety', 'stress', 'conflict' and 'worries about the past'. As Edie stood up, Lizzie remained hunched over her desk, as if shielding her own sheet. From an angle, Edie noticed two completely different words circled on her best friend's sheet: 'self-confidence' and 'insecurity'. A second later, Edie noticed Lizzie circle a third word before carefully folding the paper in two. The word was 'relationships'.

In the girls' toilet, Edie splashed water over her face to freshen up. As she dried off, Yasmina entered and walked over to the sinks.

'How are you finding it?' she asked Edie.

'Yeah, good.'

'It's amazing, isn't it? I mean … they're amazing … Sarah and Toni … and we're learning all this cool stuff.'

'Yeah, it's really good. But it's tiring. My head's … like … spinning, and we've got another session to go.' Edie threw her paper towel in the recycling bin and made for the door: 'See you in there,' she called over her shoulder, without mentioning why she was feeling troubled – that the course was bringing back memories of her mum.

By Friday evening, Edie was exhausted. In her bedroom, she lay on the bed watching *Stranger Things* on her laptop. Somehow she'd managed, just, to keep up with her schoolwork, but the half-term break was looming in a week and several pieces were due in beforehand, including an English essay on the witches in Shakespeare's *Macbeth*, which she hadn't even started. Edie was becoming increasingly overwhelmed with juggling schoolwork and being a detective – and the list of unanswered emails and calls she needed to make for her investigative work was rising steadily.

Edie dozed briefly when her phone rang: the screen identified Ethan Stephenson as the caller. Edie sighed; she'd had no time to make any progress with Ethan's brother's biochemistry exam case, so there was no point in speaking. She let the phone drop from her hand onto the duvet, flopped backwards and closed her eyes again. But then, as if out of nowhere, something came to her.

She sat upright, readjusted the pillows, closed Netflix and opened the internet browser. On the King's College London website, Edie easily found the staff email address she was looking for and carefully composed a message:

Dear Dr Bannon,

I am a Year 8 pupil at a school in north London. I really love science, especially chemistry, and would like to become a doctor. My father is a doctor, as was his father, and I would be the first female doctor in the family! My dad studied medicine at King's College and suggested I write to you because biochemistry is so important. I also saw on the website that you teach the medical students. It would be really great if I could come and visit you, and learn about what you do in the laboratory and how to become a doctor.

Thank you.
Edie Franklin (Year 8)

Once she'd sent the email, Edie composed a text to Ethan Stephenson saying she'd come up with an idea to help his brother, Martin, but it was going to take a little time. She'd try to call him over the weekend to explain.

Invigorated, Edie then opened the Notes pages on her MacBook and started making a list of all the things she needed to do before school ended for the half-term break. She was determined to alleviate the stress by organising her thoughts and structuring her time.

Under a 'Schoolwork' heading, Edie itemised the English, art and science pieces, then remembered a maths paper that also needed finishing. She recorded how long each piece of work would take to complete alongside a proposed day. Under a new section, Edie wrote down the main detective cases she was working on.

The Case of the Long Lost Friend was peculiar, and Edie didn't quite know what to make of Donna Redmond and her strange story. Yet, the whole thing seemed too bizarre to have been made up and, to Edie, it felt like there was something important lurking within. Edie made a note to herself to be more systematic and more scientific with her investigation.

Less peculiar, but also a bit odd, was the Case of the Missing Dogs, but at least Edie had a practical plan for the next day. She also jotted down a reminder to search for other such cases over recent weeks. More straightforward, perhaps, was the Case of the (Possible) Exam Fraud, and for that Edie needed to wait for Dr Bannon's reply.

Then, there was Harry Coranger and The Case of the … what exactly? Edie was mulling over meeting Harry's dad, Heath, and what a great name that was for somebody who loved gardening and the outdoors. Lost in thought, Edie didn't hear the first call from her father, although the second from the bottom of the stairs snapped her back into the present.

Leaving various items on her bed and desk, to be worked on later, Edie washed her hands and went downstairs for dinner.

CHAPTER 6

EVERY DOG HAS ITS DAY

Getting out the house on Saturday morning without giving anything away had been easy. Dad and Eli were distracted by the excitement of watching the Arsenal vs Leicester FA Cup Final live on the giant screen at the Emirates Stadium – with about 30,000 other fans. Edie's fib about going to Lizzie's mid-morning passed unquestioned (even though Edie rejected a ride there), and the only sticky moment was when Dad had looked quizzically at an item on Edie's bedroom floor that had fallen half-out of her rucksack: 'What do you need my binoculars for?'

'Any interesting activity, Lizzie?' Edie asked quietly into the microphone on the headphones lead that connected to the phone in her pocket. Lizzie's spot on the short top edge of the large rectangular area of grass, just off a busy path, was important because the undergrowth where Quincy had gone missing was behind her.

'Zulu One here,' Lizzie responded snappily, her jokey tease eliciting giggles from Yasmina and Charlie. 'Nothing to report so far.' There was a short pause during which Edie sighed. 'Over,' Lizzie concluded. More giggles.

Edie was about to say something about sticking to the plan and taking it seriously, then thought better of it.

Edie could see her best friend clearly through the binoculars, and she actually looked the part. Sitting on the bench close to the bendy tree, Lizzie could be just one of the many teenagers out in the weekend sunshine, listening to music through wireless headphones. Some kids were with adults, some with friends; some were walking pets, others were alone. Often they were sitting down either on the grass or, as in this case, on a bench.

And that was the basic principle of a surveillance operation of this kind: careful observation without being noticed. With tracking surveillance – like when Edie followed Rachel Summers – the emphasis was on 'ghosting' (watching somebody without being seen), but in the missing dogs operation there was no particular person to watch or follow, so the focus was on monitoring the location methodically for what happens, but without being seen yourself. And that meant all involved blending in and not acting suspiciously, just as Lizzie was doing as she nonchalantly started tapping at the tablet on her lap.

Edie had rejected any disguise, use of cover or having a point person out in front, in favour of an emphasis on not drawing attention, avoiding confrontation and maintaining good communication. The WhatsApp group made keeping in contact easy and, for her next check-in, Edie switched over to video and called the team again.

'Charlie, anything happening over on your side?'

Charlie's position – on the long edge of the rectangle opposite Edie – also had a wooded area behind.

'Zulu Two reporting,' Charlie replied. 'Nothing to … er … report.'

'You're reporting that there's nothing to report?'

'Correct – over,' Charlie confirmed, keeping an admirably straight face. The video jinked as Charlie broke off a piece of her sandwich and fed it to her dog, sitting politely at her side on the grass. Everyone had immediately fallen for the cute dog, with his floppy ears and black, brown and white colouring. He seemed very sweet-natured, quietly accepting hugs and cuddles from his admirers.

'Come on,' Edie encouraged her. 'Show us Alan properly.'

'Okay,' Charlie replied, flipping the phone to camera and directing it down at her canine buddy, who was munching happily on a morsel of chicken and bread.

'Ahhh,' came the collective response. 'He's gorgeous,' Lizzie added. 'Is he a beagle?'

'Yes,' Charlie confirmed. 'We've had him since he was a puppy – for two years – and if you think he's gorgeous now, imagine what he was like then!'

As their minds wandered, Edie felt the need to kick on. 'Yasmina, anything happening down your end?'

'Zulu Three here,' Yasmina replied a little too quickly, as if waiting for her moment whilst also being a bit uncomfortable with it. 'Nothing going on this end.' She was stuck out on the very far side by the footbridge, obliged to use a large log as a seat and didn't look particularly happy on screen. 'And my bum's wet.'

'Maybe walk around a bit?' Edie suggested, keen that Yasmina stay on board until the end of the operation. Yasmina didn't look like she was about to follow the instruction. 'Okay, thanks everyone,' Edie concluded. 'Keep looking out and I'll call again on the next half-hour, at half past one. Unless, of course, something happens beforehand.' Expressions on faces told a story of lack of expectation.

Edie's problem was that her accomplices seemed to be getting fed up. After two more rounds of calls, thirty minutes apart, messages on the chat group indicated that the girls were ready to go home – an hour or so earlier than had been agreed. The snacks had all been consumed, iPhone games had been exhausted and jokes had run dry (including the Zulu reporting). Edie was about to call it all off when she noticed a man, probably in his sixties, shouting loudly from the central area of grass.

It sounded like 'Bambi! Bambi!' but he was too far off to be sure. Through the binoculars, however, his demeanour didn't appear to be of somebody crying out for a friend or a child – but of somebody calling to their dog.

'Bambi! Bambi!' came the sound again, as the man made his way in Charlie's direction.

Without hesitation, Edie threw her bits and pieces into her rucksack, slipped the bag on her back and set off speedily across the grass. With one hand holding the binoculars to keep visual track of the man, Edie used the other hand to call the group, her headphones still in her ears.

'There's a man in the middle … on the grass … yelling for his dog … I think,' Edie panted. 'He's heading towards

Charlie and I'm following. If anyth …' but Edie's sentence was interrupted.

'Hey, Alan, stop! Alan! Alan! Come back!' Charlie shrieked. In answering her phone, Charlie had lost hold of Alan's lead, and he'd suddenly started barking fiercely and torn off into the undergrowth behind where she was sitting. Edie switched visuals from the man to her friend, who was now standing and looking panicked.

'Alan!' Charlie screamed again, as she set off after him into the wooded area.

'No, don't!' Edie yelped. 'Don't go alone – remember what I said!' But Charlie, who'd left her personal belongings on the bench, paid no attention and soon disappeared from view. Whilst commanding the other girls on the call to help, Edie burst into a run, dodging people and animals alike – and getting some unfriendly stares in response. She temporarily lost sight of Bambi's owner, and then, halfway across the large expanse of grass, she noticed him duck into the wooded area only twenty metres to the left of where Charlie had entered.

Arriving half a minute later at Charlie's bench, Edie stopped for a moment to catch her breath. With Yasmina and Lizzie still on their way, Edie couldn't wait. She took a quick puff of her asthma inhaler, grabbed Charlie's phone from the ground, and entered the undergrowth via a narrow track between two large oak trees.

'Charlie!' she shouted as loud as she could. 'Where are you?' No response. 'Charlie!' Edie repeated, increasingly worried.

Still nothing, so she tried another tack: 'Alan! Alan!' From deeper in the wood Edie heard a bark, so she set off in that direction. Pushing her way through the bushes, a thorny branch scratched her cheek and nettles stung her hands, but, undeterred, Edie pushed on and shouted again. 'Alan!' This time the bark was nearer and easier to follow – straight ahead and a little to the right. After two more rounds of 'Alan!', Charlie came into sight in her pink fleece, crouched down low and hugging the dog.

'Naughty boy!' Charlie berated him (at the same time as showering him with kisses), as Edie arrived.

'Are you okay?' Edie asked, kneeling down to join in the stroking.

'Yes, I'm fine. But Alan gave me quite a shock! Naughty boy,' she repeated lovingly.

'What's he eating?' Edie queried, observing something red in Alan's mouth and a few similar cubes scattered nearby on the ground.

'He must've found this meat here – it's like steak or something,' Charlie answered, removing the piece from Alan's mouth and throwing the rest away. 'Just like that dog over there,' she pointed.

Edie followed Charlie's finger and, a few trees over, Edie saw the man who'd been running across the grass searching for his own dog – which clearly he'd found. Edie stood up and took several paces nearer so he could hear her.

'I'm glad you found your dog,' she said.

'Thank you,' the man replied from a kneeling position, gently patting his own pet. 'He does that sometimes, despite his terrible vision … bolts off … He seems to have found something to eat. Weird, though, there were a couple of men lurking around here – they took off when they saw me.'

Edie glanced around but there was nobody else to be seen.

'Or maybe they got scared when they heard him,' the man added, looking down at his large, beloved dog. 'Mind, his bark's worse than his bite. Looks and sounds fearsome … but he's a softie really.'

From the corner of her eye, Edie saw Yasmina and Lizzie arrive and comfort Charlie. 'He's a beautiful dog,' she told the man. 'An Alsatian, isn't he?'

'No. Well … yes, sort of,' the man responded. 'People often call him that, though … to us … he's a German shepherd.'

'What's wrong with his eyes?' Edie asked innocently. 'They look misty.'

'Early cataracts,' the man replied, gently patting the dog's tummy. 'Unfortunate, but he's a lovely fella.'

Edie paused for a moment before backtracking: 'You named a German shepherd Bambi?'

The man laughed, before correcting her: 'His name's not Bambi – it's Rambo!'

Back home, it was five o'clock and Edie had a couple of hours before babysitting. She received a call from her dad to tell her that Arsenal had won the FA Cup Final, and that he was celebrating with Eli and other fans – singing football chants and enjoying football talk – in a cafe in Finsbury Park, close to the stadium. Moods were high. From Edie's perspective, it meant she had an hour before they'd be home.

Edie took out her laptop and sat cross-legged on her bed. The afternoon had been far more eventful than she'd imagined, although not more eventful than she'd hoped. In terms of the missing dogs operation, Edie had acquired valuable information which she transferred to her laptop: the dog stealers seemed to be still at large, although nobody had managed to get a clear look at the two men; they lured the dogs with chunks of meat, which was broadly consistent with what Mrs Solomon had suspected; and the abductors didn't appear to be intending to harm the dogs. Edie couldn't be sure about the last part, but it was a hunch.

There was something that was niggling Edie, though. Something about the afternoon, something about what had happened. She reviewed the events in her head but to no avail. If anything, the repeated thinking was scrambling her thoughts rather than providing clarity. It was as if a clue was there but just out of reach.

Out of reach for now, anyway.

To distract herself, Edie opened Outlook and pressed 'New Message'. In the 'To' domain Edie typed in Rabbi Gabel's email address, which she used for communication about her bat mitzvah preparations. As it was Saturday – the Jewish Sabbath – Edie wondered whether she should be writing to the rabbi at all, but quickly decided it was more important to give advance notice of something she wanted to discuss in their lesson.

Just before Edie closed Outlook, a new email appeared. Initially, she thought Rabbi Gabel had replied incredibly quickly, and then realised that the message was from Dr Bannon, the biochemistry lecturer at King's College. He was happy to meet Edie, although it would have to wait until the half-term week. Edie closed down the laptop, lay flat on her bed and within moments was asleep.

Forty-five minutes later, Edie was awoken abruptly by a banging sound. In her dream, Heath Coranger was hammering a nail to seal a small wooden box. He was in his beautiful back garden, amongst all the vegetables, and Edie had a strong feeling of wanting to know what was inside the box. As he bashed away, the expression on Heath's face appeared to be a warm and friendly, but he also looked suspicious.

'Sweetheart,' Dad whispered, continuing to knock as he entered Edie's bedroom. 'It's quarter to seven, and you've got babysitting in fifteen minutes.'

'Sorry, I must've fallen asleep.' The laptop was precariously close to the edge of her bed, so Edie moved it nearer to her body. The computer contained valuable information that she couldn't afford to lose, and Edie reminded herself to back up everything on her external hard drive. It wasn't the first time she'd made that particular mental note, but the task was so boring that Edie kept on delaying.

'Okay … thanks Dad, I'm up,' she said, rolling off the bed into a standing position. 'Just give me a few minutes.'

'Fine, try not to be late.'

'I know. Did you have fun with Eli?'

'Fantastic,' Dad replied, taking a step towards his daughter. 'Wonderful time and a great result.' He peered closer at Edie's face. 'What's that scratch on your cheek, luv?'

'Oh, nothing.' Edie dismissed him quickly. 'It was … my nail … while doing a face scrub. Now, can I have some privacy to get ready, please?'

Dad looked unconvinced but left the room. Good spirits made him less inquisitive.

Hair quickly brushed, change of clothes, face freshened with tap water and key items shoved into her rucksack. At one minute before seven Edie rang the neighbours' bell.

Edie heard the soft pattering of small feet before the front door began to open, very slowly, accompanied by child-like voices, the male instructing the female on how to open a door. Edie looked down to find Max, in full Batman suit, pushing the door, whilst Olivia, in cute pink pyjamas, stood on tiptoes and held on to the latch.

'Edie!' they chorused together.

Olivia wrapped her arms sweetly around Edie's left leg, whilst Max tugged at her arm. 'Can we play a game?' he asked. Before Edie had a chance to answer, Olivia had a different idea: 'No!' she exclaimed. 'Read *Bear Hunt* to me!'

'Sorry about that, Edie,' Max's dad interjected from the hallway. 'And kids … you shouldn't be opening the front door alone.'

'But I wasn't alone,' Olivia explained. 'Max was with me.'

'What I mean is … you shouldn't be opening the door without me or mum with you. I've told you before.'

Max's dad ushered Edie into the house as she tried, unsuccessfully, to close the door behind her.

'Let me do it,' he intervened. 'It's a bit broken and doesn't close properly. Once the door was left wide open for a couple of hours before anyone noticed. There's a knack …' He performed a strange two-handed manoeuvre with the latch. 'That's it … must get it fixed.'

As the door shut behind Edie, the children were still clinging on – both to their babysitter and their own particular plans for the evening.

'I can do both,' Edie suggested. 'Play a game with you,' she glanced at Max, 'and read a book with you, Olivia.' The toddler beamed.

'Well, that's very nice of Edie, isn't it, kids? Now come upstairs with me to get ready for bed first – teeth and hands – then Edie will come up. I know Mummy wanted to speak to Edie about something first.'

'Scott, is that Edie?' shouted Donna from her bedroom. 'Tell her I'll be down in a second. Put her in the lounge – and bring the kids up to their rooms.'

Scott gave Edie an eyebrows-raised look conveying that he was going to do all of that anyway. Edie smiled, took the initiative and settled herself on the comfortable slate-grey sofa. Two minutes later, Donna was sitting next to her, having quietly closed the lounge door.

'Thanks for your email in the week,' Donna began. 'You said you've established that Rachel did indeed move to Canada, then to California and then back to Toronto.' Edie nodded, then Donna probed more insistently than she'd anticipated. 'Exactly what sort of online searching did that involve, Edie, and has she changed her name?'

Edie didn't want to give too much away – not right now, anyway – so she decided to steer the conversation elsewhere. 'What I'd find really helpful please, Mrs Red … I mean Donna … is if you could provide me with a list of all the places you've been to over the past two or three weeks. Or as many as you can remember, and the times of day when you were at those locations.'

'Good idea,' Donna replied. 'So you can triangulate and see if she's been at the same places as me at the same time? Does that mean you've spoken to Rachel yet – that is, if it is her?'

Unsure how to reply, Edie was let off the hook by Scott yelling from the kitchen that they really needed to leave.

'Okay, Edie. I can do that for you. It won't take me long as I keep a diary. I'll cover the past two … no, three weeks, up until when … up until today?'

'Yes. Up until today would be good.'

'Well, the last part's easy. I spent most of today in Cambridge – I took the kids there to see the canals and punts … my old haunts, favourite spots … all the beautiful buildings. Tiring, but we had a lovely time.'

Edie felt a fluttering in her chest. 'You went to Cambridge today?' she enquired tentatively.

'Yes, I just said so. Scott was busy and it was something to do – an outing – we decided last night over dinner. I even managed to have a spin around the Fitzwilliam Museum. Not really for the kids, but I love it there.'

Edie's palms began to sweat at the name of the museum. 'Is everything okay, Edie? It's just that you've gone a little pale.'

CHAPTER 7

A SIMPLE TWIST OF FATE

'Another good night', Edie scribbled in the dream notebook. No fraught, lifelike reminders of a time, or a person, surfacing unpredictably in that subconscious state. It was a quarter past ten when Edie awoke, refreshed, with the May spring sunshine spilling through the window. The blind was still broken.

Edie got out of bed, grabbed a bowl of dry bran flakes and a glass of orange juice from the kitchen, and sat at her desk. Her lesson with the rabbi wasn't until early afternoon, before judo, so she had some free time. First, Edie got her schoolwork out of the way as per her new timetable – boring except for the geography essay on the effects of loss of biodiversity. Then Edie turned her attention to the far more important subject of her detective investigations.

On her desktop computer, Edie opened the internet browser and once again typed in 'missing dogs north London', below which a long list immediately appeared. Edie was familiar with the stories in already visited faint font and nothing new of obvious interest appeared, so Edie tried a slightly different phrase: 'stolen dogs north London'. Again, a lengthy list, largely things she'd seen before, but two new pieces appeared at the top. Edie was about to click on the first one when the doorbell rang.

Expecting an Amazon delivery of a new piece of spying equipment (which had cost most of her savings and Edie didn't want Dad to know about), Edie jumped up. At the top of the stairs, however, it was clear that Dad had beaten her to the front door. But it wasn't a delivery driver.

'Good morning, Donna' Edie heard Dad announce before inspecting his watch. 'Or rather' – he shook his head as if surprised with himself – 'I should say good afternoon.'

'Hi, Mark,' Donna replied coolly, uninterested in the time of day. 'I hope you're having a good Sunday.'

'So far, so good. How's the babysitting going? Is everything okay?'

'Absolutely fine,' Donna said. She held out a large white envelope: 'Please can you give this to Edie. It's some of her homework that she left last night.'

Confidence when lying, Edie observed, was key to believability.

As Dad accepted the offering, Donna looked past him, as if instinctively checking her surroundings. Edie was sure she'd been noticed, sitting on the top stair, yet Donna said nothing. From her raised vantage point Edie could see – over Dad's right shoulder – that there were red capital letters on the front of the envelope, possibly her name. Dad turned over the envelope, ran his fingers over the back flap and realised that it was sealed shut.

'Thanks very much, Mark,' Donna closed down the brief conversation. 'Enjoy the rest of your day.' And with that, their enigmatic neighbour turned on her heels and was gone.

Dad closed the front door, turned round and encountered Edie at the bottom of the stairs. 'This is for you,' Dad stated with an undertone of curiosity. Did he actually believe Donna's ruse about its contents?

'Thanks,' Edie replied quickly, trying to derail any lurking doubts. 'I need this to finish my geography homework.' In a flash, Edie was back upstairs in her room and tearing open the envelope.

Inside, there were three sheets of folded A4 paper – no letter, no note and no sign of to whom the information might refer, as Donna had used initials instead of full names. Initials that, on scrutiny, Edie assumed related to individuals: 'DR' presumably referred to Donna and 'SR' would be her husband, Scott. It was as if the document was created by somebody accustomed to protecting information from interpretation by others. Somebody familiar with keeping secrets.

On her bed, Edie laid out the three sheets of paper, each one containing a table for one of the three preceding weeks. Each day was subdivided into boxed time periods and, within every period, there was a note about what DR was doing, where and with whom.

Edie carefully read all the meticulously drafted text. Assuming what was written was accurate, she should now have what she needed to be able to (somehow) cross-check against Rachel Summers' movements over the same weeks. Quite how Edie was going to get that information was far from clear. Recalling something from the last PoWaR class, she decided not to try and solve that problem now. When her mind was settled, and probably when she least expected it, the answer would come. Edie filed away the tables and returned to her immediate task: stolen dogs.

Edie opened the first item on the internet search list, dated two days earlier. An article from the online edition of the *Camden New Journal* described a man who claimed his dog had been abducted in Regent's Park, close to London Zoo. The man, reportedly a dentist, was convinced that his beloved Labrador retriever had been taken because, in six years, the dog had never strayed. The police, however, saw things differently: Benny had been tied to a railing whilst the dentist used a public toilet; the lead had likely loosened, and the dog was probably enticed away by the smells of nearby animals. Yet, in a busy part of the park, nobody had seen anything. It seemed suspicious to Edie.

About to click on the second story, Edie was interrupted by a WhatsApp message alert on her phone:

Lizzie: Hey. What's up?

Edie paused from looking at the computer list.

> Edie: Not much. Done homework now working on cases. You?

> Lizzie: Nothing really. Just hanging. Playing hess with Ava.

> Lizzie: Chess, playing chess. With my sister.

Edie smiled. She loved Lizzie's younger sister, who was the junior school chess champion. Neither Edie nor Lizzie had ever beaten her.

> Edie: Didn't think you meant playing hess! Are you winning?

> Lizzie: No!!! Lost four games in a row.

> Lizzie: What are you up to later?

> Edie: Bat mitzvah class and judo in the afternoon. You?

All the previous messages had followed quickly one after another, but now there was a pause. Edie watched 'Lizzie typing ...' appear on her phone screen, but it disappeared after a bit and no new message arrived. Whilst waiting, Edie checked her emails and other social media on her phone, then returned to WhatsApp. Expecting a long message, Edie was surprised by what emerged.

> Lizzie: There's something I'd like to talk to you about. Can we meet later?

Edie felt concern rise within her. She didn't hesitate.

> Edie: OK, sure. Will call you later. When I'm back.

Lizzie: XX

Edie: XX

Almost as soon as Edie finished her kisses, Dad shouted up from the bottom of the stairs: 'Edie, we're gonna be late! Need to leave in five!'

'Okay!' Edie yelled back, her tone a semi-automatic response to Dad pressing her. 'I'm coming!'

About to leave her room, Edie noticed the desktop computer was still whirring and the last website she'd visited was still open. Edie didn't like other people prying into what she was working on, so she grabbed the mouse to close down all the remaining browser tabs. In doing so, Edie realised that she still hadn't checked the second new story on the list about missing dogs. There wasn't time now, but as Edie clicked the cross in the top right-hand corner, she noticed the two-line blurb below the story title. The breed of dog was a basset hound.

At the synagogue, Edie was ushered by a bossy older woman towards one of the seats in the corner of the main administrative area, close to the rabbi's office. Edie felt awkward sitting there, in full view, as synagogue staff carried on busily with their routine activities. Eventually, the door to Rabbi Abby Gabel's office opened and a nervous-looking boy, younger and shorter than Edie, sped out and made his way swiftly towards the exit.

'Hello, Edie,' beamed the rabbi, as she beckoned her next pupil through the doorway. Used to the rabbi's brisk manner, Edie quickened her step and took the chair on the opposite side of the desk to the rabbi.

'So, how are you, Edie?' Rabbi Abby asked, then followed immediately with another question. 'And what exactly is on your mind … I mean, with the email you sent me?'

In the modern Reform Jewish world, there were now many female rabbis, although Dad remembered when he was a child and all the rabbis were men. Something else that had changed was the naming of rabbis. Whilst it used to be customary to only refer to the rabbi by their surname – Rabbi Gabel, for example – nowadays, it was normally the title and first name. Like Edie's dad, who was called Doctor Mark at the surgery (except by the older patients who found it disrespectful), Edie's bat mitzvah teacher was known as Rabbi Abby. Edie found all the B's a bit of a mouthful, but that was how Rabbi Abigail preferred to be addressed.

'I'm fine … thank you. I've done all my bat mitzvah homework from last week …'

'Oh, good. Pass it over.'

Edie handed the written material to her over the desk. After a cursory peek, and an affirmative raising of the eyebrows, Rabbi Abby placed the pages to the side and folded her hands. 'So, Edie, tell me more about what you mentioned in your email.'

'Alright,' Edie sighed nervously. 'Thank you for letting me talk about this. I know it's not my bat mitzvah work, but it's important.'

'Not to worry,' Rabbi Abby interrupted. 'Anyway, lots of things in philosophy overlap with Jewish learning – and with Jewish ethics – so it's not totally unconnected.' The rabbi consulted her watch. 'But we've only got forty-five minutes, Edie, so what exactly is it you want to discuss?'

Edie pulled some photocopied papers, a notebook and a pen from her bag. 'Okay,' she started, 'you know how you told me that you studied philosophy at university before becoming a rabbi …'

'That's right,' Rabbi Abby interjected again. 'At Oxford. Loved it!'

'Right, well, I thought you might be able to help me with a philosophical problem.' Edie hesitated, unsure of herself.

Rabbi Abby looked intently at her pupil. 'I assumed as much, Edie, from your email. Tell me, what exactly is your philosophical problem?'

Suddenly, Edie felt embarrassed, but the opportunity would be missed if she didn't continue. 'Well,' Edie began gingerly, 'I'm trying to understand the difference between *fatalism* and *determinism*. I've been reading some of my mum's old philosophy books, but it's difficult … and I've got stuck.'

'Well, you've come to the right place!' the rabbi declared cheerfully. 'And something you won't know, Edie, is that I did a masters in philosophy straight after my undergraduate degree, and my thesis was on the connection between determinism and spiritualism. But what's the purpose of this new learning? What are you hoping to find out?'

'Oh, right,' Edie responded. 'It's for a special project.'

'Hmm … a special project. And would that be a school project?'

'Not exactly.'

'And might it be a project related to your detective work?'

'Well … yes.' Edie admitted.

'Fantastic!' Rabbi Abby beamed. 'I love a problem with a purpose – and your detective stuff is way more exciting than bat mitzvah homework! Spit it out then and we can get cracking!'

Edie relaxed a fraction. 'Okay, I'll try to explain. I'm trying to find out if things that happen in the world are meant to be … are destined to happen, no matter what. In Mum's old philosophy books, and online, I've read about these ideas – fatalism and determinism – but I don't really understand them.'

Edie took a breath as the rabbi looked on, before adding: 'If you can explain the basics to me, maybe I can see how it all relates to my case.'

Rabbi Abby paused, which didn't happen often, before smiling. 'Fine, Edie,' she replied, in a serious but also playful kind of way. 'Let's do that.'

The rabbi cleared away some items from the centre of her cluttered desk, then beckoned Edie towards her. 'Come closer, Edie. Round this side of the desk.' Rabbi Abby found a sheet of A4 paper from a drawer and grabbed a pencil from a pot. She lay the paper in the middle of the desk at an angle, so Edie could see it, and then drew a straight line across the page.

'Okay. This line represents the spectrum of possibilities – or beliefs if you like – about why things happen in life. On this end of the spectrum are the views of FATALISM.' She drew a small vertical spike on the far left end of the line and wrote the word in capitals above it. Closer to the middle, but still on the left-hand half of the line, she then wrote 'DETERMINISM'. 'I'll come back to these words in a minute, Edie, but, broadly speaking, they are the beliefs that what happens in life is already determined – is destined to happen.'

The rabbi then moved her pencil to the far right-hand side of the horizontal line. 'Here, we have those who believe the opposite,' Rabbi Abby continued. 'It's called INDETERMINISM' – which she also wrote in capitals – 'because it's the opposite of determinism.'

Edie scrunched her forehead. 'Okay, but what exactly does indeterminism mean?'

'That life is arbitrary. That what happens is largely chance – or luck, if you prefer. From where you're born to when you die, and everything that goes on in-between. It's all …' The rabbi hesitated and looked up. 'It's all … what's the right word … *random*. Yes, random,' she added triumphantly.

Edie waited a few seconds. 'That seems sad. Everything happening by chance and for no reason.'

'Well, some people might feel that, but others – maybe you've heard of the existentialist philosopher Jean-Paul Sartre – believe that the randomness provides a motivation to live life to the full. They believe in the importance of enjoying and getting the most from life at every opportunity, as you never know what will happen next.'

Edie was about to question that view, but didn't get in fast enough.

'There's even some evidence in physics that subatomic particles – particles smaller than an atom which make up the universe – can behave randomly. Anyway, enough of that for now ...'

Rabbi Abby moved her pencil back to the far left-hand side of the line. 'Are you still with me, Edie?' She nodded eagerly. 'Good. Well, back over here are the opposing viewpoints of fatalism and determinism. And what do you think the opposite of things happening due to chance might be, Edie?'

Caught off guard, Edie did what people often do to bide time when cornered: she repeated the question. 'The opposite of random?'

'Yes.' The rabbi grinned. 'The opposite of random. Let me give you a clue. Another word for random is unplanned. So, what's the opposite of *un*planned?'

'Planned?'

'Correct! A-plus!' teased Rabbi Abby. 'And who – or what – do you imagine the "planner" might be?'

Edie flushed. She didn't like being put on the spot like this. 'God?'

'Yes! Top marks again!' Rabbi Abby tapped her pencil on the paper. 'As I said earlier, at this end are those who believe that everything that happens in life is already determined, or fated. That what happens is somehow already decided. And the most commonly held view of *who* is doing all the planning, who is deciding what happens, is God. This is fatalism.'

'Do all religions believe that?' Edie asked, just about following the explanation.

'No, but a lot do, both ancient religions and modern day. The Romans and Greeks, for instance, believed in the power of three goddesses, the Fates, to decide people's destinies. And, in Islam, fate is felt to be the decree of Allah.'

Intrigued, Edie asked: 'What about Christianity?'

'Well, yes, more or less. Christians believe that only God can control a person's fate, and that God has a plan for each of us. Have you read *Hamlet*?' Edie liked Shakespeare but shook her head. 'Never mind. But Christians also believe that human beings have *free will* – which means the ability to decide what to do, but they tend to act – to exert that free will – in accordance with God's desires. Christians also believe that God only cares about the big and important decisions and will intervene for those, but isn't interested in whether you put your left or right sock on first! I know, it's complicated!'

Edie was about to agree, but Rabbi Abby had another question for her. 'God isn't the only possible planner, though, Edie. Can you think of anything else that could be responsible for our fate? Another clue: imagine Punch and Judy.'

Edie's mind went completely blank for several seconds until an unexpected thought crept in. 'I was watching *The Matrix* with my brother last week, and in the film the whole world isn't real. It's a giant computer program into which our minds are inserted, which makes it look real to us. But, in fact, everything that happens is controlled by the computer program. And by whoever, or whatever, created the program.'

'I'm impressed, Edie. You're absolutely right. Philosophers have argued that what happens in the world might not be fated by God, but could be controlled by some kind of super-scientist.' Rabbi Abby paused, put down her pencil, raised her right hand in the air and started wiggling her fingers. 'Or by a sort of puppet master – pulling all the strings – and we are all just the puppets.'

Edie was feeling increasingly bamboozled and slightly discomforted by the idea that she could be somebody's puppet. Plus, she hadn't even got to the strange coincidences of the case yet.

'It's this section, though, Edie' – Rabbi Abby placed her pencil halfway between the centre and far-left end of the line – 'that's the most interesting. If you don't believe that everything that happens is by chance and you don't believe it's all directed by God and fated, then you probably sit around here. And this is where I would place determinism.'

Edie was confused. 'I'm sorry, Rabbi Abby, but I don't understand.'

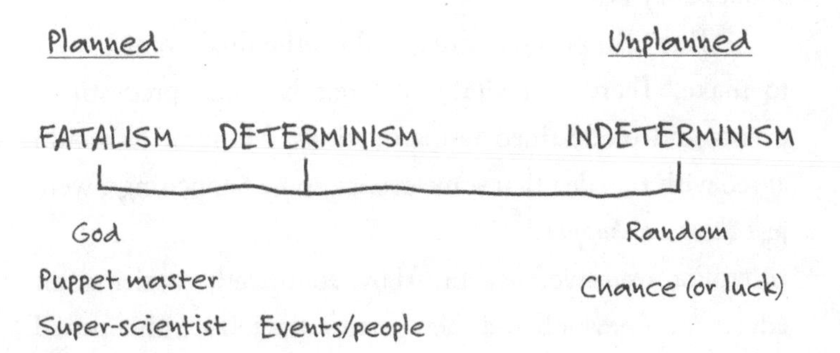

'Well, you asked me about fatalism and determinism, and we've talked about the first, so now let's discuss the second. People who believe in determinism believe that what happens in the world is already decided *in some way*. But there are variations of determinism. Strong determinism is like fatalism, only it's the super-scientist rather than God.'

Edie was perplexed. 'But that's not how the world works, is it?'

'No. I agree with you, Edie. I don't believe that the universe operates like a giant machine or computer. But we haven't got long and I want to tell you about a softer form of determinism, as it's really important.' Rabbi Abby looked intently at her pupil and wrote two words lower down on the paper, away from the line: 'EVENTS' and 'PEOPLE'.

'Here' – the rabbi tapped the paper again – 'with this softer kind of determinism, people believe that there is a difference between events and people. Or, maybe better, between events and *human actions*.' Rabbi Abby lowered her voice as if to emphasise the significance of what she was about to say next.

'This is important, Edie, and it's the final point I want to make. There is a vital difference between predestined events and predestined human actions. Many of us would agree with the idea that some events, some happenings, were just *meant to happen*.'

'For example,' Rabbi Abby continued, 'noticing an advert for a new job and then getting the job – as happened to me with this role – or finding the perfect puppy. Things that people often say were, or weren't, *meant to be*. As if they were predestined events. Already decided.'

'But do people really mean it when they say something was meant to be?' Edie probed. 'Do they really mean it was *actually* predestined?'

'Perhaps not always,' Rabbi Abby answered honestly. 'But I think, yes, people often do mean it.'

Edie braced herself. 'And would that include meeting somebody?'

'Absolutely!' Rabbi Abby retorted immediately. 'Bumping into somebody on holiday or an old boyfriend at a party could definitely be that kind of event. While some people would think such a meeting was just a coincidence, others might feel it was meant to be.'

This was now right at the heart of the Rachel Summers case, so Edie pressed on. 'And what about if two people, who hadn't seen each other for ages, keep turning up at different locations at the same time, although they don't actually meet?'

Rabbi Abby put the pencil down, sat back in her seat and eyed Edie carefully. 'That's a very specific question, Edie. Would it, by any chance, have something to do with the case you mentioned?'

Shuffling in her seat, Edie decided to open up. 'Yes, sort of. Sounds a bit crazy, I know, but I'm investigating why two women seem to keep missing meeting each other at certain locations and – if they actually are just missing each other – whether they're meant to meet for some reason.' Edie suddenly had another thought. 'Or a reason why they're not meant to meet.'

'Hmm,' Rabbi Abby considered, looking less than convinced. Momentarily, Edie regretted her disclosure; she was more comfortable keeping her cards close to her chest. 'Sounds a bit hoaky,' Rabbi Abby replied. 'But, yes, I guess that could be an example. A bit like the film *Final Destination*. Have you seen it?'

Edie shook her head.

'Well, in that film a bunch of high school students miss a plane that crashes, but it turns out they can't escape their fate as death catches up with each of them in the days that follow.' Edie's face changed from engaged to forlorn. Rabbi Abby paused, realising the implications of her words.

'Are you saying my mum's death was meant to happen ... was inescapable?' Edie posed.

'No,' Rabbi Abby responded immediately and very gently. 'Absolutely not.' She reached across the desk and took Edie's left hand in hers. With her thumb the rabbi gently stroked the back of Edie's hand. 'Your mum was an incredibly brave woman, who took on people and organisations much more powerful than she was. Took them on for their wrongdoings. And she did it all for the sake of justice, not a big pay cheque, and because it was the right thing to do.'

Edie's expression turned to one of pride, albeit sad pride, which allowed Rabbi Abby to carry on whilst still stroking Edie's hand. 'Edie, your mum was killed by evil men who would stop at nothing, not even murder, to protect themselves. Her death wasn't meant to be – at least not in my book. It was a brutal deed brought about by people who knew exactly what they were doing and who were completely responsible for their own actions.'

The rabbi waited for a response, but Edie remained quiet. Rabbi Abby placed Edie's hand delicately on the desk. 'All of which – if you don't mind, Edie – leads me back to what we were talking about before, to the softer form of determinism.' The rabbi indicated a point on the line, halfway between the far left and the middle.

She continued: 'The idea behind this form of determinism is that while there still is an overarching predestined framework within which the world operates, there is also scope for human actions to play a part in determining how life unfolds.'

Rabbi Abby paused. 'You look confused, Edie.'

'No, I'm okay,' Edie replied tentatively. 'Just ... what do you mean by "how life unfolds"?'

'Well, this is where something called free will comes in, Edie. Within this largely predestined universe in which we live, human beings have choices – and, indeed, make choices – in terms of how they act and what they do. That's free will. And those choices can, to an extent, play a part in shaping the direction in which things happen around us. The direction in which life unfolds.'

Leaning back in her chair, Rabbi Abby looked pleased with herself at remembering the complicated philosophical ideas.

Edie wasn't quite finished. 'So,' she pursued, 'people can shape what happens even if the main things are already decided?'

'Yes,' Rabbi Abby confirmed. 'To a degree. When you leave the synagogue today' – she glanced up at the clock and noticed how late it was – 'you might decide whether to go and buy a Twix at the newsagent or go straight home. That's you exercising your free will, Edie. In other words, you're making your own decision about what to do. That particular action of yours is unlikely to dramatically change the overarching direction in which the world is heading, but it's your action and will affect you and some others in some small way.

'But with free will comes something called moral agency. Some actions we take have a moral or ethical dimension – meaning they may be good or bad – and human beings can choose which path to take. The men responsible for your mum's death acted badly, very badly, with implications for your family and for many others close to you. Through their actions, those men shaped the direction of your lives. They were responsible – only them, and it doesn't mean your mum's death was somehow predestined.'

Rabbi Abby let the moment sit, providing space for Edie to digest all the information. She could sense the young girl's mind ticking over, although she wasn't expecting Edie's riposte.

'But Mum's death led me to becoming a detective and to solving the crime that Mum had been investigating … so maybe her death was meant to be, maybe there was a purpose?'

Rabbi Abby could hear the concern in Edie's voice and also see it in her frown. Trawling her philosophy lecture memories, she eventually answered: 'You're right, Edie. It's true that certain things have happened since your mother's death and, indeed, because of your mother's death. And who knows, with your detective work you could go on to solve bigger crimes, crack even bigger problems and maybe even save the world from climate change! But that's not quite the same as your mum's death being predestined.'

The uncertainty on Edie's face suggested a different tack might be needed. 'When your mum and I chatted about the Three Principles ...'

'You spoke to Mum about that?' Edie interjected.

'Yes,' Rabbi Abby replied, taken aback. 'Sorry, I thought you knew.'

'No. I mean ... yes, I knew about Mum's interest in the Three Principles, but I didn't know she talked about it with you.'

'Oh, yes,' responded the rabbi with a deliberate lightness. 'We attended a few courses together and had a number of conversations – in this very room ...' – she gestured – 'I'm a big fan, and use the Three Principles understanding as part of my own learning and development, and also in my teaching.'

Edie was surprised. She knew Mum had attended courses and programmes, so it wasn't a revelation that somebody else – even the rabbi – did likewise. Rather, it was the disconcerting realisation, again, that other people had their particular relationships with Mum. It sometimes felt as if those particular bonds diminished Edie's own extraordinary relationship.

'So,' Edie wondered, 'how are the Three Principles helpful in what we were talking about?'

'It's the Principle of Mind. The idea that we're all part of something much bigger than ourselves, something beyond the comprehension of our limited human brains. An energy or life force to which we're all connected, and which we're all part of. Most of the time we aren't even aware of the connection, but from time to time we sense it. And this thing that's bigger than us – this life force or Principle of Mind as it's also called – is responsible for all the beauty and love in the world, as well as all the extraordinary happenings.'

Edie was captivated. 'So,' Rabbi Abby added, 'it remains the case that those criminals were solely responsible for your mum's death. But, as time passes, the ways of the universe – of mind – might become revealed, for instance, by you starting a detective agency.' For the final flourish, Rabbi Abby beamed and slapped her palms on the desk. 'And perhaps even saving the planet!'

Edie smiled as Rabbi Abby peeked again at the clock on the wall. 'It's time, Edie,' she announced. 'We've had quite a chat, but the lesson is over for this week. Isaac Gold will be waiting outside – he's got his bar mitzvah in a couple of weeks.'

Edie packed up her bag quickly, and at the door turned round: 'Thank you, Rabbi Abby. That was really helpful.'

'A pleasure. Next week we'll be back on your bat mitzvah pieces, okay?' The rabbi winked as she added: 'Although, you'll have to tell me how the case is going!'

Her head spinning with all the philosophical ideas, Edie forced herself to concentrate through judo – not least because she didn't want any more bruises. Edie even managed to catch Sensei Dominic off guard with the speed of her Harai Goshi, a new hip throw the teacher had introduced. This time, it was Dominic who ended up on the floor with a sore knee.

Back home, Edie listened to Lana Del Rey on her bed, interrupted by Dad shouting that dinner was ready. Instinctively, Edie checked for messages before going downstairs. Crap, she thought, seeing Lizzie's message sent just recently, at 19:03.

Lizzie: Thought we were gonna meet up? XX

Edie: So sorry! Long day. Can I call u after dinner? X

Lizzie: No. I wanted to meet and talk like I said.

Edie: FaceTime? x

Edie had time to tidy up her desk and get her bag ready for school by the time Lizzie eventually responded.

Lizzie: DW. See you at school

CHAPTER 8

HIDDEN SECRETS

A bad night. The opposite of the previous one. No dreams, but Edie woke at ten past four in the morning.

She'd forgotten to get back to Lizzie and Ethan about things that were clearly important to them, and she hadn't been in touch with Mrs Solomon for a while, despite knowing about the older woman's loneliness in hospital. It wasn't good enough. Edie was disappointing others and thereby disappointing herself. Under-promise and over-deliver, Mum had advised, yet Edie was failing. She needed to turn things around and was determined to start right now.

At six, Edie got dressed for school and, very quietly, went downstairs. At the front door she checked the alarm keypad. Thankfully, Dad hadn't put the alarm on overnight, otherwise the loud beep that sounded when the alarm was inactivated would have risked waking Dad and Eli. An idea had germinated in Edie's mind whilst lying in bed, although the seed of the idea must have crept in when Edie saw Dad working in the lounge the previous evening.

More and more, Dad was using Mum's study on the first-floor landing when he needed to work at home, but he sometimes looked uncomfortable in Mum's old work space, still filled with all her belongings and photos. So, now and then, Dad took his laptop into the lounge instead, which provided an emotional escape. And that's where Edie had seen him the previous evening, hunched uncomfortably in an armchair over his work laptop.

Edie silently left the lounge door ajar, sat on the sofa, picked up Dad's laptop from the coffee table and opened it up on her knees. Clicking the 'Start' button jolted the machine out of hibernation, and the NHS logo quickly appeared, followed by a request to enter a username and password.

Edie flipped the laptop over to reveal, as she already knew, a white label on which Dad had unwisely written all the login information. She typed in what was needed only to be advised that either the username or password was incorrect. Crap, Dad had changed something but not updated the sticky label. On a hunch, Edie tiptoed upstairs, grabbed Dad's blue alphabetised password book from Mum's study and, under 'N' for NHS, found what she needed. Back in the lounge, Edie entered 'MFranklin' followed by 'Markthedoc7?', and the laptop duly sprang into life.

On the left-hand side of the home screen Edie found a patient records system, an appointments schedule for the surgery, prescribing booklets and a database on evidence-based medicine. Not what she wanted. But in the top right-hand corner Edie noticed two icons that looked much more promising: RFH, which Edie assumed stood for Royal Free Hospital, and UCLH. These were the two hospitals that served patients from Dad's surgery, and also would be responsible for a patient who lived in Camden – like Heath Coranger.

As Edie clicked open the University College London Hospitals icon, she noticed the computer clock read 6:30 – close to when Dad would be getting up. She double-checked the lounge door was open so she could listen out. Once she'd entered the UCLH site, Edie was initially confused by the array of different hospitals listed, and it took her some time to work out that the named institutions – one for eyes, one for neurology, one for tropical diseases and more – were all part of University College London Hospitals. That was why it had an 's' at the end, although the main building opposite Euston station was just called University College Hospital (UCH).

When asked to enter a patient name, Edie typed in 'Heath Coranger' and pressed enter. Immediately, Edie was asked for Harry's dad's date of birth. On her phone, Edie opened 'Photos' then scrolled until she found the recent images of letters from the stationery tray on Heath Coranger's desk. The tax office letter had Heath's date of birth. Once entered, Edie waited a second or two for the search results to appear. The new page showed appointments, both at the main hospital building and in the Department of Oncology, which stretched back over the past six months. She clicked on the top one, opening a new page titled 'Adult Ambulatory Care Cancer Service', which solved Edie's uncertainty about the definition of oncology. To her astonishment, Edie noted the date and time: it was today at four o'clock.

Footsteps down the flight of stairs from Mum and Dad's bedroom – well, Dad's bedroom – to the toilet off the first-floor hallway; a creature of habit, Dad always had a pee after waking up, then went back to bed before properly getting up fifteen minutes later. As soon as Edie heard him climbing back up the stairs, she closed down the computer, put it carefully back in its place and returned to her own room. Four in the afternoon, Edie thought: that meant bunking off her last lesson.

'Are you going to read it?' Yasmina asked at lunch, her voice raised due to the din. The girls were seated as a foursome, two by two, at one end of a long table in the school dining hall.

'No,' Charlie answered immediately, before checking herself. 'I mean, I know it's important and all that, but the book sounds really boring. Why, are you?'

'Yes!' said Edie and Yasmina together, then looked at each other and laughed.

'I am,' Edie added. 'Ms Dylan said it's the most important book ever written about the climate emergency. Even more important than *An Inconvenient Truth* or the sequel she's showing after half-term.' Edie took a mouthful of her vegan burger.

'Depressing book title, though,' Lizzie chipped in, pizza slice in hand. '*The Uninhabitable Earth.* I mean, who would want to live here anyway if it's uninhabitable?'

'That's the point!' Yasmina countered. 'There won't be a planet to live on if we don't change things.'

'Speak of the devil!' said Charlie in a hushed tone, indicating with a slight turn of her head a teacher who had come through the main doors and was now walking down the central aisle, close to the girls' table. Automatically, Edie and the others looked in the suggested direction before leaning in closer. 'She's so scruffy,' Charlie added. 'Hard to believe she's head of department.'

'Or so passionate about her cause,' Lizzie interjected. 'Maybe it's all an act to make us feel sorry for her.'

'Appearances can be deceptive,' Edie countered. She tried to catch Lizzie's eye but Lizzie looked away, avoiding her. 'She's just a good person,' Edie continued, 'committed to preserving the planet and saving humanity.' At that very moment, Ms Dylan turned her head and smiled at the four pupils, as if she'd sensed their conversation. Embarrassed, the girls sat back in their chairs. Edie finished her burger, ate an orange and then asked Lizzie if they could walk up the hill together.

On Broadlands Road, the longer route back to school to avoid the masses, Edie took her opportunity. 'I'm sorry I forgot to call yesterday, Lizzie. It's just that I've had a lot to do and, y'know, with my bat mitzvah preparations and everything …'

'It's not that,' Lizzie interrupted. 'Your bat mitzvah homework doesn't even take very long. You told me that. You're caught up with your new cases … stupid missing dogs. The detective stuff – that's the real reason. That's why you forgot.'

Edie was about to deny Lizzie's accusation, then realised it was pointless. Her best friend was right. And she felt Lizzie was hurting. 'Can we slow down?' Edie asked, feigning breathlessness. 'Sorry, my asthma's been bad … pollen in spring … and the hill.' Edie stopped, sat on a garden wall and took two puffs from her Ventolin inhaler. As Edie held in her breath, Lizzie joined her on the wall – slowly and somewhat reluctantly.

After thirty seconds, Edie let the air out. The day was windless and the sky cloudless. She reached for Lizzie's hand. 'Is everything okay?' she asked softly. That was all it took: Lizzie burst into tears. Edie tried to pull her sobbing friend close but there was resistance, so she waited for Lizzie's shaking to abate.

'What's wrong?' Edie asked quietly.

'It's my Mum and Dad,' Lizzie admitted eventually.

'What about them? Are they getting a divorce?'

'Maybe, I don't know. They've been arguing a lot, and I hear them talking in the bedroom. They whisper, but I can still hear what they say – or some of it. Dad's had a lot of pressure at work … been in bad moods for weeks, maybe months. Mum thinks he doesn't love her any more … wants him to see the GP for depression, but he refuses.'

Edie listened intently before a pause gave her an opportunity. 'You said that things are a bit better now. That's good, isn't it?'

'Sort of,' Lizzie responded, still staring at the ground. 'Yes, they're not arguing so much, and even cuddling sometimes, but they've come up with a plan.'

'What kind of plan?' Edie asked, seeing the concern visible on Lizzie's face.

Lizzie looked up. 'They say they need a change … we need a change, as a family. Dad's got a job offer in the United States and they think we should all go.'

'What?' Edie exclaimed, upset for Lizzie and also realising the implications for their friendship. 'Where?' she asked, worried. 'And when?'

'Washington,' Lizzie answered. 'And soon. July. As soon as summer term ends.'

As Edie exited the school gates, Mr Bowling marched past, raising his bushy eyebrows inquisitively. She offered a doctor's appointment as an excuse for leaving early and didn't linger long enough to be challenged.

On the bus down Highgate Hill to Archway, Edie had two quick phone calls to make from her seat at the front of the top deck. First, Edie dialled the Royal Free Hospital, where the switchboard operator passed her through. Her call was answered almost immediately.

'Ward 6 East. Sister Gemma speaking. How can I help?'

'Oh, hi,' Edie said, surprised to be reunited with the kind nurse. 'This is Edie Marble here. You helped me, like a week ago, when I sort of passed out.'

'Yes, of course. You were visiting Mrs Solomon, the woman who'd been attacked. How are you?'

'I'm fine, thanks. The doctor says it was a panic attack. She's told me what to do if I get another one. I was wondering about Mrs Solomon – how she is and if I can talk to her.'

The silence lasted a few seconds. 'I'm not sure I should say anything – medical confidentiality and all that – but I realise how much you care about her, and I know that Mrs Solomon liked you and wanted to see you again.' As Sister Gemma paused, Edie feared the very worst – but was wrong. 'I'm afraid Mrs Solomon had a stroke last Friday, and had to be transferred out.'

'What?' Edie cried. 'I don't understand. I mean, she was fine when I saw her … recovering from her injuries.'

'I know, Edie. You're right. She *was* doing well, but this kind of stroke – it's called a subdural haematoma – can happen several days after a blow to the head. We had to send Mrs Solomon over to University College Hospital for an operation.'

'Oh no! How is she?' Edie asked despondently.

'I don't know, I'm afraid. You'd have to call there: try the neurosurgical critical care unit. I'm so sorry to be the bearer of this news. I know Mrs Solomon thought you were really sweet, kept talking about you after you'd left … and that strange incident with the man stealing her phone.'

Edie gathered up her bag and descended the stairs as the bus neared Archway, from where she planned to take the Underground. 'Okay. Thank you very much, Sister Gemma.' Her mind distracted, Edie clicked 'End call' at the very moment the nurse was saying goodbye. Edie had run out of time for the second call to Martin Stephenson, but she wasn't in the mood any more.

A fresh idea had germinated, though.

Blue-green glass, shimmering in the afternoon spring sunshine, covered the frontage of University College Hospital on the Euston Road. Six stops on the Northern Line had deposited Edie at Warren Street station in good time, and now she stood outside the main hospital entrance at a quarter to four – still fifteen minutes before Heath Coranger's medical appointment.

At reception, Edie checked the precise title on the Notes pages of her phone and then asked the bored-looking assistant for the Ambulatory Care Cancer Service. Edie had looked up the meaning of 'ambulatory', which was an outpatient clinic where people received cancer treatment without having to actually stay in hospital.

'That's for adults, you realise,' the receptionist advised, fiddling with a curl of hair whilst looking distractedly out on to the main road.

'Yes, I know,' Edie replied. 'It's my uncle. I'm meeting him there.'

'Alright. It's in the Cancer Centre – different building. Back out those doors,' she pointed, 'round the corner in Huntley Street. Second floor.'

'Thanks,' Edie said curtly, legging it out the main entrance as directed.

By the time Edie reached the correct clinic in the Cancer Centre, she was out in a sweat – not helped by the hoodie worn on top of her school uniform and pulled over her head to avoid being recognised. Edie still had a few minutes, so she slipped into the women's toilet. Inside, Edie splashed water on her face to freshen up, then unzipped her backpack. From the bag, Edie removed the matchbox-sized item she was hoping to use shortly and placed it carefully in her pocket.

Confidently, Edie exited the WC, took a few steps into the waiting room and sat in a discreetly positioned chair, shielded by a concrete floor-to-ceiling pillar. From a nearby coffee table, Edie picked up a *House & Garden* magazine and started flicking through absent-mindedly. Whilst her fingers turned the pages, her eyes surveyed the area.

There weren't many patients around and Harry's dad was easily identifiable with his casually bedraggled appearance and give-away hair. Sitting at a right angle a few rows in front, Heath Coranger was visible to Edie, but she doubted he would notice her. The way his coat and recycled mesh bag were thrown carelessly over the adjacent seat suggested that Heath was familiar with his surroundings. At five past four, Edie's suspicion was confirmed when a nurse appeared from a door marked 'Outpatients Cancer Treatment', went over to Heath and struck up a friendly conversation. He replied and she laughed.

Despite the softness of their voices, Edie heard the nurse indicate that the doctor was ready. Heath said something in reply, looked over towards the toilets, then pointed at his coat and bag on the chair. The nurse nodded and gestured that it was safe to leave his belongings there. As the nurse advanced towards the consulting room, Heath got up and made for the toilet. This was Edie's chance, but she needed to be quick.

As soon as the toilet door was shut and the red 'Engaged' sign visible, Edie stood up. Nonchalantly, she headed towards where Heath had been seated, stopping at the chair next to the one on which his coat and bag were placed. Edie sat down, picked up a *Good Housekeeping* from the table and opened the magazine at a random page. Whilst appearing to read, Edie cast a look around the waiting room: there were around ten other people present – patients with their loved ones – and none appeared the slightest bit interested in what she was doing.

Edie removed the audio surveillance device from her pocket, careful to keep it invisible in her clenched fist. The bugging device she'd bought didn't need to be turned on; the battery inside meant it was ready to go. Surreptitiously, Edie moved her hand over the chair's armrest and deposited the listening device into Heath's jacket pocket. There was risk involved as he might stumble across it, but Edie felt the risk was worth taking.

From behind Edie there was a sudden yelp, making her heart leap. Instead of spinning round immediately, Edie waited a good ten seconds before slowly turning her head. A woman in her seventies, in an old-fashioned, yellow-and-brown checked wool coat, was fussing over a similarly aged man in a wheelchair, who had spilt a cup of tea. The woman was attempting to mop the liquid from his lap with a grey scarf, patting away before attending to the mess on the floor. The incident provided a convenient distraction for Edie, who slipped away back to her former seat just as Heath emerged from the washroom. He grabbed his belongings, put on the jacket and headed for the Outpatients Cancer Treatment door.

Choosing wired headphones over AirPods, because of the more reliable connectivity, Edie placed the earbuds casually in her ear and called the device telephone number she'd previously entered into her Contacts as 'Can Be Heard'. To anybody in the waiting room, she looked like another teenager habituated to music or podcasts rather than a private detective (of sorts) illegally tapping in to somebody else's confidential conversation. Such is the life of a supersleuth, Edie thought.

Having already checked the device at home, Edie was confident it would work in the hospital. But she wasn't prepared for the degree of sound interference and interruption – presumably from the walls and doors – as well as the scratchy noise from movement inside Heath's pocket. As a result, even with closed eyes, a furrowed brow and maximum concentration, Edie could only pick up bits and pieces of the conversation between Heath and the doctor.

Doctor: How .... feeling .... Coranger?

Heath: .... tired .... no appetite.

Doctor: .... got .... blood resu .... not so .... white cells .... infection .... and bleedi ....

Heath: .... do? .... bone ma .... biopsy?

Doctor: Not .... on .... symptoms ....

Heath: .... options?

Doctor: Not .... the NHS.

Heath: .... any other poss ....?

There was a short pause as the doctor seemed to

do something, perhaps on the computer. Edie used the opportunity to adjust her headphones, then move to a seat closer to the treatment room door, receiving a smile from the man in the wheelchair on the way.

Doctor: .... only .... private .... United States .... maybe Cana .... experimenta .... successf .... trials ....

Heath: .... cost?

Doctor: .... ty thousand .... approxima ....

Heath: .... don't .... money.

Doctor: .... palliati .... nursing .... your son.

Heath: (muffled sound of crying) .... long .... have?

Doctor: Hard .... months.

Edie heard somebody blow their nose, then a gently soothing woman's voice. She imagined the nurse comforting Heath, before the scrape of a chair on the floor suggested he was ready to be given his treatment. Ten minutes later, with the audio reception much improved from a different room, the nurse told Heath she'd be back in an hour, and he should press the red button if he needed anything.

Edie ended the call to the device, grabbed her bag and hastily made her way out of the Cancer Centre and back to the main hospital reception.

'Huh! You again.' The reception assistant greeted her coldly.

'Yes. Me again.'

'So, what do you want now?' she demanded.

'The neurosurgical critical care unit, please,' Edie asked politely.

'Well, that's not in this building either, I'm afraid.' She paused, looking Edie up and down. 'Anyway, why aren't you in school?'

'It's my grandmother. And I haven't got long, please.' She gave the fed-up assistant her most sweetly pleading smile.

'You uncle *and* your grandmother,' the receptionist said, unconvinced. 'Well, some would call that pretty unlucky.' She sighed wearily before adding: 'You need the National Hospital for Neurology and Neurosurgery, over in Queen Square, other side of Southampton Row.' She gesticulated with a hand. 'Fifteen minute walk, maybe twenty.'

'Crap!' Edie reacted with frustration. 'Isn't anything actually in this building?'

Before the receptionist could reply, Edie spun round and exited through the revolving doors. On the Euston Road, she reinserted her AirPods, typed the destination into Google Maps, put on one of her Mum's old Spotify playlists and pressed 'Go'.

The first song to play was 'Fight Test' by The Flaming Lips, but Edie hardly registered its relevance as a Scottish voice guided her across communal gardens and through the maze of Bloomsbury backstreets. The sun warmed Edie's head and heart, and she felt good. When 'There is a Light

That Never Goes Out' by The Smiths came on, Edie sang the words as she'd done with Mum, dancing round the kitchen table on a Friday night after dinner. A couple more tracks followed and then, as Edie arrived at Queen Square, 'Meet Me There' by Nick Mulvey began – a song they both adored.

Edie entered the square, sat on a bench and gazed around at the verdant surroundings and children playing on the grass.

The lyrics brought a tear to her eye.

Inside the National Hospital for Neurology and Neurosurgery, Edie made her way through labyrinthine corridors, passed busts of famous doctors and took the lift up to the neurosurgical critical care unit. The family waiting room was immediately to the right – a sea of sorrowful faces. She pushed the button to gain entry to the clinical area and was buzzed in. A nurse pointed compellingly at a sign on the wall, and Edie realised she needed to don a plastic apron, cap and surgical mask.

Once clinically attired, Edie stepped tentatively into a largish room which looked straight out of *Grey's Anatomy*. There were about ten beds, spaced well apart, each of which contained a patient in a critical state. Machines beeped, lights flashed, ventilators pumped, drips fed life-sustaining fluid and staff zipped around with both purpose and calm. For half a minute Edie was hypnotised, until snapped from her trance by a woman in a white coat asking whom she was looking for.

'My grandmother, Violet Solomon,' Edie replied.

'Oh, she's one of mine,' replied Dr Babinski, as per the name tag on her lapel. 'Come with me.'

Edie followed Dr Babinski to a bed in the far corner, where Violet Solomon lay unconscious and oblivious to all the activity around her.

'Really sad, this one,' Dr Babinski started. 'I understand she was doing quite well over at the Free after her assault. A number of days later, apparently, she started feeling dizzy and sick, then a headache, and the CT scan showed a subdural haematoma. She was unconscious by the time they got her over here.'

'Excuse me, Dr Babinski,' Edie said through her mask, as the doctor picked up the clipboard at the end of the bed with information on the patient's condition. 'But what exactly is a subdural haematoma?'

'My apologies. Let me explain – and call me Sophia, please.' Edie's eyebrows lifted responsively. 'After a head injury – sometimes several days or even two or three weeks later – blood can leak between the thin cling film-like layers, the meninges, that surround the brain. The blood can collect in the space between the brain and the skull, the subdural space, causing a clot or haematoma, as we call it.' Pointing towards the thick bandages on the side of Mrs Solomon's head, Dr Babinski continued: 'We did an operation on that side of her skull, where the scan showed the haematoma was. We drilled some holes and were able to remove most of the clot and relieve the pressure on Mrs Solomon's brain.'

Edie grimaced at the notion of the brain surgery. 'Will my grandmother be okay?' she asked, biting back on the guilt of her deception.

'Hard to say, but I hope so. We've got her in an induced coma for now – that means drugs are keeping her unconscious so her brain can rest. But the operation went well, and scans since then have showed no further bleeding. There is, of course, always the chance of some brain damage, but let's hope for the best. We'll know more in a few days when she regains consciousness.'

'Thank you,' said Edie, comforted by the more optimistic prognosis. 'Would it be okay if I had a few minutes alone with her?'

'Yes, of course. Just don't touch any of the tubes or equipment.'

'I won't.'

Edie sat on the bed next to Mrs Solomon as the doctor moved on to another patient. She gently held Mrs Solomon's hand, careful not to displace the clip on her right index fingertip measuring the blood oxygen level. Mrs Solomon's hand was frail, her skin paper-like and dry. Intravenous tubes had been inserted into both forearms just below the elbow, sealed in place with bloodied, see-through adhesive pads. Mrs Solomon's eyes were taped shut, and her chest rose and fell rhythmically as air was pumped artificially into her chest via the plastic tube in her mouth, strapped tightly in place with a bandage that wrapped around her neck. Facial bruises, from the original injury and also the operation, created a battered appearance.

It was a sorry sight, yet also a wonder of modern medicine. The body kept alive by technology, without which Mrs Solomon would be gone. Edie frowned. So much for the physical body, but where was the spirit of Mrs Solomon now, her life force, the essential spark that is the energy of all life?

Without loosening her grip, Edie gently stroked the back of Mrs Solomon's hand with her thumb. She looked at the surrounding medical paraphernalia and her eyes settled on the cabinet near the head of the bed. On the top, next to some sticky tape and gauze, stood a large framed photo of Quincy, Mrs Solomon's beloved brown-and-white springer spaniel, sitting contentedly on the garden grass.

The adorable shot fired a jolt of determination through Edie. 'I'm going to get Quincy back, Mrs Solomon, trust me,' Edie spoke aloud. 'And when you're better – and you *will* get better – we're going to take Quincy for a walk, together.'

At the very moment that Edie said the last word of her sentence, she felt a change of pressure around her fingers. Her hand had been squeezed. Just a fraction, and only for a second, but the sensation was unquestionable. Edie glanced up at the unconscious patient's face, but it remained utterly impassive. Edie wondered if she should alert Dr Babinski, but then anticipated that she'd be told it was just a reflex or Edie's own imagination.

But Edie knew otherwise, and the eerie experience raised her spirits and steeled her resolve.

Edie was back at the Cancer Centre in the nick of time. The chemotherapy treatment had finished quicker than expected and, on turning the corner into Huntley Street, she saw Harry's dad exit the building. Edie called the device, and the immediate rustling sound reassured her of its place in the pocket of the jacket that he was once again wearing. Headphones in and hood up, Edie followed her quarry.

Near Caffè Nero in Grafton Way, Heath Coranger stopped, leant over the kerb and wretched. He quickly pulled himself together and carried on at a surprisingly good pace up busy Tottenham Court Road. Heath Coranger was clearly used to his outpatient treatment, and he was also tough. As he descended the escalator at Warren Street Underground Station, Edie closed the distance for fear of losing him – and also losing her precious spying equipment, which she needed to retrieve.

In the cramped Northern Line carriage, it was easy for Edie to stay inconspicuous. At Camden Town, as half-expected, Heath got off the Tube and ascended the escalator, but he then took a surprising direction – up Parkway rather than towards Camden Road and home. Edie kept fifty metres back and called the device again after it had disconnected when underground.

At the corner of Albert Street and Parkway, Heath paused, checked his watch and then headed into the Spread Eagle pub.

Crap, Edie muttered under her breath. How on earth was she going to get the device back now, as children weren't allowed inside pubs unaccompanied?

She looked at her watch. It was just past six o'clock and the pub was already heaving, inside and out. Perched on the end of an outdoor pub bench, facing away from the other customers at the table, Edie peered disconsolately through the window, wondering what to do. Suddenly, she caught sight of Heath amongst the indoor throng as he took a place in a discrete booth, not far from her own position outside. Three, possibly four, others were already ensconced at the table in the booth, segregated off conveniently from the lively crowd. They were clearly expecting Heath, as they shuffled on their seats to accommodate him. Heath removed his jacket, hung it on a peg at the end of the booth, then sat down and took a sip from a glass of water.

With her vision partially obscured by drinkers milling about inside the pub, Edie found it hard to decipher exactly who else was at Heath's table. Two, maybe three, appeared to be men, their arms more visible than their faces as they picked up pints of beer from the tabletop. Edie peered in harder: was there one woman in the far corner? Possibly, but Edie couldn't be sure.

Edie switched her attention to sound and turned up the volume on her phone. With the device – still in Heath's jacket pocket – further from the centre of the group the audio was even worse. It was also picking up muffled words from those standing nearby. Edie grabbed a notebook from her bag, applied all the concentration she could muster and wrote down the snippets she heard.

Heath: .... hospital .... son .... not good ....

Male voice 1: .... sorry .... the plan .... no .... to waste .... derailed (?) ....

Heath: .... don't know .... not the ans .... viol .... now .... change .... planet .... X ....

Male voice 2 (sounds angry – maybe Jarrah?): .... stick to .... R .... don't know what they're .... twice .... show them .... sent .... bogs .... alone ....

Male voice 3 (or possibly 1 again): .... dom (?) .... jack (?) .... (very unclear).

Voice 3 (likely female, very faint): .... count .... in ....

Several things then happened simultaneously. In a louder, angrier tone Heath spoke incomprehensibly before Edie caught the word 'toilet' and then noticed him march off in that direction. At her own table outside, Edie's attention was diverted by a waitress bringing gin and tonics to the girls now sitting next to her. The distraction led Edie's eye to a man in his forties, standing by the main pub door reading a notice, accompanied by a girl of Edie's age. The young girl pointed to something on the notice, after which they both entered the pub. This was Edie's chance.

Phone and headphones thrown into her pocket, Edie was up in an instant and tailed the likely father-and-daughter pair into the fuggy interior. She was so close that she could easily be a friend of the other child. Smells of beer and sweat pervaded the raucous atmosphere. Jostled, Edie picked a path through the customers towards the nearby booth. A guy in his twenties, carrying three pints of lager in two hands, bumped into Edie and splashed beer onto her school blazer.

Ignoring his apology, Edie closed in on the group in the booth. A quick look over her shoulder revealed Heath coming out of the toilet, so there was no time to lose. Head down, Edie negotiated the last couple of metres to the booth, resisting the temptation to look at those seated – except for one split-second glimpse.

Edie slipped her hand into the pocket of the jacket hanging on the peg. Crap: nothing. Edie manoeuvred to reach into the other pocket, where she was utterly relieved to find what she needed. Out came the device, and out went Edie hastily from the pub.

Catching her breath as she walked back down Parkway, Edie was certain that one of the men was Jarrah. And the profile of the woman looked weirdly familiar, although Edie really couldn't be sure.

Edie had a problem, though. A serious problem. Unbeknownst to Edie, her brief glance at the table hadn't gone unnoticed.

CHAPTER 9

ENCOUNTER

The bi-weekly repeating timetable meant double maths first thing on Tuesday. As much as Edie liked the subject with its inherent logic, and had a soft spot for the bumbling Mr Bowling, two doses whilst still waking up was pushing it. At mid-morning break, Edie grabbed a Dr Pepper from the Triangle Café and found the quietest corner possible of the open-air quadrangle.

From the Notes pages on her phone, Edie checked her to-do list. First up, speak to Ethan Stephenson. On WhatsApp, Edie opened the most recent message from Ethan and tapped the phone icon. Ethan answered immediately and, after apologising for taking a while to call, Edie shared the outline of her plan to help his brother (she hadn't worked out the details yet), including the appointment she'd made to see Dr Bannon at the university during next week's half-term. Edie asked how Ethan's brother, Martin, was doing and what exactly he'd been told.

Martin already knew of Edie from his brother – including her role in understanding their dad's death and unravelling the associated corporate crime – and Ethan had merely shared that Edie was helping with a couple of things. Otherwise, Martin was just upset about the curtailing of his summer backpacking trip to India and concerned about being expelled from medical school if he failed the biochemistry re-take exam. But Martin was coping, and had recently started a part-time job in a shop in Oxford Street to help pay for university.

Next, Edie googled the number for the National Hospital for Neurology and Neurosurgery in Queen Square and was transferred by switchboard to the neurosurgical critical care unit. Dr Babinski was on duty and took Edie's call. Unfortunately, 'no change' was all the doctor could offer Edie as an update, although she did jot down Edie's mobile number and promised to call should there be any significant developments.

With five minutes before lessons restarted, Edie felt she had just enough time for her final call. But it was tight. She went back to her Notes pages and found the telephone number sent to her following her email enquiry to the Confederation Against Planetary Extermination (CAPE). She tapped in the number for the group's London office and a woman soon answered.

'CAPE, good morning. How can I help?'

'Hmm, I have a question about membership,' Edie offered hesitantly.

'Let me pass you through.'

Edie took the phone away from her ear to check the time, which showed only three minutes before end of break. She bit the skin next to her right thumbnail, winced as the tear hurt more than she'd expected and then inserted her headphones.

'Hello, CAPE membership, London office ...'

'Oh, hi. I'd like to join CAPE ... support the next campaign, maybe join the peace community group too ...'

'Okay,' the male telephonist said patiently, slowing things down. 'One step at a time. First thing, would you be an adult or youth member?'

'Youth,' Edie answered too hurriedly. 'But my uncle's a member ... if that helps.'

'Right,' said the telephonist suspiciously. 'And who might your uncle be, if you don't mind my asking?'

'No, not at all,' Edie replied. 'His name is Heath Coranger.'

In the few seconds of strained silence, Edie noticed only a minute remained before the next lesson. 'Heath Coranger,' the man eventually repeated. 'Your uncle. Hmm ... Well, then you'll probably know that Mr Coranger has been expelled from CAPE, along with some of his friends. Their views were felt to be ... how shall I put it ... too extreme. A fight even broke out between members at a recent meeting ...'

Shocked, Edie spluttered: 'Sorry, I have to go now, thank ...'

'Hold on! What did you say your name was?'

But Edie had already ended the call, just seconds before the bell rang.

Edie caught up with Lizzie on the walk back up Broadlands Road from the lunch dining hall. Unusually, she was talking to Ella and Allegra.

'Hiya,' Edie aimed awkwardly at Lizzie. 'How are you doing today?'

'Fine,' Lizzie scowled, turning her face away from Ella and Allegra.

'Oh, sorry.' Edie immediately grasped that she shouldn't have indicated that something was amiss within earshot of the others. Lizzie clearly hadn't told anybody else about her parents or about Washington. Edie couldn't seem to do anything right at the moment.

Softly, Edie continued: 'I wasn't thinking … didn't realise …'

'You should've realised!' Lizzie snapped. 'Like I said, you're so caught up in your own stuff, you don't really listen. And that won't make you a good detective!'

It hurt. Hurt Edie badly. It was brutal coming from her best friend. But Lizzie was right. Edie had been absent: she wasn't being a good friend, she hadn't been finding the necessary time and she didn't always listen properly to others. Instead, she listened to what suited her.

All set to respond, Edie's attention was diverted by a hand on her shoulder.

'Hi, Edie,' a male voice interrupted.

Caught unawares, Edie replied tentatively: 'Oh … Hi, Harry.'

Harry's deliberate look at the other girls was acknowledged as a request for some privacy, leaving Harry and Edie to walk alone. Lizzie's point had been proven.

'You didn't reply to my message,' Harry asserted.

'Sorry, I've been busy with school stuff … and some other cases,' she added defensively.

'Well, have you had any ideas about my dad's situation?'

Thinking on her feet, Edie remembered something her mum had said about answering with a question when put on the spot and unsure what to say. 'How's it going with your dad and that organisation, CAPE?' she asked.

Harry thought for a moment. 'He hasn't talked about CAPE for a while, now you mention it, but he's still spending a lot of time with those guys. And behaving oddly. Didn't come home till very late last night … bit drunk, I think, and went straight to bed. Normally, he checks in to see how my day was.'

'And how is he?' Edie pressed clumsily.

'Okay, I think,' Harry answered uncertainly. 'But … like I said … he's not been eating or cooking much. And we've always liked doing that together.'

Edie quickened her pace, keen to get back to school and avoid further conversation. She suddenly felt so guilty about her knowledge, but she didn't know what to do with it. Was it her responsibility to let Harry know?

'Have you actually asked him if, like, everything's alright?' Edie felt conflicted and sick to her stomach about her deception.

'Yes. Well, sort of …' Harry hesitated. 'He says he's fine, but he's not telling me something. I can sense it.'

At the school entrance, Edie turned to face the troubled boy. His expression was one of deep suffering and she felt even more awful. 'Keep talking to your dad' was all she could feebly advise. 'Maybe he'll reveal something.' Harry looked on quizzically as Edie, desperate to alleviate his pain, stumbled on. 'Look, I'm investigating *something*, and I'll tell you when I know more.'

Harry's blank expression turned serious, irritated at being given such a measly crumb. 'What do you …?' he started in an exasperated tone, but Edie was already through the gates.

Edie tried to avoid the Parkland Walk, although the verdant footpath was by far the nicest route to and from school – filled with greenery, birdsong and the smell of nature. Bad memories were the obvious cause of her avoidance. Today, she sped along, ascended the incline to the exit on Crouch Hill, turned left and was soon standing on the porch of the Alba Hotel. Once buzzed in, she was greeted at reception by the same woman with the dyed-blond hair, now sporting a green dress with matching nails.

'Ah, hello again, dear. Back to book a room for your grandparents?' the manager enquired.

'No,' Edie replied sheepishly. 'Not that. I was wondering …' Edie suddenly felt a bit silly, as if her plan made more sense in her head than in reality. 'I was wondering if I could speak to one of your guests. Her name is Rochelle. I bumped into her outside on the street last week, although she may have left by now.'

'Surname?' the manager asked with a frown as she tapped the keyboard.

'Maybe Summers … but maybe not,' Edie suggested tentatively.

The manager looked up with misgivings. 'Well, we do have a guest here, for a little longer, whose name is Rochelle. But that's not her surname. She's in her room – I'll ring.'

Before Edie had a chance to change her mind the call was done, and a few minutes later, Rochelle was standing at reception looking bemused. Edie hinted at needing privacy, so they found a table in the far corner of the breakfast room, out of earshot of the manager.

'It's a bit of a surprise to see you again … Edie, I think you said your name was? Is this about the accident the other day, when we bumped into each other? Or Canada?'

Edie took a moment, just like her mum used to. 'No, it's not that …' she started, looking down at the table, embarrassed by her upcoming bizarre explanation. Edie fiddled with the placement of a fork on a napkin before lifting her gaze to this woman she hardly knew: a supposed long-lost friend of Max's mum, another woman Edie hardly knew.

Suddenly, something changed. Having been anxiously unsure of how she would begin this conversation, in the very moment that Edie sat at the table, looking across at the prominent facial mark, Edie found what she needed. Or what she needed came to her, just like her mum used to tell her: that you have what you need inside you. Just have faith that it will appear rather than worrying that it will not.

'Have you always been called Rochelle?' Edie began.

The expression on the face opposite her provided an answer. 'What's this all about?' the woman eventually asked, clearly unsettled. 'And who exactly are you?'

'My name is Edie Marble' came the calm reply. 'And I live close to here – just around the corner, in fact.' To avoid sounding accusatory, Edie took her tone down a notch. 'I'm guessing that Rochelle hasn't always been your name?'

'No, you're quite right there. Rochelle wasn't my birth name.' She paused, her expression shifting to one of irritation. 'I don't know how exactly you know that,' she continued more forcibly, 'but now is the time to tell me. Otherwise, I'm off. I'm in no mood for games.'

'This is not a game,' Edie replied, ready to divulge more. 'I go to Highgate Hill School, near here, but I also work as a detective.'

'A detective,' the woman sniggered. 'But you're just a kid. What are you, some kind of Nancy Drew?'

Edie absorbed the familiar comparison but held her nerve. 'There was a police killing of a hitman close to here a few months ago, in the Parkland Walk ...'

'Yes,' Rochelle interrupted. 'I heard about it from the manager.' She gestured vaguely towards the reception area. 'A case about a pharmaceutical company ... something about a genetically engineered virus. A schoolgirl was a heroine ... a local heroi ...' Rochelle paused, piecing it together as she spoke. 'That's you?'

'Yes, that's me,' Edie replied proudly.

The woman was now captivated. 'There's a plaque on the Parkland Walk – a tribute. The manager told me to have a look. Underneath that weird goblin sculpture coming out of the brickwork.'

'It's a spriggan,' Edie corrected. 'But, yes.' The woman looked impressed as Edie continued. 'Since then I've started my own detective agency.' She took out a business card and handed it over. The woman smiled.

'Okay, detective Edie. Please tell me what this is all about.'

Rapport now established, Edie took a deep breath. 'I will, absolutely. First, though, *are* you … or *were* you … Rachel Summers?'

'Yes,' the woman replied categorically this time. 'I have no idea how you know that, but it's not a big secret. I emigrated from this country a long time ago and wanted to reinvent myself, so I changed my first name to Rochelle. Similar, I know. But I always liked the name Rochelle. And I didn't like Rachel. The name or the person.'

'Thank you … Rochelle,' Edie said awkwardly, her notebook now out. 'And did you know someone at Cambridge University called Donna Redmond?'

Rochelle's response surprised Edie. 'You're right again, detective, I did go to Cambridge. But I didn't know anybody of that name.'

'You didn't?' Edie grabbed her notebook from her bag and scrabbled through the pages, checking names and wondering what had gone wrong. Her search was interrupted, helpfully.

'I did know a girl at university called Donna. But her surname was Corringer, not Redmond.'

'Coranger!' Edie repeated, ashen-faced. 'Can you … can you spell that please?'

'Yes. C – O – DOUBLE R – I – N – G – E – R. Are you alright, Edie?'

'Okay, sorry. *Corringer*, with two R's and an I? You're sure?'

'Yes, absolutely,' Rochelle insisted.

Edie's heart stopped racing quite so fast, but it still felt very odd. And then it clicked: Redmond was Donna's married name. Edie's next question was obvious: 'Did you also know somebody at university called Scott?'

Rochelle's jaw dropped, the name connecting with painful memories. Frustration rising, she snapped: 'I haven't heard that name in fifteen years, and I don't particularly care to. So, you'd better start telling me something, right now!'

'Okay, Rachel … sorry, I mean Rochelle. I just needed to check that you are the person that I thought you might be, which you obviously are.' Rochelle fidgeted irritably in her chair. 'This is going to sound very strange,' Edie declared, 'very strange, but I'll try to explain. Donna Redmond … or Corringer as you knew her … lives on our street, a few doors from me. She married Scott Redmond, so I know her as Donna Redmond or Mrs Redmond.'

At the mention of Scott and Donna being together, Rochelle started to bite her lip. But there was only one way for Edie to go now – onwards.

'Donna has hired me as a detective because she thinks she's seen you on a number of occasions over the past couple of weeks – in different places at different times. At first, she wasn't sure it was even you, then she became more certain, especially when she saw you recently in Crouch End.'

'What?' Rochelle cried, loudly enough to draw the manager's attention. 'What the hell are you talking about?' Edie could sense the thoughts churning frantically inside Rochelle's head by the bewildered look in her eyes. 'Donna married Scott, and they live around here?'

'Yes. In Cecile Park, a few houses down the road from me.' The ensuing silence allowed Edie to take out Donna's document describing her recent activities. It also contained personal details such as Donna's address. 'Rochelle,' Edie continued, 'I know this is very weird, but can I ask you where exactly you were on a few occasions over the past couple of weeks?'

'Okay,' Rochelle agreed reluctantly.

'Right.' Edie turned the document so that it was facing Rochelle, then pointed to a rectangle representing a date on the chart. 'Were you watching a mime artist on the square at Covent Garden on this day?'

Rochelle let out a gasp of exasperation. 'Well, I *was* in Covent Garden a couple of weeks ago, but I need to look at the calendar on my phone to check.'

'Yes,' Rochelle affirmed moments later. 'I was indeed there that day, and I remember the mime artist.'

Meanwhile, Edie was preparing her next question: 'What about this day?' Edie indicated on the chart. 'At a Pret in Vauxhall … around lunchtime?' Rochelle checked her phone, then nodded faintly.

'Initially, Donna thought you might be following her. But then she realised that was impossible. She works for the government – security services – so maybe she's used to watching out for being tracked.'

Edie added a tick to the chart to confirm the presence of both women and cross-checked a couple more dates with the baffled Rochelle. Then she came to the most recent occasion. 'And were you at the Fitzwilliam Museum in Cambridge last Saturday?'

Now Rochelle looked spooked. 'This is ridiculous!' she exclaimed. 'Yes, I was there. I told you I was going to research my book. But I didn't see anyone I recognised, let alone Donna.'

'Well, she was there with her children on the same day.'

'They have children?'

'Yes. A boy called Max, who's four, and a two-and-a-half-year-old girl called Olivia. They're very cute.'

Rochelle frowned and let out another soft gasp, as if imagining a different world that could have been. 'Why didn't she speak to me then?'

'She didn't see you. I only realised afterwards that you had both been there on the same day.'

'Well …' Rochelle shook her head. 'This is completely crazy, and I've had enough now. What's also ludicrous is that this – what you're suggesting – is the subject of my book, *Serendipity*, which I told you about.'

'Yes, I remember. But doesn't that make it all easier to believe?'

'No!' Rochelle cried, drawing the manger's attention again. She stood up from the table and added firmly: 'Quite the opposite. My book is fiction, *Miss Detective*, and this is reality! It's preposterous. Art mimicking life. Or life imitating art! Whichever, it's time for you to leave. And right now.'

Edie wasn't surprised by Rochelle's incredulity, but she was taken aback by her hostility. She packed up her bag but held her ground. 'I think Donna would like to see you and talk this through,' she offered gently. 'Would you like to come and meet her, Scott and the children? I can take you.'

'Absolutely not!' Rochelle said angrily. 'They ruined my life once and I won't let it happen again. They're the last people I'd like to see. Now, please go!'

Edie stood and made to leave but then stopped. 'Maybe you'll change your mind. Please email me if you do,' she added, pointing to her business card on the table, which also included her address. 'Donna lives ten houses up the road from me – closer to here.'

'I won't be *changing my mind*,' Rochelle sneered. 'I've told myself for fifteen years that I never want to revisit that period, those people. That won't be changing, and I'll be going home to Canada at the weekend, as planned.'

As she made her way across the breakfast room, Edie turned around a last time. 'Changing your mind is only a thought away,' she counselled, remembering something from the first PoWaR lesson. 'It's much easier than people think. Just a single thought away.'

The remark sounded much more condescending than Edie had intended, and the ire in Rochelle's face suggested utter disdain for the patronising thirteen-year-old.

The class settled in their seats so quickly that Toni didn't even need to raise her hand. Edie couldn't remember the last time the class had been so respectful and so punctual. Mrs Plunkett, Ms Dylan and a new biology teacher – whose name Edie couldn't remember – joined as observers at the back of the class.

Sarah introduced the session, called 'Our Incredible Psychological System', and started by showing slides of some of the systems behind life – the solar system, photosynthesis in plants, the respiratory system – and how they are all powered by some form of energy.

'Does anybody know what that energy is called? The energy that keeps those systems going?' she asked the class. With nobody responding, Sarah explained: 'Well, in physics they call it the formless energy behind life. In biology they call it life force, which is similar to qi in Chinese medicine. And in ...'

An arm was raised at the front, so Sarah stopped mid-sentence. 'Yes, Daniel?'

'Isn't it ... like ... God ... as well?' he asked.

'Yes, that's true, Daniel, and thank you for bringing that up. In different religions the energy behind life can often be imagined in relation to God. But we're not going to be talking about that in this course, just the idea that there is energy behind all these systems – and that includes our *psychological system*. But first, Toni wants to ask you about a particular energy, or force, that we all know about. Gravity.'

Toni took over. 'Right, does anybody know the formula for gravity?' There was no response from the class.

'Does anybody know the equations for acceleration and deceleration?' Billy Barnes's mate, Andy Roberts, was about to raise his hand for a joke, then decided against it.

'And does anybody know how to calculate the trajectory of an object moving in a parabola?' Nobody even understood the question.

From her skirt pocket, Toni pulled out a tennis ball and immediately threw it across the room. In the third row, Allegra instinctively reached for the ball, seemed to have made a clean catch and then managed to drop it on the floor – to oohs and aahs from her amused classmates. A boy nearby picked up the ball, stood up and cockily threw it back overarm, cricket bowling style, to Toni – who did make a clean catch, for which she received a round of applause.

When the excitement had settled, Toni explained the point of the exercise.

'All of the systems we've talked about have *intelligence* built in to them – and you don't need to know how everything inside the system operates for it to work. For example, you didn't need to know the formula for gravity in order to catch the ball. Well, sorry, in Allegra's case maybe you did,' Toni teased gently. Chuckles erupted from numerous children, including Edie, who had quite enjoyed Allegra's lapse.

'Okay,' said Toni once the noise had subdued. 'This is important, so please listen carefully. Like gravity or electromagnetism, the force – or energy – behind the psychological system is *Thought*. It is Thought that powers the psychological system. Now, in this slide' – Toni clicked the remote – 'we use a capital T for Thought because we're not talking about an individual thought you might have – say, what you're having for dinner. No, we mean the Power of Thought, the invisible energy that *enables* us to think, that allows those individual thoughts to come to life.'

Toni paused for a few seconds. 'Thought is constant. It is always present, like gravity, but what we think about changes from moment to moment. And, this is vital, *we feel what we think*. That's where our feelings come from – from our thinking.'

Toni allowed time for the class to digest what she was saying, then continued playfully: 'Now, I hope none of you are feeling too bored!' Their facial expressions suggested not. 'Good! But, even if you are feeling bored, that can change in a moment, when your thinking changes.'

After a few seconds Toni nodded at Sarah, who stepped in.

'Now, let me ask you all a question: did any of you ever have a comforter when you were younger – something that made you feel better or more secure? Maybe helped when you didn't feel so good?'

'A blanket,' a girl shouted from the back of the room.

'Yeah, a teddy bear,' Lizzie chipped in, surprising Edie.

'A Humpty Dumpty that my au pair made me!' Yasmina shouted out.

'And the boys?' Sarah asked. 'Don't be shy.'

'Billy had a dummy!' Andy Roberts shouted, to hoots of laughter. 'Still does!'

Once the class had calmed down, Sarah put up a fresh slide. 'We can laugh about it now,' she began, 'but those things felt important to us when we were young – we felt insecure without them – but *what if they've just been replaced with a new set of things*?' Everyone went very quiet as she indicated on the slide the images of money, popularity, food, social media and more.

'Yeah,' piped up Daniel. 'But getting lots of likes on a post *does* make me feel good. I know it does.'

'What if it just *seems* like it makes you feel good? What if … just imagine … those "likes" *weren't* actually responsible, and you *didn't* need them to make you feel that way? Wouldn't that be a bit of a relief?'

Before Daniel had a chance to counter, Sarah instructed each member of the class to throw into a bucket, which was being passed around the room, strips of paper depicting the modern comforters from which they'd like to be free. Twenty suggestions had been printed on perforated strips on a sheet of paper on each desk, but Sarah said they could write down others if they preferred. Edie ripped off pieces saying 'good results', 'looking good' and 'gadgets' and chucked them into the bucket.

Once they were settled, Toni resumed. 'Our intelligent psychological system has *everything* we need built-in,' she emphasised. 'Just like a cut on your skin repairs itself, so the psychological system has everything that is needed to look after each of you, through *whatever* life throws at you.'

As Toni's last phrase worked its way through Edie, she began to feel unsettled. But the facilitator wasn't quite finished. 'We call what is built-in our *innate* qualities. We're born with them and every human being has them – and here are seven that we feel are particularly important.' She flicked to a new slide and read out each quality: 'Wellbeing, resilience, wisdom, gratitude, compassion, love and peace of mind.'

Toni then grabbed a snow globe off the desk – which contained seven small blocks featuring those seven words – and shook it hard, causing the snow to come alive inside the dome. 'When our minds get really busy, when they get agitated, we lose track of those innate qualities and instead we *outsource our wellbeing* – meaning that we believe our wellbeing depends on those things you've all just thrown in the bin.'

Can you join your innate qualities to their correct meanings?

Peace of mind	a deep feeling of calm
Love	a deep feeling of being thankful just because
Wellbeing	a feeling that we can handle life because of the way we work
Resilience	a deep feeling of caring
Wisdom	a strong feeling of connection/much bigger than just liking
Gratitude	a deep feeling of wellness
	the amazing thinking we have that lets us learn stuff, know what to do, solve problems and get over our hurt/anger

You could have heard a pin drop in the room, but Edie's mind was all over the place. Distracted and upset, her attention finally returned as Toni was wrapping up the session. 'So, please, over the weekend, just think a little about this – that we all have *everything* we need within us to deal with life.'

Edie's hand shot up, almost without her even realising it. Her mind was a jumble and she didn't know if she was sad, mad or distressed.

'Yes, Edie,' Toni asked, confident of the children's names.

'But Miss … I mean Toni …' Edie started, her voice sounding confused. 'Do you mean we have everything inside us to deal with your parent getting really ill or even something like your mother dy…?'

In a flash, Sarah was by Edie's side. With a hand on her shoulder, she murmured softly: 'Yes, Edie. We mean exactly that – to deal with life, no matter what challenges we might face.'

CHAPTER 10

(LUCKY) ESCAPE

Edie pulled a tummy-ache sickie on Friday, meaning the half-term break began a day early. She needed the extra day to delve deeper into the developing threads of her investigative spider's web.

With Eli at school, Edie would have (gladly) been alone in the house all day, but Dad came to her room before morning surgery to tell her otherwise. After checking on his daughter's health (he even took out his stethoscope to listen to Edie's lungs, which meant he was taking things really seriously), Dad explained that because Mama and Papa had tickets to go to the Royal Botanic Gardens at Kew, their weekly housekeeper Grace would be staying with Edie until her grandparents arrived mid-afternoon. Edie's protestations proved futile.

At half past nine, Edie ambled downstairs in her comfy fleece dressing gown and Buffy slippers to find Grace busy in the kitchen, unloading the dishwasher.

'I can do that, Grace,' Edie offered. 'You don't need to.'

'No, you need to rest. Your dad said so. Do you want some breakfast? Or something to drink?'

'A coffee would be nice, Grace.' Edie smiled. 'Thank you. Two sugars today, please.'

Whilst the kettle boiled, Edie walked through the playroom, unlocked the back door and stepped out onto the decking. Immediately, Edie knew something wasn't right. Günther's double-storey hotel home was at an angle; not a good sign as it was heavy and took some effort to shift. Most worryingly, the cage door was ajar.

This corner of the garden was in perpetual shadow due to the high house walls on both sides, and Edie gazed with unadjusted eyes into the dark cage interior. Hay was scattered randomly, which was unusual for the tidy guinea pig. A wooden bridge-like play structure had been knocked over – and Günther was nowhere to be seen.

On the decking in front of the cage was a small pile of faeces. Edie's heart sank. One of the many foxes that patrolled the garden must have managed to open the cage door. What a horrible way to go.

Edie started crying as she inspected the rest of the small urban garden. Both top and bottom levels seemed normal at first, although one flowerpot on the lower level had been knocked over. Then Edie noticed the wooden owl, handmade from twigs, had been displaced from its perch. Another sign of the foxes who didn't like its presence.

Distressed, Edie sat on a wicker chair, where Grace could see her through the French doors from the kitchen. Their eyes met, and Grace knew something was wrong. She quickly went outside.

'He's gone,' Edie repeated after their extended cuddle had ceased. 'I love him so much and I killed him … I must've left the cage door open … and let him get eaten by a fox!'

Grace tried to placate Edie. 'It's not your fault – it really isn't. You always lock the cage door – I've seen you – it's just unlucky ...' Her voice trailed off, uncertain what else to say.

Edie started bawling and Grace pulled her close again. The embrace continued for a few minutes, Edie's mind racing with guilt and memories. First she'd lost her mum and now her precious pet.

'What's that noise?' Grace cried suddenly.

'What noise?'

'That noise ... the scraping.'

Now Edie could hear something too, and both sets of eyes darted around the garden.

'It's coming from round there,' indicated Grace, 'by the hutch.'

They charged around, reopened the cage door and checked everything inside again, including the little house where Günther slept. No sign of her friend, but the scraping sound continued.

'It's coming from underneath the decking,' Edie exclaimed. 'I can get in there from below!'

Edie tore down the stairs to the lower garden, opened the tiny gate under the main decking, then got down on her hands and knees to crawl the distance to reach the spot beneath Günther's cage.

It was very dark and Edie wished she had her iPhone with its torch. Slowly, her eyes adjusted and she was able to recognise old flower pots, a broom, tennis balls and a lot of spiders' webs. All relatively nearby.

In the far corner, however, Edie could just make out a small round object, which could easily have been a punctured football or even a mound of soil. Or, just possibly, Günther.

As Edie's vision acclimatised further, she was confident that the object was her furry friend, shaking and panting. She let out a huge sigh of relief, quietly informed Grace through the slats that she'd found him, and then beckoned Günther towards her with her fingers.

The guinea pig refused to move, and Edie feared he was injured, perhaps mortally.

Then, comforted by Edie's voice and smell, Günther stepped warily the few inches towards Edie, and within moments she had him cradled in her hands.

Delicately, Edie crept backwards until she was out from under the decking, and then went back up the garden stairs and sat with Grace.

'He must've got through that hole in the corner of the upstairs deck, behind the cage, to escape the fox,' Edie speculated. 'He must've fallen down the last bit. But I think he's fine – just a couple of scratches.'

'Clever guinea pig!' proclaimed Grace.

Edie smiled. Günther was possibly smart, but he'd also had a lucky escape. Or was it luck? she pondered. Maybe his demise just wasn't meant to be. Either way, there would be another lock on his cage tonight.

And what about all the other chance happenings that seemed to be swirling around Edie? Could she make sense of them, even change their trajectory? There was only one way to find out: the cases needed to progress and maybe then all would be revealed.

Lying on her bed after clearing out Günther's cage and settling him down, Edie plotted her next steps. She wasn't seeing Donna until after lunch, so Edie started with the plan she'd intended to share with Harry in person at school. She waited until morning break, when pupils were allowed to use their phones, and called Harry's mobile number, hoping he'd pick up.

'Yo, Edie,' Harry answered. 'How are you?'

'I'm fine, Harry. Just a bad stomach.'

'Oh, okay. Glad it's not serious.'

Edie suddenly had the unsettling thought that if she hadn't taken the day off school, she wouldn't have found Günther and he might not have survived.

'Edie, are you there?' Harry asked after a prolonged pause.

'Yes, sorry. I was just wondering if you'd had a chance to check again with your dad that everything's okay … like with his health?'

A short silence was followed by a tetchy reaction against unwelcome interference. 'I told you: I've already asked him, and he said he's fine. Why would I ask him again?'

Edie needed a different tack, otherwise Harry might dig his heels in even more. 'You don't have to …' she proposed more tentatively. 'It's up to you, of course. But you said you thought he might have lost weight and … I guess, if it was me … I wouldn't mind somebody who loved me double-checking if everything was alright.'

The softer approach worked. 'I could do, I guess,' Harry acquiesced. And then the reason behind his prickliness came out: 'I've been even more worried recently. I heard him being sick in the toilet the other day. On and off for ages.'

'Right,' agreed Edie. 'So, it can't hurt to ask again. You're just being kind.'

'Yeah, okay, I'll do it over the weekend. When the time's right.'

Harry paused for a moment, then added: 'Actually, I'll have to do it tomorrow as Dad said he'd be out on Sunday … with those friends of his from CAPE again. Or *supposed* friends. I don't like them …' Harry paused, as if thinking. 'By the way, have you had any more ideas about what's going on with that side of things?'

Now Edie was where she wanted to be in the conversation. 'Yeah. Don't you think it would be good to know where they've been going? Where they spend the whole day with the car? And what exactly they've been doing? You said you've asked your dad but he's not given you a proper answer.'

'That's right,' Harry responded, as the bell for the end of break rang in the background. 'And, yes, I would like to know what they all get up to. I've been worried, as I told you. Look, I've gotta go – it's next lesson. What are you suggesting?'

'Can you come round here tomorrow morning? I've got an old iPhone 8 that I don't use any more, but it works fine.

I've bought a new SIM and I'll have it fully charged. I've also got some strong brown sticky tape that my dad uses for packaging. I'll give you that too.'

'And what exactly am I supposed to do with it?'

'You'll need to strap the iPhone securely to the bottom of the car – there are lots of pipes under there – as late as possible before your dad leaves with his friends on Sunday. Make sure the phone stays turned on when you attach it. I've got the Find My iPhone app on my own phone linked to that one, so I can see exactly where they go – at least for a few hours until the battery runs out. And it really doesn't matter if the phone gets damaged or broken.'

Edie waited, uncertain how Harry might feel about tracking his own father.

'That's a great idea – I like it,' Harry said. 'See you tomorrow.'

Edie wasn't supposed to leave the house, but she knew that Donna worked from home on Fridays. After lunch, Edie messaged her neighbour, lied to Grace about needing a walk before Mama and Papa arrived later, and then walked the hundred metres or so along the road to the right.

As Edie approached the house up the garden path, she noticed that the front door was a fraction ajar. Regardless, she rang the doorbell and waited on the doorstep.

Max's mum answered. 'Hello, Edie. It's nice to see you. Come in.'

'Hi, Mrs Redm … I mean Donna. You know the door was open a little,' Edie pointed.

'Yes, I know. Scott said he'd fixed it yesterday. Annoying. He's rubbish at DIY. Thinks he's good, makes a big deal of it, like most men, but his repairs never last. I'll have to get the locksmith in. Anyway,' she ushered, 'do come in. Sounds like we've got things to talk about.'

Sheepishly, Edie followed Donna into the lounge and sat on the sofa. It seemed like a good time to talk as nobody else was in the house.

'So,' Donna began, taking the seat right next to Edie. 'What's the update? I assume you have some news regarding my problem … and our arrangement?'

'Yes. Well, sort of,' Edie began with hesitation.

Donna's eyes brightened, her focus stronger. 'Good, let's hear it then.'

'So,' Edie continued haltingly, 'first I checked out the Alba Hotel where you said this woman was staying. I was having a look around inside, checking the register on the computer while the manager was distracted, and found a first name with an initial R, which could've been Rachel. Different surname though. Then a woman came down the stairs who I thought *might* be Rachel – because she had a mole on her upper lip – so I followed her all the way into Waitrose.'

'Okay,' chipped in Donna with clear interest. 'And?'

'Well, I was watching Rachel at the checkout when you suddenly tapped my shoulder.'

'What!' exclaimed Donna before the implication clicked. 'Oh, I see, we were there at exactly the same time but didn't meet again.' Donna looked perplexed.

'Yes, and what's more, I'm sure she didn't follow you. She was just buying some groceries, and you happened to be there too.'

Edie paused whilst Donna processed the information. Edie could sense her neighbour's mind whirring, and could feel the discomforting energy of Donna's mixed emotions of confusion, irritation and maybe even mistrust. Perhaps that's what happens when you're a spy: you learn not to trust anybody or anything. There's always a reason behind events, it's just a question of working it out. Only this conundrum was proving tricky to resolve.

All of a sudden, the quiet was disturbed by youngsters bickering. Max charged into the room, bedecked again in his beloved Batman suit, his sister Olivia trailing behind with a toddler's tottering gait.

'My ball!' Olivia cried.

Max ignored her as he kicked a small pink ball around the lounge. Olivia chased after the ball but her older sibling always got there first, at which point he gleefully booted it to the other side of the room. As the ball whizzed past, Edie noticed spinning Barbie images on the surface.

'My ball!' Olivia repeated, now wailing whilst her brother laughed.

Donna leapt out of her seat and grabbed the ball from under a side table. The look on her face immediately caused her son's giggles to cease.

'Enough,' she stated sternly. 'Stop it right now, both of you, otherwise it's straight to bed.'

'Sorry, Mrs Redmond,' apologised the au pair who had appeared in the doorway. 'I went to the bathroom and … they've been difficult today … and, well, sorry to disturb you.'

'No problem, Christina,' Donna replied. 'Maybe give them their bath early today, please.'

Christina scooped up the children. 'Yes, of course.' Edie liked the new au pair, who had arrived recently from Poland, but Christina represented a rival for babysitting.

With the children upstairs, Donna firmly closed the lounge door and returned to her seat.

'I don't have long, Edie, so please tell me what else you've found out.'

Something about her neighbour's manner always seemed to make Edie feel jittery. Was that something else you learned as a spy? Stay detached and aloof and the other person will feel uneasy – and be more likely to make a mistake.

'Okay,' the young detective continued. 'I bumped into Rachel when I was walking to school. It was just luck or a coincidence – my route goes past her hotel and we collided as she came down the steps. I was knocked over and she helped me up. Then we chatted and she told me she's a writer.'

'A writer?' Donna interrupted. 'I didn't realise … well, I guess, how could I? She did the college magazine at Cambridge, but I don't recall her being much of an author. What kind of books?'

'Fiction. She told me about the book she's writing right now about things – good things mainly, I think – happening for reasons beyond luck. Beyond chance. Or, if I understood correctly, outside chance, as in beyond the idea of chance … if you get what I mean.'

'I'm not sure I do exactly,' Donna retorted perfunctorily. She had the voice of somebody who preferred facts over fiction. 'If you're talking about serendipity, that's not something I particularly believe …'

'Yes, serendipity,' Edie interrupted. 'That's the title of her book. And, here's the thing: she went to Cambridge the same day as you did last week. She came over from Canada to research her book and she went to that museum.'

'The Fitzwilliam?' Donna's face paled.

'Yes, the Fitzwilliam Museum, on …'

'The same day I was there,' Donna completed the sentence. Stony-faced, she stared across the room at a crimson-and-black abstract painting, seemingly transfixed by the swirling lines, although Edie imagined that wasn't the case.

Edie was about to relay the conversation she'd had with Rabbi Abby about determinism and fate, but the opportunity was cut short. 'It's all mumbo jumbo,' Donna announced boldly, redirecting her gaze towards Edie. 'There's got to be an explanation behind all this nonsense. What else did you find out?'

Edie fidgeted uncomfortably. She hadn't been looking forward to this part. 'I went and met Rachel at the hotel a few days ago. I thought it was best just to confront her, tell her everything and see how she reacted.'

'Right!' Donna countered, her tone unimpressed. 'It doesn't sound very sleuth-like detective work,' she added sarcastically. 'And did it help you to get any answers?'

Edie chewed the skin around her left thumbnail. Honesty seemed best. 'Yes and no … It *is* her, Rachel, the woman you knew from university. But she thought the whole story of the locations sounded crazy … didn't really believe it or get it … and found the connection to her new book very odd. That's when I found out about her museum visit. Then she got angry. She said that she had no interest in seeing you at all, that she was going back to Canada in a few days anyway and then she asked me to leave.'

'Hmm,' grunted Donna, discontented. 'That approach didn't seem to work out very well, did it? Oh well, I suppose that's the end of that. Very peculiar.' She stood up purposefully, ushering Edie towards the front door.

'Right, thank you, Edie,' Donna said dismissively. 'Now I have to get on with my day.'

Unexpectedly rebuffed, Edie complied meekly. She considered asking about her final payment as she left, but decided otherwise. It just didn't seem right, or not the right moment.

Friday evening turned out to be a surprise. A very pleasant surprise.

Mama and Papa arrived late afternoon as expected. Whilst Papa read the paper in the lounge, Mama sat with Edie in the kitchen for some time, showing her photos on her phone from earlier in the day at Kew Gardens. Edie loved seeing Mama inside a semicircular gazebo that was completely enveloped in pink-purple wisteria.

Of the various indoor spaces at Kew, the Waterlily House particularly appealed to Edie: the large, plant-covered ponds offered a tranquillity to counter Edie's busy mind. One photo showed Papa pointing very excitedly at something on top of one of the giant, flattened circular leaves that sat perfectly afloat on the water. It was just a frog, Mama clarified, nonplussed by the fuss.

The picture that Edie liked the most, though, was of one of the oldest trees at Kew. As Edie turned the phone on its side, Mama explained that, unusually, this tree lay fully horizontal. Near its base – at the far right-hand edge of the photo – was an arrangement of brickwork, which had become entangled with the tree over time. And now tree and wall were forever inseparable, like Edie felt about herself and the spirit of her mum. Enmeshed for eternity.

Mama wasn't sure what kind of tree it was, possibly a Japanese pagoda, but she remembered that it was transplanted in 1762 when it was just a few years old. Astonished, Edie imagined everything through 250 years of history that this warrior of nature had witnessed since the reign of King George III: British convicts sent to Australia, Nelson winning the Battle of Trafalgar, the invention of the steam engine, Queen Victoria's reign, two world wars, the discovery of antibiotics in-between and the incessant wrecking of the planet through climate change.

Edie then watched TV with Papa whilst Mama prepared a meal. Around seven o'clock, Dad arrived home from evening surgery and half an hour later Edie, Dad, Eli and Edie's grandparents all gathered around the kitchen table. It felt wonderfully normal to Edie – a traditional Jewish Friday night family dinner, except for the one missing person.

Mama said the prayer to bring in the Sabbath, hands over her eyes to shield them from the light of the candles as she recited it, after which Papa led the prayers for wine and challah. Tonight was truly special as Mama had baked her very own challah – salty, sweet and with an abundance of poppy seeds.

After the delicious dinner (chicken soup, roast chicken and apple pie) was finished, Edie stayed at the table with her grandparents whilst Dad and Eli cleared up.

'I went down the Parkland Walk the other day,' Papa announced unexpectedly. 'First time since … since … well, you know what.'

Edie was taken aback. 'Why did you go?'

'I don't know exactly. It just felt like I needed to be there.'

Dad looked over briefly, then carried on washing a saucepan.

'Did you go, Mama?' Edie's question was greeted with a shake of the head.

'So, which part of the Parkland Walk did you go to?' Edie enquired.

'The actual spot. To see where all the horror ended with my own eyes.'

'You mean where that statue comes out of the wall … the gargoyle?' Mama asked, having seen a photo of it.

'It's not actually a gargoyle,' Papa corrected. 'I've been reading up about it – on the plaque on the Parkland Walk and on the internet.'

'So, tell us what it is,' Mama said.

'It's called a spriggan,' Papa explained, 'and it's a mythical goblin-like creature from Cornish folklore – hundreds of years ago originally – known for its grotesque features, love of causing mischief, incredible strength and the ability to swell in height from one metre to three.'

Edie smiled to herself knowingly. She'd done similar research herself.

'Sounds horrid!' Mama cried.

Papa was in his stride, though, and had more information to impart. 'The world-famous horror writer, Stephen King – you'll be a bit young to know him, Edie – wrote a short story after walking past the spriggan, called "Crouch End". I read it on Kindle – it was pretty scary but very good.'

'Wow, you have been busy,' commented Mama. 'I didn't know you'd been up to any of this.'

Edie's mind was on a different track. 'How did you feel when you were there, Papa? Were you angry?'

During the short silence that followed, Edie became acutely aware of the loudness of the hum from the fridge.

'I was sad, Edie, of course. Terribly sad about what happened. But I wasn't angry, no.'

Edie waited. She'd been having some dark thoughts about the perpetrators of Mum's murder and had been experimenting, as they'd discussed at the last PoWaR session, with letting go of the hatred that emerged from time to time.

'Mama, and you too, Papa,' she took a different tack. 'How did you cope after the war, with how awful the

Nazis had been … all your family members that had been murdered? How did you manage to get through all of that?'

'Well,' Mama responded. 'That's a good question. Some survivors managed to move on and create new lives, much better than others.' Mama glanced at Dad, as if needing his endorsement to continue.

'What I wanted to ask is …' Edie hesitated, a tear forming in the corner of her eye. 'Were you able to forgive those who caused such harm?'

With the edge of her finger Mama sweetly caressed away the tear, allowing Papa to come in. 'People often ask that,' he said softly. 'Do you forgive the Nazis for their actions? But it's not really about forgiveness – forgiveness is almost the wrong word. I don't *forgive* the Nazis for what they did, as in I don't *excuse* them for their behaviour, as if it's all in the past and forgotten. No, definitely not.'

Edie looked confused. Mama, as was often her way, finished off what her husband seemed about to say. 'What we learned, my darling, is that you can't afford to live with the hatred. Acceptance is essential, somehow, as resistance is the biggest cause of long-term emotional distress.'

A puzzled look on Edie's face encouraged Mama to elaborate. 'Holding on to the hatred – the revulsion about what happened – is soul-destroying, in that it literally destroys your own soul … it risks ruining your own life, your future, beyond whatever occurred in the past.'

'Life, with all its challenges, is here to be lived,' Papa emphasised. 'One has to find a way of letting go.'

Upstairs, Edie felt calmer than she'd done for a while. The extra day off had been valuable in terms of her spirit and her pet, although she was unsure how much the cases had actually advanced.

Before going to bed, Edie had a cursory end-of-the-evening look at emails to her detective account. One stood out, marked 'Personal', which she clicked to open. Greeted by a message from an unidentified sender, her post-dinner calmness immediately disintegrated.

> Edie Marble: Keep your nose out of other people's affairs otherwise you, your family and your precious guinea pig will suffer. There will be no more warnings. And there will be consequences if you share this message.

CHAPTER 11

LONG WEEKEND

Edie tossed and turned through the much of the night, not falling asleep properly until five o'clock, after which she slept soundly through Saturday morning, mind and body in need of rest. When she opened her eyes, the bedside table clock read 12:47. Through the still-broken blind, the brightness of the middle of the day lit up Edie's room as she reached for her phone.

There were several WhatsApp messages already, including a jokey one from Yasmina on the Kenwood dogs group chat asking if they could bring the crack surveillance team back together for one last mission, to which Charlie responded that runaway Alan wouldn't be joining, as he was now in training to be a police dog. Further down, a message from Lizzie about the upcoming meeting with Dr Bannon didn't sound good:

> Not sure I can help with that visit to the biochemistry guy. Too much to do. Will LYK.

Edie was digesting the somewhat dismissive tone as she read a very recent message from Harry:

I'll be at your house at 1. Need to talk.

Edie jumped out of bed, charged into the bathroom, brushed her teeth and showered in record time (four and a half minutes). She'd just finished pulling her hair back in a tie when the doorbell rang. As Dad approached the front door, Edie screamed from the top of the stairs that it was for her and not to worry. Suspicious, Dad smiled up at his daughter and said that he was practically at the door so he might as well open it.

'Hi' Edie heard from out front as she raced down into the hallway. 'Is Edie in?'

'I've got it, Dad,' Edie snapped, pushing past her obstructive parent.

'Hi, Harry. Sorry about that. Come in ...' Edie regretted her brusque behaviour, but Dad calmly retreated.

'Can I bring my bike in?'

'Sure, just leave it in the hall,' Edie said, pointing to a wooden console table on which sat a jade dish for keys. 'Here, rest it against this table.' Harry obliged, scraping the wood with a handlebar and then apologising profusely.

'It's okay, really,' Edie reassured him. 'Let's go upstairs.'

In the bedroom, Harry paced awkwardly by the window whilst Edie sat on her bed. He looked troubled so Edie just waited. Eventually Harry settled enough to speak.

'It's my dad,' he began. 'I spoke to him this morning. Edie, he's not well – not at all well. He might even die ...' Harry struggled with the words, turning away towards the window to wipe away his tears.

'I'm so sorry,' Edie ventured eventually, feeling dreadful again about her concealment. 'That's awful. What's wrong with him? Is he getting any treatment?'

With his back still to Edie, Harry replied with his own question rather than an answer. 'You knew all along, didn't you, and you didn't tell me?'

Harry's tone was accusatory and he sounded betrayed. There was nothing for Edie to do except to come clean.

'Yes, I did. I'm *so* sorry,' Edie pleaded. 'I just didn't know what to do.' She explained about the letter in the bin and searching her Dad's medical records, but she left out the trip to University College Hospital and the listening device. Evasively, she claimed she didn't know exactly what was wrong with Harry's dad, and then tried to defend why she hadn't mentioned anything earlier. But it was pointless. Harry was now facing her, and from his expression the damage had already been done.

Yet, despite the broken trust, Harry was still hurting and desperate about his dad.

After a tense silence, it was Harry who spoke first.

'He's got something called multiple myeloma … it's like a blood cancer … had it for months and didn't want to tell me. Didn't want to upset me. I told him that was ridiculous, that I knew something was wrong anyway, but he just shrugged his shoulders.'

'I guess he didn't want to worry you,' Edie suggested supportively, keen to start repairing the additional hurt she'd caused. 'Maybe he thought there wasn't much you could do.'

'Yeah, but he's been getting chemo by himself at the hospital. That's so sad.'

After a moment Edie offered a different explanation. 'Or very brave.'

Edie saw how tired Harry looked. And dishevelled, as if he'd just thrown on the jeans, dirty trainers, creased black T-shirt and hoodie.

'I guess so,' Harry finally agreed, more composed but still cold. 'He's always been so strong … a rock through everything … and he likes to deal with stuff himself … not bother anybody else. I just wish he'd told me.' Harry took a couple of steps and sat down on Edie's desk chair.

Edie found it weird seeing somebody else in the seat where she spent so much time. 'Well, now that you do know,' Edie enquired softly, 'what are you going to do?'

'Help him. Support him as best I can. Maybe go to appointments … not exactly sure yet.'

'And maybe ask him what he'd find most helpful?' Edie wondered out loud.

'Yeah, I'll ask him that … in relation to his health. But I'm not sure he really knows what to do about his mates from CAPE – Jarrah and Sven – the ones you met, and some others.' Edie nodded, conscious that this wasn't the right time to let on about her other findings. 'I think he's had some kind of argument with them … fallen out with them over something. He told me this morning … I'm pleased, to be honest. He's intending to tell them today that he's had enough.'

Eagerly, Edie asked: 'Did you do what we talked about with my old iPhone?'

'Yes, I strapped it under the car, to a pipe near the exhaust. It was quite easy. I did it first thing this morning before Dad was up. And they headed off just before I came here to … wherever they go. So, I guess we should find out in a bit.'

Downstairs, Edie made them both a sandwich and they sat in the garden. Harry remained distant and the atmosphere was awkward. As soon as possible, Edie led them back upstairs, closed her bedroom door and opened the Find My iPhone app on her own iPhone. They peered at it expectantly.

First, a beating radar ball showed Edie's own location in Crouch End. From the list underneath, Edie selected 'Edie's old iPhone', and the map scooted instantly out of London, past Oxford and stopped where a new mini iPhone icon was pulsing in a field in the middle of nowhere. Edie zoomed out too far, noticing the town of Burford, then zoomed back in again slowly, revealing that the nearest village was called Swinbrook.

'I think I know this area,' Edie remarked. 'We went there for a weekend once as a family to visit some old friends of my parents. It's an area in the countryside called the Cotswolds.'

Dad declared Saturday to be takeaway-and-movie night. Eli was delighted and Edie grateful for the distraction, although they inevitably argued over what food to order. Eli wanted Nandos, Edie fancied Japanese, and Dad and Emmeline said they didn't care. Eventually, they settled on Thai and at eight o'clock were all seated in the lounge around the TV, plates on laps.

The next problem was choosing a movie. An action film was Eli's predictable preference, although Edie said she couldn't face watching any of the *Taken* or *Bourne* films again. Dad suggested a thriller, Edie pleaded for something gentle and Emmeline suggested a comedy. With the food getting cold, they finally decided to watch *A Dog's Purpose* – Eli begrudgingly threatening the PlayStation if he was bored.

As it happened, the film proved perfect; adventurous enough for the youngest and heart-warming enough for everyone else. Halfway through the movie, a beautiful English springer spaniel appeared momentarily in the background of a scene.

'That looks like Quincy,' Edie observed, just below audible range.

'What did you say, luv?' Dad asked.

'Nothing,' she replied.

In one scene, a golden retriever was sniffing around the outside of a house and the owner was telling a neighbour about the dog's incredible sense of smell. He could find anything, the woman declared – an old pair of lost socks under the bed, a mouse beneath the decking, a fish buried years ago in the garden. No wonder the police like to use them.

The sensation of an insight – a new realisation – is of a spark ignited deep inside. It feels like sight from within, of seeing something fresh for the very first time. Edie recognised the feeling from when she'd solved her mum's clues and the associated grizzly crime, and she felt it again on the sofa watching the film. The feeling was magical and also mildly disquieting.

With the spark kindled, Edie's mind tumbled from one idea to the next without any conscious control. Gradually, something more concrete began to take shape and then settled.

Edie attempted to excuse herself. 'I've just got to go upstairs ...'

'Why?' Dad asked, perplexed. 'You love this movie. And it was your choice.'

Regardless, Edie stood up, said she'd be back down in a bit and insisted the others carry on watching. Heads turned but no one tried to stop her.

Upstairs in her bedroom, Edie closed the door firmly and went straight to her desk. From her rudimentary filing system, she retrieved the folder she'd titled 'Missing Dogs'. Inside, Edie found the newspaper printouts she'd accumulated about the cases of dogs locally that had disappeared over the past few weeks.

Instead of looking at factors such as location, time of incident or the owner's account, Edie just looked at the breed of dog: English springer spaniel, Labrador, two beagles. Plus, Alan was tempted. After jotting down several breeds, Edie googled 'What kind of dogs are used as sniffer dogs?' The breeds of the missing dogs all featured in the top ten list.

Was this whole thing something to do with drugs, Edie wondered, and not about random abductions? The breeds were being targeted deliberately.

After her realisation and the ensuing work, Edie felt exhausted. She fibbed to the TV-watchers downstairs that she had to speak to Lizzie on the phone and withdrew again to the sanctuary of her room.

By ten o'clock on Sunday morning Edie was up, showered and ready for the day. Despite the lingering unsettling feeling from the nasty email, she'd been invigorated by her discovery the previous evening and the possibility of solving one of her mysteries. She was determined to push through Sunday's routine stuff and then get on with the next phase of her investigations.

Judo was cancelled, however. Sensei Dominic was ill and instructed Edie instead to practise the latest moves at home, either by simulation alone or with a willing accomplice. She'd found the latter in the shape of Eli, who enjoyed being tossed around the room for the first part of the afternoon, acrobatically exaggerating the impact of Edie's throws.

Due to a family matter, Rabbi Abby asked to do their Sunday bat mitzvah session by Zoom. Edie was clearly distracted and the session wasn't going particularly well. Three quarters of the way through, Rabbi Abby switched from working on the biblical text to asking Edie about her detective cases.

Edie decided against telling the rabbi about the email threat (otherwise Rabbi Abby would tell Dad, he'd call the police and it would all implode), but did share that she was worried about pursuing one particular case, and didn't like fear getting in the way of something important.

The kindly rabbi's words sat with Edie for the whole day and beyond: 'This links to what we discussed the other day, Edie, about what is meant to be and about things beyond our human understanding. It's important not to live in fear of life's experiences and feelings, otherwise, it's not a life fully lived. Be sensible and careful, of course, but if one stays focused on what is going on now, then the universe has a remarkable knack of serving up what is needed. Of providing you with exactly what is required at any given time. Of looking after you. And, most importantly, you'll be open to actually seeing, and accepting, whatever that may be.'

Almost as soon as the session was finished, Dad came into Edie's room. The late afternoon plans to visit Mum's bench – with the dedication plaque – in Highgate Woods were off as something urgent had come up at the surgery.

Edie mooched around the house, finding it hard to concentrate. She was keen to get on with the next phase of her investigations, but the weekend seemed to be dragging. Playing with Günther helped for a while, then she delved into her computer city-building game, *Cities: Skylines.* After half an hour, she realised she needed to get out of the house.

Grabbing her laptop and various notebooks and folders, Edie told Dad she was meeting Lizzie at Costa in Crouch End. Another fib, as Lizzie had declined to meet because of 'other plans'. On the short walk there, Edie had an uneasy feeling of being followed but checks over her shoulder revealed nothing.

At a corner table at the back, Edie sat alone with a salted caramel Frostino. Out of her rucksack she retrieved what she needed to get on with her schoolwork, put her head down and tried to focus.

After an hour – and in spite of the hectic late Sunday atmosphere – Edie felt that she'd accomplished more than she anticipated. The only problem was this enduring unsettled sensation. Was it just the email or was it something else? On a few occasions when she'd looked up from her work, Edie imagined that other customers were observing her.

Needing the loo, Edie asked a safe-looking middle-aged woman on an adjacent table if she would kindly watch Edie's belongings. 'Absolutely,' the woman responded, she'd be pleased to help. Two minutes later, however, when Edie returned, the woman had oddly disappeared. Thankfully, Edie's computer and bag were still there.

Back at home, Edie went straight to her room and unpacked her rucksack on her bed. Last to spill out, from the very bottom, was a white envelope. No writing on the front, just an envelope – with something inside. Suspecting the item had got there accidentally when she'd shoved in some other stuff earlier, Edie was surprised when she opened the envelope to reveal a folded sheet of paper. It read:

Edie,

At some risk, I have used various connections to get you this note – a warden I have befriended plus my dear old trusted secretary, Margaret. Assuming you may not be pleased to hear from me, I will get to the point quickly.

I fully understand why your father turned down my request to see you. There are, however, two reasons why I wished you to visit me – one personal and the other very grave. Hence, this unorthodox method of contacting you. The first reason is to say that I am truly, truly sorry, from the depths of my soul, for the pain I have caused you and your family. There is no excuse for what I did and I deserve to be here, imprisoned, and nowhere else. I hope one day to be able to explain to you in person how I have been seeing the world in a different way, but for now I can only offer my deepest remorse.

The second point, which has required the secrecy of this note, is that when you are in prison you hear about what is happening outside in the criminal world, or about to happen. In the woodwork room two days ago, I heard inmates talking about an incident planned for this week in London. A serious attack, maybe terrorism. Then I overheard two other prisoners talking similarly in the refectory yesterday. Something bad is definitely about to happen, possibly to do with climate change.

I can't tell the guards or the police, otherwise I will be branded a snitch and assaulted, even killed. So, I am telling you. I read about the Brave People Awards in the newspaper, for which you are a most deserving candidate, and I am confident you will work out what to do. And I am trying to put my evil wrongdoing to right.

Thank you - and good luck.

Regards,

Peter Goswell

The last thing Edie needed was another note, and especially not one from this disgusting man. She was glad her dad had refused a request for a visit, and pleased he hadn't even mentioned it to her. But the content of the note was fascinating.

CHAPTER 12

SWINBROOK

Monday morning felt like déjà vu, a repeat of three months earlier when Edie had shared her findings about Mum with Lizzie and Eli prior to the trip to Finsbury Park Tube Station. Only this time Eli was in no shape for a further adventure.

'That's really weird,' Lizzie remarked after Edie told her about the case of the long-lost friend and all the chance encounters. Lizzie was the first to have arrived at Edie's house, before Eli was up or Grace had started work.

It was nine in the morning, the first day of the May half-term break, and they were sitting in the playroom.

'I know!' Edie replied, and then tried to explain all she'd learned about fate and determinism from her conversation with Rabbi Abby.

Edie had already given Lizzie more details about the missing dogs case as well as an outline of the exam fraud case. By sharing her personal experiences, Edie hoped to pull her best friend back in closer. But it didn't work.

'Well, I'm not convinced,' Lizzie retorted about the apparent coincidences. 'No hard evidence,' she added flatly. Edie was disappointed but, deep down, she knew Lizzie was probably right.

Edie then tried to talk about Lizzie's family situation at home, but was repelled with a brisk 'no change' comment. Edie hadn't been forgiven for her inattentiveness, but at least Lizzie was here and they hadn't fallen out. Yet.

Next to arrive was Ethan, accepting the quid pro quo arrangement Edie had presented over a WhatsApp message. As Edie was helping Ethan with his brother's medical school exam problem, it felt fair that he would assist the detective with her latest investigation. Given the long drive ahead, Ethan asked for a strong cup of coffee. As Edie made him a drink, the doorbell rang again. Lizzie answered and Harry entered with his bicycle – this time more careful not to damage the console table.

'I didn't realise that others were ...' Harry mouthed to Edie at the other end of the hallway. He pointed in surprise towards Lizzie and the now visible Ethan who had emerged from the playroom, then decided against saying anything further.

'We need a driver,' Edie responded, 'and Ethan' – she looked at him – 'has kindly agreed to help.' Ethan took a gulp from his coffee and vaguely nodded. 'And you know Lizzie from school. She's my best friend and confidante ... and well, we're always looking out for each other.' Lizzie blushed and made as if it was nothing, although deep down she liked being described in this way, especially openly to others.

Grace arrived as Edie was explaining the plan to the team in the playroom. Edie fibbed that they were going to Hampstead Heath to spend the day at the funfair that had arrived for the half-term week. It was the same lie that Edie had told Dad and proved similarly successful. Thankfully, Eli still wasn't up, as he'd have seen right through it.

Edie grabbed a packet of ginger nut biscuits from a kitchen cupboard, filled her and Eli's water bottles, picked up her keys, stuffed it all into her rucksack and announced to the E-team that it was time.

'Come on everybody. Let's go!'

In the small, two-door Renault Clio, Lizzie and Harry sat in the back, Harry's longish legs cramped behind the driver's seat. Edie took the front passenger seat next to Ethan, who put her in charge of directions. Edie typed 'Swinbrook' into the navigation app on her phone, which calculated that it would take an hour and thirty-seven minutes to drive there.

Edie wedged her phone on the centre of the dashboard so Ethan could see it easily, then sat back as they set off on another journey of the unexpected. In the back, Harry and Lizzie chatted for a while before their voices went silent. Edie looked over her shoulder to see they'd both withdrawn into the inner worlds of AirPods.

As they ascended the North Circular flyover towards Staples Corner, Edie caught sight of Brent Cross Shopping Centre to her right. She remembered the many shopping trips with Mum. The purpose was usually for school clothes, although Edie always managed to persuade her mum into buying her something fun too. Or maybe, Edie now thought, it wasn't persuasion at all, and Mum had always been intending to treat her daughter. Edie smiled.

Once they'd reached the M40 motorway, Ethan passed his own phone over to Edie. 'Pick something from Spotify for us to listen to. I don't mind what – the journey's still another hour.'

Edie gladly accepted and opened Spotify on Ethan's phone. She clicked 'Playlists' and scrolled through the ten or so that Ethan had created. She was drawn by the title of the very first list, though, and scrolled back up again.

'What's this one?' Edie asked. '"Outside Chance".'

'Oh, that's my latest,' Ethan replied, keeping his eyes firmly on the road as the speedometer hit seventy. 'Still not that much on it.'

Intrigued, Edie carried on: 'Why did you give it that name?'

'Well, this might sound a bit odd, but the name – and the idea – came after a conversation I had with my brother last week.'

'You mean Martin, with the exam problem?'

'Yes, Martin. I've only got one brother,' he teased.

'What was the conversation?' Edie asked, looking at Ethan's profile. He was nice-looking with unusually prominent cheekbones.

'Martin told me last week that he'd met this girl, Ashley, at medical school. Actually, not met, they'd known each other for a while as they're in the same year, but they just weren't in the same friends' groups. But now they're going out together ... the last few weeks. He'd always thought she was so peng, but now he's crazy about her. Says it's the best thing that's ever happened to him. Thinks he might even be in love!'

'After a few weeks!' Edie scoffed, too strongly for her own liking.

'I know!' Ethan concurred, smiling. 'Sounds unbelievable, but that's what he told me.'

Edie gave it some thought. 'And how did they meet?'

'Here's the eerie part,' Ethan responded. 'And how it links to the playlist. He met her because she also failed the biochemistry exam, one of the few other medical students to write about the exocrine pancreas – correctly. They were sitting outside their tutor Dr Bannon's office, got talking and then went for a drink in the uni bar afterwards. And now it seems they are, well, in love.'

Edie flushed at the mention of Dr Bannon – who she'd lied to in her emails and was due to visit the following day – but she was captivated. 'So, they wouldn't have met if they hadn't both failed the exam?'

'Most likely not,' Ethan agreed. 'And that's what Martin was talking to me about. The unlikely set of events that led to him meeting Ashley, which he now feels was meant to be. That it wasn't just chance. And I get what he's saying.'

Edie shivered in her seat. 'So, the playlist ...?'

'Oh, yeah, sorry. So I started making a playlist with songs about stuff that's meant to be. You know, fated. Not all the songs, but some of them. And I called it "Outside Chance". It's been fun. Stick it on if you like.' Ethan waited but Edie did nothing, so he carried on. 'The lyrics of the first song – "Something Changed" by Pulp – are amazing … All about what the world might look like if two lovers hadn't actually met. But it starts with him saying he wrote the song *before* they met, as if it were destined.'

Stupefied, Edie looked back down at the phone and pressed 'Play'. The song made Edie cry, but she concealed her tears by looking out through the side window. As the track ended, Edie glanced over her shoulder to check on the back-seat passengers. Lizzie looked asleep, but Harry stared back intently. Edie was unsure if he was genuinely listening to anything through his AirPods, or if he'd heard her whole conversation with Ethan. Harry said nothing, and could easily still be angry with her. Was that jealousy in his eyes, though, Edie wondered?

Edie scrolled through the playlist – the name of one of the bands, Goat Girl, made her smile. She leant back, closed her eyes and for the next hour let the music drift over her, the steady hum of the tyres on the motorway enhancing the dream-like experience.

The lyrics of each song spoke to Edie, telling her something – about her short journey through life, about everything that had happened with Mum, about where she was at right now, about the importance of trusting herself. Maybe the significance wasn't exactly what each artist had intended, but Edie found meaning in the words. They made sense to her as lines from different songs became entangled:

> Don't be afraid, don't try to run away ... life could have been very different but then

something changed ... for a minute there I lost myself ... nothing is quite as it seems ... serpents in my mind ... we're absolute beginners with eyes completely open ... I can think what I want, I can feel what I feel ... I could be the one ... that don't kill me can only make me stronger ... I'm looking for the magic ... the only thing that stays the same is that everything must change ...

'We're here,' Ethan announced as he indicated to turn right off the busy A40, snapping Edie from her trance. A signpost directed them down a narrow, single-lane country road towards the village of Swinbrook, one mile away.

Edie turned off the hauntingly beautiful song, 'Phantom Walls', and placed Ethan's phone on the dashboard. Shortly before reaching the village, Ethan pulled over into a layby. Edie and Ethan twisted around to face the rear-seat passengers.

'So, what's the plan?' Lizzie asked semi-interestedly.

Harry was the first to respond: 'Well, we know where my dad's car went from tracking Edie's old iPhone.' He pulled his own phone from his pocket. 'I took a screenshot of the location and sent it to myself. Here ...' He held out his phone and pointed at the icon just off-centre to the left. 'This is where the car stopped moving. This looks like where we should search.'

'Seems like it's not far past that church.' Lizzie pointed to the lower left of the screen, then scrunched up her face quizzically. 'But that seems to be the middle of a field?'

From the dashboard Ethan retrieved his own phone, opened Google Maps to show 'My Location' and then placed his screen next to Harry's. 'Look, we're here now,' he indicated on his own screen. 'And Harry's dad's car's position' – he compared the two screens before pointing to the top-left corner of his own – 'was over here.'

Ethan adjusted his own map, then used two fingers to enlarge it. 'It looks like Harry's dad parked near a small building just there ... on the edge of the village, by the fields. It might be a small track into a field.' He examined closer: 'Does that say Faws Grove?'

They all peered in with curiosity.

Edie broke the silence. 'So, here's the plan. We park the car here' – she pointed – 'by the church. Not too close to the actual building, so we're not seen. Ethan, are you okay to stay in the car, in case we need to make a quick getaway?' The driver nodded begrudgingly.

'Harry, Lizzie and I will walk the last part, round the back of the village to that building on the map. See what we find. Split up if necessary. We'll set timers on our phones for thirty minutes, so even if we separate, we know we have to be back at the car before the time is up. No later, else that means trouble. We have each other's numbers and should call if there's any problem. Any danger.'

Mention of the word 'danger' made it all feel suddenly more real. Not a game or a bit of fun, but an expedition with risk – although risk carried excitement. Edie placed her right hand out and the others each put a hand on top: they were all in, no turning back now.

Ethan restarted the car and crossed the small, pretty bridge over the River Windrush. It was disconcertingly quiet. 'In an absolute emergency – if something happens or someone gets lost – we meet there ...' He pointed at the Swan Inn. Silence suggested assent, so Ethan continued slowly round the bend and pulled in close to St Mary's Church, near the centre of the village.

'What are we looking for?' Lizzie asked, concern now etched into a frown.

Edie wondered if it had been such a good idea bringing her best friend along. She didn't want to make her feel even worse.

Edie placed a hand comfortingly on her best friend's shoulder as she got out the car. 'It'll all be fine,' she tried to assure her. 'We're looking for anything unusual, anything that doesn't look right. Or strange behaviour.'

All three set their phone timers. 'See you in thirty minutes or less,' Edie told Ethan as they set off around the churchyard.

Whilst the church looked majestically ancient, the side roads around the back of the village contained a strange mixture of building styles. Initially, most of the homes were pretty cottages in classical creamy Cotswold stone: some were smaller and cutely squat, others grand and sprawling with dry stone walls protecting manicured lawns. Yet, just a hundred metres back from the main street, many of the homes had a more twentieth-century appearance.

'I prefer the cottages,' Lizzie commented, pointing at a tired bungalow, dull grey and run-down, probably built in the 1950s. Peeling paint covered half the exterior.

Edie held her phone out in front of her, trying to steer the group down side roads towards the place where they believed Heath's car had ended its trip.

'Left here,' she directed, noting the street sign on the corner. 'Brook End.'

Harry and Lizzie didn't look convinced.

'And let's try right here,' Edie added, fifty metres further on. 'Handley Lane,' she noted aloud again.

'We've already been walking for six minutes,' Harry grumbled. 'Do you even know if we're going in the right direction?'

'Yes,' Edie replied assertively. 'Look.' She showed him her Google Maps page, tilting the phone slightly to the left. 'We're here, and we're heading for ... here. Just a couple more turns, I think.'

'There's nobody around,' Lizzie interjected. 'I mean really nobody. And it's a weekday. Where is everyone?'

'There was that woman back there in her front garden, cutting the roses,' Harry corrected.

'Yeah,' Lizzie said. 'But she went indoors as soon as you said "Hi". It's kinda creepy.'

Oblivious to the conversation, Edie carried on. 'Left here, then first right again and we should be there.'

The others dutifully followed and they ended up on a nameless lane, narrower than the ones since the church, and marked with a 'no through road' signpost at the entrance. The sky darkened ominously as they set off down the lane.

'Look.' Harry pointed to wheel tracks on the ground. 'A car's certainly been down here. And it rained a few days ago, so it must've been since then.'

'Who are you? The Lone Ranger?' Lizzie jested.

'No,' Harry replied with a smile. 'Tonto.'

Edie swallowed her irritation with Lizzie's flirting and kept up her concentration. 'There.' She gestured towards a small building a hundred metres ahead at the very end of the dead-end lane. 'That's the place, I'm sure.'

Eight-foot hedges on both sides of the lane created a tunnel-like feel, a horror film vista funnelling them towards the cabin-in-the-woods at the end. Now, halfway down the lane, the only options were to go either forwards or back from where they had come.

They slowed their pace and heightened their awareness. All of a sudden, there was a loud thrashing sound and a pheasant burst through the hedgerow on their left. The speckled brown-black bird, its red and green head bobbing furiously, was followed closely by a fox, who stopped in surprise at all the people.

'Shoo! Get away!' Harry put himself between the two animals and attempted to usher the predator away. At first, the fox was having none of it, holding its ground and staring intently at the teenager. But when Harry raised his voice, the fox reluctantly sloped off.

'Well done, Harry,' a male voice congratulated him as the pheasant disappeared through the shrubbery opposite.

Edie turned around, surprised to see Ethan. 'Sorry, it was too boring waiting in the car. And I thought you might need help.'

Edie was irritated that her plan had been broken, but she was also upset with herself for being so distracted that she'd not heard Ethan's footsteps.

The incident, however, put Edie and her accomplices even more on edge, and their pace slowed further as they approached the building. Constructed in the same drab, mass-produced council housing style, the single-storey home stood spookily alone, enclosed by tall hedgerows that wrapped around the back of the building.

Yet, there was more to this space than was initially apparent. First, Edie noticed two estate agent signs lying flat on the ground to the left. Placing a finger to her lips to advise the others to be quiet, she tentatively made her way over and took some photos. Both signs had the same design and included the name and phone number of the agent. One read 'For sale' and the other 'Available to let'. Muddied, wet and damaged in places, the signs had evidently been horizontal on the ground for some time.

Edie beckoned the others over to join her by the wall of the house. Harry and Ethan came quickly, Lizzie lagged apprehensively.

'Look,' Edie whispered as she pointed to the side window. 'Inside here …' She placed her face close to the glass, hands cupped to see more clearly behind the net curtains. 'Somebody lives here or has been staying here. Maybe more than one person – see the coffee cups on the table – and there …' – she gestured to the floor – 'it looks like maps.'

Edie leant in even closer, her forehead now touching the cold glass. 'Are they actually maps?' she murmured aloud. 'More like drawings. Blueprints?'

'Like when they're planning a bank robbery in a film,' Lizzie offered quietly.

Edie's eyeline caught something else unusual on the floor, next to the sofa. A tangle of wires and, was it, batteries? Edie turned to face her best friend and was about to say something.

'Over there,' Harry hissed, indicating the back of the house. 'Looks pretty new to me.'

Edie followed Harry's finger to a motorbike parked discreetly away from the gravelled yard.

Careful not to make too much noise on the stone chippings, they circled the rear of the house.

'Cool motorbike,' Lizzie whispered, looking around anxiously. 'It's an odd shape, though.'

'It's an electric motorbike,' Harry explained. 'And this is a pretty new one. They can look a bit strange – no exhaust pipe. I visited a showroom with my dad a while back, but he chose an electric car in the end.'

Edie thought through the implications. Whilst the house looked run down and derelict externally, inside it appeared to have been recently used. And the presence of the electric motorbike suggested that at least one of those users might be still present. Edie noticed a structure set back into a break in the hedge at the rear of the house.

'Is that a shed?' Ethan said softly, seeing what Edie was staring at. The quartet wandered over silently.

The outhouse was the size of a very large garden shed. Well concealed by the overgrown hedge, closer inspection revealed double-glazed windows set into the slats at the front as well as a wooden veranda to the side, with an awning providing some waterproof cover. Under the canopy and abutting the house was a stack of logs, in front of which stood a hefty tree stump. The surface of the stump was covered in multiple cut-marks and crevices. Embedded frighteningly in the stump was a large axe.

'I don't like this,' Lizzie admitted. 'Something's not right. The logs are wet – like they've been here for a while. And the axe. It's scary. Let's go back.'

Edie tried to pacify her. 'It's okay, Lizzie. It's probably been there for ages.'

'We're only at sixteen minutes,' Harry announced in agreement, checking his phone timer. 'We can look around a bit more.'

Despite the presence of a padlock, Edie tugged at the shed door: unsurprisingly, it wouldn't budge. She moved to the nearest window and again cupped her hands to her face and pressed against the glass to see inside. In the centre of the room, two makeshift tables were just discernible.

On the tables sat an array of various-sized plastic containers, many with labels, as well as flatter packages seemingly wrapped in film or tape. Tools of various descriptions, including screwdrivers and tweezers, were scattered around on the tabletops, alongside boxes of nails and screws. Beakers and other measuring flasks completed the murky picture.

Edie placed her phone camera against the glass and took some photos, zooming in on key items. Harry broke her concentration.

'Faws Grove,' he stated, staring at an old-fashioned waymarker a few metres over to the right. 'Half a mile, apparently.' Overgrown trees made the sign easy to miss, and also semi-obscured the adjacent narrow footpath to which the directional arrow of the sign corresponded.

Edie observed large footprints on the ground, recently trodden despite the middle-of-nowhere location of the track. Her detective instincts were tickled.

'What's that?' Lizzie suddenly blurted out, worry obvious in her tone. The others stopped what they were doing to listen.

'I don't hear anything,' Harry replied. They waited.

'There it is again,' Lizzie reiterated, and this time Edie could also hear the unmistakable sound of approaching footsteps.

Certain in the knowledge that there was only one location from where the noise could be coming, the foursome tiptoed the last quarter of the house perimeter, staying close to the hedgerow for cover, until they were able to see down the lane from which they'd arrived. Approaching the house from the lane with determined pace was a tall figure, probably a man, wearing black leather motorcycle trousers, jacket and boots, face hidden by a black-and-grey helmet with the darkly tinted visor down. Presumably, he had been disturbed by something earlier and was preparing to take off on his bike.

The image was menacing.

'Shit, I told you we should leave,' Lizzie mumbled.

'We'll be alright,' Edie hushed. 'Just let me think.'

Harry seemed momentarily paralysed.

'Let's go down that track to Faws Grove,' Edie proposed. 'I remember the map – then we can loop back round to the village.'

The footsteps were sounding more distinctive, more disturbing and closer.

'I'm *not* going down that track!' Lizzie insisted too loudly. 'We don't know where it goes – or if you can even get through to the end – and if he follows us, we're stuck. I'm hiding behind there.' She pointed to the woodshed.

'You really will be trapped if he finds you there.' Edie worried for her friend. She was uncertain if Lizzie's choice was based on merely doing something different to herself.

'He won't find me,' Lizzie contended. 'You do whatever … but that's what I'm doing.'

Edie looked to Harry for back-up: 'And you?'

'Track,' he replied. Perhaps his irritation with Edie was diminishing.

'Please, Lizzie,' Edie implored a final time. 'Let's keep together.' But her best friend was already making for the woodshed.

'I'll stay with Lizzie,' Ethan proposed. 'Make sure she's okay. Just stick to the plan and we'll see you back at the car.'

Edie thanked Ethan as he headed off.

With the footsteps sounding very near the top of the lane, Edie darted down the track to Faws Grove, her hands brushing away overhanging vegetation. She was closely followed by the captain of the school football team.

After a couple of minutes of panicked running, Edie and Harry reached a junction with a small country lane.

She had a naturally good sense of direction and guessed that turning right would probably lead back round to the village. But, instinctively, Edie felt she needed to cross straight over, on the continuation of the same track. A new waymarker indicated that Faws Grove was now only a quarter of a mile away.

'That way,' Harry proposed, pointing right, hardly panting given all his sporting fitness.

'No, straight ahead,' Edie commanded with little scope for negotiation. A thudding sound from the track behind them clinched the deal, and Edie caught sight of a helmet bobbing intermittently above the hedge about fifty metres back. The person clearly didn't want to be recognised.

They continued down the track at speed for another couple of minutes until reaching a stile. Edie clambered over, losing her footing as she descended.

'Ow!' she exclaimed, clutching her lower leg. She took several further steps before turning to face Harry, now on the top of the stile. 'I think I've sprained my ankle,' she said with apprehension.

Harry jumped down athletically, drew Edie's arm around his neck and reassured her. Edie wondered if he'd forgiven her or whether he was just naturally gallant.

The track ended abruptly inside the border of a small wood, or copse, and Edie assumed they'd now entered Faws Grove. Through a gap in the dark clouds, sunbeams glinted in latticed rays between the trees, creating an atmosphere that Edie would have found magical if they weren't being chased by a possible madman.

Harry led them deeper into the wood. 'Come on. We can hide where it's darker.'

Edie limped, debilitated by her ankle, but with Harry's support they weaved between trees, keeping off the woodland tracks. Dry leaves and twigs crunched underfoot, but they pressed on, staying as quiet as they could. Edie was heartened that she could see the edge of the grove on most sides, the brightness of escape a symbol of hope and safety.

'Huh?' Harry grunted suddenly. 'What the hell is that?'

Heavily concealed in the centre of the wood, well off the footpaths, stood another shed-like building, similar in size to the one by the house but more ramshackle. It would be invisible to walkers sticking to the track – not that this remote woodland likely attracted many ramblers. As they approached silently, Edie thought that it looked more like a forest hut, complete with a small front door – a witch's home out of a Grimms' fairy tale, missing only smoke from the chimney.

'We need to have a look,' Edie stated in a hushed tone.

'Why?' came the perplexed response.

'Just a feeling' was all Edie could offer, as Harry keenly scouted the surroundings for any sign of Helmet Head.

'Well, be quick as we've got to get out of here. I'll keep a lookout.'

Edie checked the hut's single front window, but it was filthy, plus it was too dark – outside and in – to see anything. Hobbling, Edie made it to the front door, where a padlock barred her entry. She shoved and there was a creak.

'Quickly!' Harry insisted.

Edie rammed the door again and this time it budged, opening a few inches until prevented from further movement by the padlocked latch. Immediately, the smell hit Edie: pungent and acrid, the odour was distinctively of animals.

'That stinks!' Harry recoiled. 'Can we *please* go now!'

'One moment.' Edie flicked on her iPhone torch and shone it through the crack in the door.

A low-grade whining accompanied the lighting up of the hut interior, and Edie was taken aback by what she saw. At least two living dogs were visible, with a third curled up on the floor. All three were muzzled to avoid attracting attention, and those on their legs looked scared. Otherwise, however, the hut was surprisingly well kept: scraps of food, dog biscuits and a half-full water bowl littered the small floor space. The limited amount of faeces meant the place was cleaned out regularly, which was presumably when the muzzles were removed to allow the dogs to eat. The smell was acrid, nonetheless.

'What the ...!' Harry exclaimed, checking over his shoulder.

'There are dogs in here,' Edie explained. 'We've got to get them out.'

'No, we don't – not now! They're not ours and we have to get away.'

But Edie wasn't paying any attention to Harry's protestations. Instead, she was transfixed. Was that Quincy in the corner? Edie took a few quick photos before Harry grabbed her assertively.

'We're off … right now. Look.' Harry pointed. 'He's over there and clearly searching. Let's head in the opposite direction, behind the trees as much as possible.' Edie saw the figure fifty metres away, moving with purpose.

Again, Harry wrapped his right arm around Edie's waist and slung her left arm around his neck. 'Let's go!' They set off together, advancing in five-metre bursts, ducking behind trees in-between, Harry ensuring he kept his eyes on Helmet Head whenever possible.

After two or three minutes, they were at the edge of the copse, albeit a different section to where they'd entered. Stopping to catch their breath, Edie could make out Helmet Head at the witch's hut, a ray of light reflecting off his (by now she assumed it was a man) helmet. He looked at the door suspiciously, perhaps noticing the damaged hinge, before making a 360-degree inspection with heightened intensity.

And then the inexcusable horror happened.

Harry's phone timer rang. The 'Radiate' ringtone at high volume. Edie had put her phone on silent when they were at the building, but Harry clearly hadn't.

Adrenaline flooded Edie's body as Harry fumbled clumsily to turn it off. But the damage was done. Helmet Head caught the direction of the sound and was now staring right at Edie.

'Run!' Harry directed, grabbing Edie's hand once he'd silenced the phone.

Edie knew she'd just have to put up with the pain of her injured ankle, and they set off across a small field in the direction Edie was confident led back to the village. As they neared the same narrow lane they'd hit further up earlier, Edie looked behind her. Although the leather gear and heavy boots were affecting his running speed, Helmet Head was a third of the way across the field and gaining ground. But that wasn't the worst of it.

'Oh my God,' Edie yelped fearfully. 'He's got the axe!'

She prayed that Lizzie was safe. Ethan too.

Even Harry looked scared now, but he was brave and level-headed. 'We need to get back to the village … where there's people … Let's go left.'

After a hundred metres, the lane arced to the right and they were upon the village, but strangely there still wasn't a person in sight. The lane straightened, with an occasional cottage on either side, and Edie considered ringing a doorbell for help. That would eat up time, however, with the prospect of no answer. Edie looked behind them again. Helmet Head was still gaining ground, holding the axe in front of him with two hands as if ready to wield it.

With Harry's support, Edie continued her limping run, the pain masked by the adrenaline of fight or flight and her spirits revived by the sight ahead.

'Look! It's the church,' Edie screeched, noting the relief on Harry's face.

A minute later, the exhilaration of reaching the church was met with immediate deflation: Ethan's car was nowhere to be seen. Edie stopped momentarily but the thudding footsteps, albeit slightly less audible, meant that Helmet Head was still close.

'The pub!' Harry screamed. 'The emergency location … they've gone to the pub car park.'

'Oh my god,' Edie blurted out. 'I don't know if I can run any further.'

Harry stared directly at her. 'Yes, you can,' he asserted. 'We're not giving up now.'

He was right, and that was all Edie needed. Never give up. Never say die.

The lane wended round two further bends, and with the pub now visible, Edie realised she couldn't hear any chasing footsteps. She chanced another look over her shoulder.

'He's gone,' Edie proclaimed.

They both stopped and listened. Nothing. Not a sound, allowing them to slow to a jog and then walk the final stretch.

Situated next to the historic bridge over the River Windrush and surrounded by spacious gardens, the pub was clearly closed and deserted, but in the car park – to Edie's utter relief – was the Renault Clio. Ethan opened the passenger door from the inside, and Edie breathed a huge sigh of relief at the sight of Lizzie seated quietly in the back.

Harry clambered quickly into the rear and Edie jumped into the front passenger seat. Leaning back, Edie squeezed Lizzie's hand tenderly.

'What happened? Where on earth have you been?' Ethan asked.

'Tell you later. Let's just get out of here,' Edie replied.

'No, tell me now,' Ethan repeated. 'We've been worried since we got away from that guy in the motorcycle outfit …'

'Please!' Edie pleaded. 'Just drive. I'll tell you on the way.'

The impasse lasted half a minute or so.

'Over there!' Harry yelled suddenly. 'Look, by the cricket pitch.'

The field next to the pub had long ago been converted into a cricket pitch, famous locally for Sunday matches through the summer. Only now it was being used disrespectfully for another purpose – as a shortcut. Barrelling over the grass was a motorbike, Helmet Head clearly the rider. He'd evidently raced back to the house to retrieve his bike. Disbelieving, they watched Helmet Head's progress towards the pub car park.

'Drive!' Edie shouted at Ethan, who fumbled for the keys in his pocket before realising they were already in the ignition.

Ethan turned the key, but the car wouldn't start. He tried again with the same outcome. Edie's eyes met Ethan's with alarm. Third time and the engine kicked into life, and Ethan sped out of the car park, tyres screeching on the gravel.

Crossing the bridge, Edie watched the motorbike change direction, heading now to the far corner of the field where it would meet the lane where the car was heading.

'Faster!' Edie urged. 'He's trying to cut us off at the crossroads.'

Ethan accelerated as much as he dared, but it was a single-track lane so they would collide with any vehicle coming round a corner. Reaching the junction just before the motorcycle exited the field, Ethan checked left and right. No cars, so he crossed the junction just as Helmet Head came right up behind them.

'Look! He's got that axe!' Lizzie cried fearfully. It was wedged between the pursuer's leg and the bike seat.

Ethan sped up despite the risk of oncoming traffic, the danger from behind clearly worse – but the motorcycle was now upon them, tailgating.

'Stop!' yelled Edie.

Ethan gasped. 'What?'

'Hit the brakes! Stop the car!'

Suddenly twigging what Edie had in mind, Ethan slammed down on the footbrake sending everyone in the car lurching forwards, saved by their seat belts. Almost immediately, there was a loud whack as the motorcycle and its rider smashed into the back of the car.

Time stood still as Ethan realised what he'd done, and all four felt momentarily numbed by the awfulness of the situation. The car had stalled from the abrupt halt, the engine dead. 'Shall I go and check on him?' Ethan asked eventually. 'Check he's alright?'

'No!' Lizzie retorted aggressively. 'Just get us out of here.'

'Oh shit! He's getting up,' Harry cried as they all saw Helmet Head slowly stand upright in the road directly behind.

'Go!' Edie shrieked.

Ethan started the engine, thankfully first time, as Edie watched the motorcyclist raise the axe forebodingly above his head. The car jolted forward at the same time as the axe crashed down on the back of the car, cracking the rear windscreen. Harry and Lizzie cowered, expecting splinters of glass.

Thankfully, the windscreen held – saved by the car pulling off – and they were away. The bike appeared too damaged to give chase. Helmet Head stared intently, removed a phone from his jacket pocket and appeared to take a photo. The car registration number, possibly?

On the journey back, they were all too stunned to talk much. Lizzie explained how she and Ethan had stayed hidden until the man went up the track, and then ran straight back to the car. Lizzie had noticed the axe missing from the stump.

Edie and Harry then shared their experiences and findings from Faws Grove.

Edie's mind, though, was whirring with various thoughts and ideas, and once safely back on the motorway she asked Ethan if she could put on some music. He gave her his phone and she restarted the 'Outside Chance' playlist.

The songs once again washed over Edie. As they closed back in on London, one stood out – an eerily atmospheric song by Quiet Hollers called 'Mont Blanc', which reminded Edie of Dad's treasured ballpoint that Mum had bought for his fortieth birthday present.

The song's sad, post-apocalyptic lyrics made Edie think of a world wrecked by climate change, but the chorus also reminded her of how everything feels changed – friendships, wellbeing, expectations – when something really bad happens. One particular lyric, however, a phrase repeated after the chorus, brought Edie's thinking to an abrupt halt.

A lump formed in Edie's throat. Goosebumps prickled her skin.

One word that she couldn't bring herself to say aloud …

CHAPTER 13

THE EXOCRINE PANCREAS

Bribery. Surprisingly effective, especially on the young.

Lizzie pulled out of accompanying Edie to King's College to meet Dr Bannon, stating in a text message the previous evening that she'd been too upset by the Swinbrook trip and needed a break from crime fighting. Edie had been half-expecting this, and was worried that their damaged relationship was now getting beyond repair.

Lizzie's withdrawal had also put Edie in a fix as she needed an accomplice for the university visit, and it was now too late to call on Yasmina or Charlie – or, indeed, any of her other friends.

Only one option remained: her brother. Eli's unashamed venality, along with his tough negotiation on payment, took Edie by surprise – especially given Eli's bleary-eyed, first-thing-in-the-morning appearance. Ceding more ground than she'd wished, Edie agreed to £25 cash plus one month of Ethan choosing all the TV programmes. In addition, he wanted the money upfront, obliging Edie to relinquish a quarter of Donna's down payment for the long-lost friend case.

But at least Edie now had an extra pair of hands and eyes. She wasn't sure exactly how it would play out with

Dr Bannon, but she had a feeling that she'd be less successful alone. The previous evening, Edie had almost withdrawn from the meeting altogether, such was the turmoil in her mind after they'd returned from the Cotswolds. Ethan – who'd decided to tell his mum that a stone had hit the rear windscreen on the motorway – had kindly deposited Edie, Lizzie and Harry at their respective homes. They were all in a state of shock about Helmet Head, and it had taken Edie some effort to calm her thoughts. She finally got some sleep after logging an online message of concern with the RSPCA about the semi-abandoned dogs.

To her surprise, though, Edie had awoken energised and purposeful, rather than tired and dispirited, and her ankle felt much better. Sadly, Lizzie didn't feel the same.

In bed first thing, Edie had formulated her strategy for the day. First, wake Eli and bribe him to be Lizzie's replacement, explaining the background of Martin's case (not everything, of course, but what Eli needed to know to be a good assistant); next, tell Dad about the trip and get his agreement; visit Dr Bannon and rectify Martin's problem, whilst also getting information for Edie's more significant case; and, finally, take all her findings down the road to Donna in the afternoon.

All quite straightforward. How could anything possibly go wrong?

With Eli now successfully on board, Dad was treated, for once, to (almost) the truth. Edie checked with him over breakfast that it was okay to visit King's College, although her justification that the trip was related to a half-term school chemistry project was complete fabrication. Edie played on her knowledge that King's was where Dad had studied medicine, bigging up the sentimental connection to such a level that the addition of her brother passed unnoticed. The only issue Dad raised was why Edie hadn't told him about the visit earlier – to which she looked deliberately surprised and faked: 'What do you mean, Dad, I told you about it last week?'

Soon after ten o'clock, Edie and Eli jumped on the W3 for the short bus journey to Finsbury Park. Renovations at the station meant they couldn't use the ramp that led from Wells Terrace to the Underground trains. Edie could sense Eli's apprehension as they walked close to the ticket counter where, a few months earlier, he'd successfully lied about losing his sister and where he'd managed to weep crocodile tears, although hours later he'd remained expressionless and dry-eyed when confronted with the horrific evidence they'd found.

Together, brother and sister descended the stairs to the Victoria Line southbound platform, deliberately going to the opposite end of the platform to where Mum had stood that fateful day. Once on the Tube, Edie again went through the plan for the visit with Eli, then they sat quietly as the stations drifted by. No headphones or music, just two kids watching the world from the rear carriage of a Tube train.

At Warren Street, they switched over and took the Northern Line to Charing Cross, where they exited onto the

Strand. Edie opened Google Maps on her phone and led the way eastbound down the wide main road in the direction of the university. It was a warmish spring day, sunshine and cloud, although Edie thought the tourists sporting only T-shirts were being overly optimistic about the London weather.

A tiny road on the right marked the private entrance to the Savoy Hotel. A memory stirred in the back of Edie's mind from when she'd seen an exhibition of Impressionist painters in Toronto on a family trip to visit Grandfather David. Mum loved Monet's oils of nineteenth-century London, painted – as she told Edie – from his room at the back of the Savoy overlooking the River Thames.

Once they'd crossed the road leading to Waterloo Bridge, Google Maps advised they'd arrived, but it took Edie a couple more minutes to locate the main entrance and the porter's lodge.

'Who you visiting, luv?' the duty porter asked, and five minutes later Dr Bannon arrived from inside the building. The grey-haired, bespectacled biochemistry lecturer escorted the children through the barriers and down a large, wide central corridor.

'Well, nice to meet you, Edie,' Dr Bannon announced rather formally. 'And who might this young man be?'

Eli bristled but held his cool. He didn't like being referred to as a 'young man', and he didn't like people posing a question about him to somebody else when he was clearly present. Eli was about to answer, but his sister got in first.

'Oh, this is my brother, Eli. He's also very interested in becoming a doctor, like our dad.' Edie paused for effect as Dr Bannon indicated they should walk up the main staircase. 'Did I tell you my dad was a doctor?' Edie asked. 'And studied medicine here, at King's College? A long time ago, though.'

The lecturer smiled. 'Yes, indeed, young lady, you did tell me that.' It was Edie's turn to resent the tone, but she recognised that Dr Bannon didn't share the arrogant smarminess of some men his age; rather his language was of an old-fashioned and kindly nature.

'Third floor. Hope you don't mind all the stairs!' Dr Bannon jested, finding himself rather amusing. 'Most of the biochemistry teaching is on the Guy's Campus, but we have labs here – which I thought would be more interesting for you,' he beamed.

By the time they'd ascended the stairs, Edie was out of breath and took a puff from her inhaler. Dr Bannon flashed his pass to open a set of magnetically locked double doors, through which they entered a narrow, white-walled corridor with a distinctly clinical appearance.

Dr Bannon guided the Franklin siblings along. To the left and right side of the corridor were administrative rooms and storage cupboards, as well as the occasional door marked with a biohazard sign. Two men in lab coats passed by, acknowledging Dr Bannon with a smile.

'Let's start in my office.' Dr Bannon held his pass against a blue door at the very end of the corridor, the nameplate stating that the lecturer was deputy head of the biochemistry department. After a soft click, he turned the handle and led the children inside.

Windowless and musty, the office was also cluttered and messy, papers and books strewn across surfaces and shelves. Yet, there was a warm and homely feeling to the impersonal space: photos of Dr Bannon's family on the walls and desk, and houseplants in assorted coloured pots.

'You sit there.' Dr Bannon pointed at two plastic chairs as he whisked items off the matching white coffee table. Dr Bannon sat behind his desk, rather than next to the children, which suited Edie as she purposefully scanned her surroundings on the lookout for anything useful that might provide bargaining power.

'So, Edie, you said you were interested in being a doctor,' Dr Bannon began, 'and your brother apparently too. What is it you'd like to know or ask me about biochemistry and medicine?'

Suddenly, Edie realised that she hadn't prepared for this part of the conversation, as her attention was focused on Ethan's brother, Martin, and his exam fraud problem.

'Is it hard to become a doctor?' was the first question that came into her head.

'Yes, of course.' Dr Bannon launched in with natural enthusiasm. 'Well, you have to do science A levels, of course. Maths, biology, chemistry, physics – any three out of those four – usually with A* grades. Different to your father's time and very competitive. Do you like the science subjects at school, Edie?'

Edie couldn't stand anything to do with physics, and chemistry held about the same appeal, although she was strong at maths. 'I love them,' she feigned with a smile. 'All that interesting stuff about gravity and acceleration and … and …' She was struggling. 'And chemicals … the Periodic Table … magnesium!'

'Right,' Dr Bannon said, unconvinced. 'And what about you, Eli?'

With the lecturer's focus temporarily on her brother, Edie continued to survey what was visible, noticing a laptop as well as a desktop computer, but all the scattered papers were too disorganised or distant to interpret.

After a brief pause, Eli did his best: 'I like the shows about hospitals and doctors on TV … *Holby City*, *House*, er … *Grey's Anatomy*.' Edie had never seen him watch any of these and was amazed he even knew the names. She was also impressed.

'Oh, yes,' Dr Bannon agreed. 'I love *House* too – all those medical mysteries and strange diseases!'

For a while, further questions and answers were blandly exchanged. Eventually, Dr Bannon asked Edie and Eli if they'd like to see the laboratories.

'Yes!' they responded enthusiastically in tandem.

Dr Bannon led his guests out of the office – closing the door carefully behind them – down the corridor, then made a left and a right before guiding them through another set of magnetic double doors labelled 'Biochemistry Laboratory A'. On entry, Dr Bannon directed them to sit on the grey stools at a benchtop. At the far end of the room, two women in lab coats were busy with large beakers by a sink.

For fifteen minutes, Dr Bannon explained the types of experiments they did in the lab before moving on to his own area of research interest – glycogen metabolism and the Krebs cycle. Edie supressed a yawn whilst Eli fidgeted in his seat. To liven things up, Dr Bannon then conducted a mini experiment in front of Edie and Eli, using magnesium and a Bunsen burner to create a flash of white light. Neither of the children was particularly impressed.

'I really need the loo,' Eli stated, having received the agreed hand signal from Edie (scratching her right ear with two fingers).

'Oh, I see. Well, I'll have to take you there ...'

'Not yet!' Edie intervened energetically. 'I was really hoping you'd explain more about ... about ...' She thought quickly. '... about diseases of glycogen metabolism. What happens when that goes wrong?'

'But I really need to go to the loo – like now – right now,' Eli pleaded.

Dr Bannon looked uncertainly between the children, and Edie seized the opportunity. 'You could just give him your pass,' she suggested sweetly.

'I'm not really supposed to do that ...'

'He'll be fine,' Edie said reassuringly. 'And we won't tell anybody about the pass. Promise!' She grinned.

'Alright, I suppose,' Dr Bannon acquiesced unsuspiciously, pulling the lanyard cord over his head. 'Take a right and the toilet is first on the left through the double doors.' He handed his pass over to Eli. 'We went past them on the way here. Come straight back after, please.'

Eli nodded and jumped off his stool. Struck by her brother's spirit, Edie's felt an incredible warmth inside, a loving feeling for Eli that she couldn't remember last experiencing.

Edie did her best to look interested as Dr Bannon wholeheartedly shared his knowledge of diseases of the metabolic system. She nodded purposefully at every opportunity as time ticked by. Five minutes, ten minutes – at which point Dr Bannon expressed concern over Eli's whereabouts, which Edie deftly deflected.

Just before fifteen minutes, Edie's phone buzzed in her pocket. 'Let me just check he's okay,' Edie said, smiling knowingly as she pulled the mobile from her jacket pocket. As Dr Bannon paused, Edie checked WhatsApp and saw a set of newly sent photos. She looked through them carefully.

'Everything alright?' Dr Bannon asked in his gently bumbling manner.

'Oh, yes,' Edie responded, at the very moment Eli pushed his way back through the doors into the biochemistry lab.

'Dr Bannon.' Edie started afresh. 'What I'm really most interested in is diabetes.'

'Ah, fascinating disease,' Dr Bannon nodded. 'I'm glad you asked. It's caused by a problem with …'

'The pancreas,' Edie interrupted. 'Isn't that right?'

'Yes, indeed! Well done, young lady, you're clearly very smart. Deficiency in pancreatic function is the cause of the problem. Well, to be more precise, one part of that organ, the …'

'The endocrine pancreas,' Edie intervened abruptly.

This time, Dr Bannon took a moment, his enthusiasm disturbed. 'Yes, indeed, you're right, the endocrine pancreas.'

'And that's quite separate to the *exocrine* part of the pancreas' – Edie stressed the difference – 'which is responsible for producing enzymes that help us digest our food.' Edie paused for dramatic effect.

The expression on Dr Bannon's face shifted to disbelief and borderline irritation. 'What exactly do you want to know, Edie?' he enquired forcibly. 'It sounds like you are already familiar with the cause of diabetes.'

Edie fiddled with the Bunsen burner on the bench, but internally she felt strong and held her ground, comforted by the supportive presence of Eli, now back on the adjacent stool. 'Here's the thing, Dr Bannon. I've not been completely honest with you.' The biochemistry lecturer watched on, his stare intensifying. 'I'm not really interested in studying medicine, although my dad is a doctor. I'm more concerned with a friend … of a friend … who is studying medicine here at King's, right now, and who failed the end-of-year biochemistry exam.'

'What the heck is going on here?' Dr Bannon exclaimed. 'First, you lied to me and shouldn't even be here, and now you're speaking nonsense. Tell me, who exactly is this *supposed* student to whom you're referring?'

'That's private. Confidential,' Edie countered, prepared for the question. 'And it doesn't really matter. What is important, though, is that this person – and a few others – wrote correctly in the exam about the much lesser known *exocrine* pancreas. Yet, they failed the exam, while everybody else, over 200 students, wrote incorrectly about the more obvious *endocrine* pancreas – and passed. Doesn't seem fair, eh?'

'I don't know where or how you got this information, but it's none of your business.' Dr Bannon stood up, red-faced. 'Now, it's time for both of you to get out of here before I call security.'

Edie, however, was not to be deterred. 'And students tried to bring this to your attention, and to the attention of your biochemistry colleagues, but you refused to engage with them or release the exam paper – presumably worried about how it would look if almost the whole academic year of students had to come back in the middle of the summer to retake an exam.'

'Get out of here, right now! Both of you,' Dr Bannon yelled, trying to nudge Eli off his stool. But Eli clung on by gripping the benchtop. 'You don't know what you're talking about, and you've got no evidence for any of this.'

'But that's where you're wrong, Dr Bannon.' Edie launched WhatsApp on her phone and opened the photos just sent by Eli. She held on tight to the phone and turned the screen to Dr Bannon. 'Here's a photo of your computer screen showing the exam paper.' She enlarged a particular section. 'You left yourself logged into your office computer. And here's another photo, zoomed in to the question about the exocrine pancreas. Very clear. And here ...' – she scrolled to the next photos – 'are some of the exam results, with names, as well as emails from staff to students denying any wrongdoing.'

'Give me that phone!' Dr Bannon shouted. 'That's private ... theft ... I don't know how you got hold of this.' He stopped, realisation dawning as he redirected his glare at Eli.

'We're not trying to cause trouble,' Edie asserted quickly, desperate to avoid the confrontation escalating any further. 'Really.'

Her comment stopped Dr Bannon in his tracks. 'So, what exactly is it you want? You're already causing trouble, and I don't want trouble when I'm only a few years off retirement.'

Edie steadied herself, enjoying holding the upper hand. 'I won't report any of this – the deliberate concealing of the truth, the lies, the harm to students – so long as you come clean as a department and own up to an error. An oversight. You'll need to reverse the results of the students who failed the exam. I don't care what you do with everybody else.'

Relieved, Dr Bannon asked what would happen if he refused. 'I'll tell the dean myself. And I'll release these photos and the story to the newspapers.'

Dr Bannon agreed surprisingly quickly. 'I'll do that,' he said, taking Edie slightly aback. 'It was wrong, I know. I've hardly slept since. But there was so much pressure from above to conceal the error. I was told I wouldn't get my professorship, for which I've waited so long.'

But Edie wasn't interested in the lecturer's sob story. 'Oh, there's one other thing,' she added. 'I need your help with something else important. Right now.'

'And what might that be?' Dr Bannon asked, even more perplexed.

Edie found the relevant photos on her phone. 'I know these are dark and a bit blurry, but I need to know what these chemicals are used for.'

Dr Bannon put his glasses on, jerked the phone in Edie's hand closer to his face and screwed up his eyes as Edie led him through the images she'd taken through the window of the Cotswolds building. 'I can't tell what the labels … and the chemistry symbols … on the plastic containers say or mean,' Edie explained. 'Or what's in those boxes on the floor … And what all this stuff would be used for.'

'Can I hold this, please?' Dr Bannon asked. 'It'll be easier.' Edie refused, but she enlarged the relevant parts of the photos. Eventually, Dr Bannon removed his glasses and looked at Edie. 'It'll be the end of the matter – if I tell you about these photos and sort out the exam stuff?'

'Absolutely,' Edie replied immediately and earnestly.

'These chemicals … these materials,' Dr Bannon began. 'Well, you've got types of fertiliser and different forms of sugars and …' He named a few other chemical substances that Edie didn't recognise. 'Well, I don't know quite how to say this, but these materials – all put together in the right way – would make …' He choked as if wary of finishing the sentence. But Dr Bannon did finish.

'They would make a bomb. A large bomb.'

At home, Edie took a sandwich lunch into her bedroom. Lying on her bed, she messaged Lizzie to see how she was doing. No reply, so she called her on FaceTime. Lizzie looked tired and forlorn, but at least she answered.

After a few superficial exchanges, Edie tried to get closer. 'I'm sorry about the trip to the Cotswolds. I didn't realise what would happen, but I shouldn't have brought you into it.'

There was a pause before Lizzie replied. 'No, you shouldn't. But that's the thing, Edie. You're always putting yourself and your stuff first. I've told you before but you don't listen.' The comment stung, but it was spoken with honesty rather than venom. And it was fair: Edie had been prioritising her own investigations. 'The guy with the motorcycle … the axe … it's too much for me right now,' Lizzie added.

The incident with Helmet Head had clearly rocked Lizzie, but Edie sensed there was more and was determined to be a better friend. 'How are your parents? Is there anything new?' she asked gently.

That was all it took. Lizzie started crying and then turned off her camera. 'They've been arguing a lot,' she ventured finally, 'and I overheard a conversation yesterday when they used the word "divorce".' Lizzie was choking back the tears. 'I can't imagine life without them being together. Without the family being together.'

For the next ten minutes, Lizzie let out how sad she was feeling and how she found it hard to imagine that spending months in Washington would solve anything.

'Can I suggest two things?' Edie posed delicately, after another break for Lizzie to blow her nose.

'Yes, okay, go on then,' replied Lizzie, her voice low-pitched and flat.

Edie thought carefully about what words to use, how best to share what she wanted to say without inadvertently upsetting Lizzie further. 'I learned some stuff from my mum and her books … and also from that class,' Edie began. 'First, uncertainty can be the hardest thing of all to deal with, and you've got so much uncertainty with your parents right now. It's as if the uncertainty causes the most stress … the most anxiety … as your mind races away with all the things that *might* happen. But, of course, they often *don't* happen.'

Edie hesitated, concerned she'd said the wrong thing, so she was surprised by Lizzie's positive response.

'Yeah, that's exactly it. I can't stop thinking about stuff … what might happen … my mind goes crazy … and then I can't sleep. It's horrible!' Lizzie paused. 'And what's the second thing you were going to suggest?'

'Oh, right.' Edie gathered her own thoughts again. 'It's that people deal better … cope better … with things that have *actually* happened, compared with the worry of what *might* happen.'

'Meaning what exactly … for me?' Lizzie asked, turning the video back on. Edie could sense her friend's brain ticking over across the link.

'Meaning that even if your parents do split up, you'll be okay. You'll be alright. Really. You'll adjust and manage … like I have with Mum. It doesn't mean it's not difficult, sometimes *so* sad, but you'll cope and you'll still be able to enjoy life. Even though it doesn't feel like that right now.'

As the words gradually sank in, Edie observed the tension in Lizzie's forehead ease. After a bit, Lizzie changed the subject and asked how the visit to Dr Bannon had gone. Edie described what had happened, to Lizzie's amusement, then explained that she had to make some other calls – important ones about her cases. Edie said goodbye and promised to call again later in the evening.

Edie lay down on her bed, relieved about the nature of the conversation. Briefly, she dozed. A weird dream about different breeds of dogs escaping Battersea Dogs and Cats Home (with a familiar-looking canine at the front of the pack) dissolved abruptly when her phone rang.

Influenced by Ethan's playlist, Edie had changed the ringtone to Dua Lipa's 'Be the One', which at least meant the jolt from her slumber was uplifting. Unknown number. She usually declined those occasional calls, but in this instance she chose to answer.

'Oh, hi,' said a serious male voice. He sounded more adult than child. 'Is that Edie? Edie Franklin?'

'Hi,' Edie replied. 'Can I ask who's speaking, please?' She looked at the clock on the phone. It was 16:45.

'Oh, yes, of course. Sorry. This is Heath. Heath Coranger. Harry's dad.'

'Right ... okay.' Edie was suddenly anxious. 'Is everything alright ... I mean, how come you're calling me?'

'Sorry, I realise this is unusual but ... it's Harry ... I'm worried.'

'What exactly are you worried about?'

Edie could hear Heath's laboured breathing down the phone, and wondered if it was his illness or concern for his son. 'He's missing. We had a sort of ... well, an argument this morning ... and he left in a bad mood. A temper, really. But it's been six hours now and I've not heard anything from him. He's not answering my calls and it's just not like Harry to be out of contact like this. Even if he's upset. And I wondered ... well ... I know you two are friends ... whether you'd heard from him.'

'I'm so sorry, Mr Coranger,' Edie sympathised, her own concern escalating. 'But I haven't heard anything from him today. I was with Harry and some other friends yesterday, but that was the last time I saw him. Maybe his phone died?'

'Maybe,' Heath concurred, unconvinced.

'Do you mind if I ask what the argument was about?' Edie enquired, aware of her intrusion into their family privacy.

'No,' Heath agreed quickly, taking Edie by surprise. 'It was to do with climate change and CAPE. Some stuff that's been going on ... people I've been working with or, rather, not working with any more. Oh, yes, I remember now ... you met a couple of them at our house.'

Heath sounded truthful and Edie was tempted to ask him about the others at CAPE. But she remained wary over what to divulge, so redirected the conversation instead. She took a slight risk, tinged with guilt, but a risk from the heart.

'I hope you don't mind my mentioning this, Mr Coranger, but Harry told me about your illness ... and I'm ... well, really sorry. And I hope you're doing okay.'

A slight pause, causing Edie to wonder if she'd overstepped the mark. But, as she was increasingly learning, if you speak from a place of genuine care and concern, people tend to respond positively.

'I don't mind you mentioning it, Edie. And thank you for your kind words. To be honest, I'm glad that Harry is speaking to somebody about it all. And not bottling things up. That's really important.'

'Is there any chance of … like, a cure?'

Heath sighed. 'We'll see. The NHS care is amazing – really amazing. People forget how lucky we are with our health service. They're doing everything they can. Otherwise, well … the United States … maybe. Time will tell.'

A difficult silence ensued, which Edie eventually broke. 'Well, if I hear anything from Harry, I'll be sure to get him to call you. And … if you hear anything from him … would you mind letting me know, please?'

'Of course,' Heath affirmed, and they said their goodbyes.

After the call, Edie took a moment and then checked through her contacts. Edie's latest dream was leading her towards something she felt she already knew, perhaps from the moment they'd all watched that film.

At 'B' Edie found what she needed and called PC Jessica Brearley. The police officer had encouraged Edie to call whenever she needed to, and after biding her time, now was the moment. PC Brearley answered immediately and sounded pleased to hear Edie's voice. Edie explained her hunch that the recent surge in stolen dogs across north London wasn't random. That particular dogs, certain breeds, had been targeted, and Edie suspected they'd been selected for a distinct purpose. A criminal purpose. But she wasn't ready to share everything.

PC Brearley said she'd make some calls, do some checking and get back to Edie.

Before Edie knew it, dinner was announced.

She wandered downstairs into the kitchen and arrived at the same time as Eli appeared from the playroom. They exchanged knowing glances that carried an understanding that the morning's activities in central London wouldn't be mentioned.

Although the back door was wide open, smoke from the burgers in the frying pan filled the kitchen. Dad was preparing one of his cycle of ten dishes: home-made turkey burgers in a brioche bun, with fried onions and lashings of ketchup. Edie felt her tummy rumble: she was hungry and this was one of her favourites.

At the table, they all battled away at the greasy, dribbling, delicious burgers, kitchen roll at the ready. Dad spoke first, a splodge of mustard at the corner of his mouth, which he wiped away when Eli pointed it out.

'Only two days to the Brave People Awards, Edie. Any further thoughts about what you'll spend the money on if you win?'

'You better give *me* some money,' Eli interjected, with a combination of cheek and seriousness.

'I'm not going to win,' Edie said incredulously.

'You might,' Dad countered. 'So best to be ready … to be prepared … including your speech. There'll be TV cameras there, you know.'

'Really?' Eli wondered. 'Will I be on TV?'

'Probably not you. But Edie might be – especially if she wins.'

Edie suddenly realised that she'd hardly given the event a thought – and she certainly hadn't written a winner's speech. She'd been so distracted with other happenings.

'I heard on the news this evening,' Dad added, 'that they've raised the national threat level to substantial – meaning a terrorist attack is likely. And we got an email today from the award organisers saying that they're expecting protests at the British Museum.'

'Why there?' Edie asked innocently.

'Not sure. It could be to do with the sponsors of the event – Brent Petroleum.'

'I thought BP just meant "Brave People".'

'It does, my love,' Dad answered. 'But Brent Petroleum have sponsored it all, including the prizes. Sorry, I thought you realised. They're a massive global company that produces petrol. Their comms team have obviously had fun with the title of the event.'

Edie looked on, aghast.

CHAPTER 14

SERENDIPITY

Edie woke up late again, sleep elusive until the early hours. Immediately, she checked her messages. Nothing from Harry, which was her biggest concern. Nothing from Lizzie either. There was an interesting message, however, from Edie's police officer friend:

PC Jessica Brearley: Have made some progress. Will call you later.

There was some nice support too from friends at school:

Yasmina: Can't wait for tomorrow! Good luck. You're gonna win!

Charlie: Really proud of you. Thnx for inviting us to the British Museum. Can I bring Alan?

And a bit of a surprise:

Allegra: I know we haven't been the best of friends, but it's pretty amazing that you've been nominated for the prize. X

An even more surprising message from a new number, although Edie recognised the face in the icon:

> Unknown: Hello, Edie, it's Mrs Plunkett here from Highgate Hill School. I just wanted to let you know that the school is very proud of what you have achieved, and we wish you the very best of luck for the awards tomorrow. Regards. PP

Edie momentarily wondered what Mrs Plunkett's first name was, then moved to the final message. Another unknown, this time without any image in the icon. Edie clicked the message which created a black screen with the word 'Enter' in the centre. Thinking it was some kind of joke, Edie clicked on the word. A skull and crossbones expanded gradually to full screen size, at which point it exploded and blood trickled down the screen. Accompanying the horrible image was a voice, unpleasantly gruff and threatening:

> Keep out of the way. Save your life. Keep out of the way. Save your life ...

The horrid voice repeated the lines over and over, like something from a horror movie, and Edie was unable to pause it. Her anxiety rose incrementally until she eventually worked out how to delete the message and put an end to the sound.

Spooked by the experience, Edie texted Donna to double-check she was still available to meet later in the day.

Edie had reached out the previous afternoon as she'd felt an urgent need to share the various entangled happenings with her neighbour from the security services. Edie had been due to go round then, but Donna had postponed until today.

Donna messaged back that any time after lunch would be fine, as she was working from home all day. Edie intended to go sooner rather than later.

Edie ate some breakfast cereal, which doubled as lunch, checked on Günther and brought him into the playroom. Her beloved guinea pig needed extra loving attention after the frightening experience with the fox. Twenty minutes of stroking his ears (which was his favourite), along with carrot and broccoli nibbles, seemed to hit the calming mark, for both pet and owner. In search of company, Edie checked on Eli next, who didn't appreciate being woken.

From her bedroom, Edie called Harry's phone again – the fourth time this morning. No answer. She tried Harry's dad. Frustratingly, also no answer, so Edie left a message asking Heath if he'd heard anything from his son – or, indeed, if Harry had returned home.

Next, Edie tried Lizzie, but that call also went through to voicemail, so Edie sent a voice text instead, saying hello and checking gently how her friend was today. The minutes seemed to be going by so slowly, Edie thought, as another time check indicated that it was just past midday. What constituted 'after lunch'? Edie contemplated briefly. It was still too early, but Edie decided she'd walk over at exactly two o'clock.

What to do? What to do? There was no delaying it any further, so Edie sat at her desk with pen and paper, her hand hovering over the page. Eventually she started writing:

> I can't believe I've won this award. I'm not sure I deserve it. All the courageous acts of the other candidates ...

No, far too cheesy.

> I'd like to thank the organisers for ...

No! Definitely not that. She hated the organisers, and she wasn't giving a lecture.

> I'm honoured to be given this prestigious award. Brave is not necessarily a word I'd use to describe myself ...

Wrong tone. And self-congratulatory in a roundabout way.

> I'd like to dedicate this award to my mother. The bravest person I know, and the one who truly ...

Edie stopped writing. She'd burst into tears if she started talking about Mum.

Something else popped into Edie's mind from the PoWaR session at school. Something about the difference between wisdom and intelligence, and the importance of trusting your inner self. Edie wasn't sure exactly what that meant, but she remembered Toni telling the class that you'd know what to do or what to say in challenging situations when the moment arrived. The words would come to you there and then, in the present, and those words would come from a place of feeling rather than intellect, and be all the more authentic for that. Avoid overthinking a situation, Toni stressed, and have faith in your own wisdom.

Edie put down her pen and rocked back in her chair.

Her mobile rang. It wasn't the call she was hoping for, but it was one she needed to answer.

'Hi, Dad.'

'Hi, sweetheart. I'm finishing a surgery so just a quick call. Please don't forget your appointment with Dr Young today. You know, the follow-up about panic disorder. It's at half past two.'

'Oh, crap.'

'What was that?'

'Nothing. It's just that I had another …' She paused. 'No, that's fine, I hadn't forgotten. I'll be there.'

'Good. Drop in and say hello if you have time.'

'Sure. If I have time, Dad. I've got schoolwork too … deadlines.'

'But it's half-term.'

'I've gotta go, Dad. I was on a call with Lizzie when you rang. See you later!'

Sitting in the playroom, fidgety, Edie pondered again who'd sent the creepy skull-and-crossbones message. In her heart, Edie felt she probably knew. Although she'd only met them once properly, she'd been immediately uncomfortable in the presence of Jarrah and Sven, Heath Coranger's CAPE friends. They were up to something. Something bad. But it didn't all add up. How could they have known that she was on to them? Edie had been careful, or so she thought.

Too many questions remained unanswered.

Then, Edie had an idea. Using her iPhone, she went to the CAPE website and searched the London region members section. She found name captions for Sven Olsen and Jarrah Guyula, whose photos matched the people she'd met at Harry's eco-house. Edie enlarged the faces and took screenshots of both.

At a quarter past two, Edie set off along Cecile Park for Crouch Hall Road surgery, passing Donna's house along the way and wishing she'd been able to go and see her neighbour straightaway. At the surgery, Edie was greeted with a kindly smile by Nikki.

'I'm sure Dr Young won't be long,' the receptionist promised. 'Take a seat and she'll call you in when she's ready.'

Edie duly took an uncomfortable plastic chair in the open-plan seating area and waited. She texted Donna to say she'd be round later than intended, and then texted again to extend her expected arrival time further. Finally, Dr Young emerged just after three o'clock and called her name.

Edie leapt up and was escorted into Dr Young's room.

'So, how have things been, Edie?' the coolly dressed young doctor questioned, after apologising for the long wait.

'Good,' Edie responded, as she sat down in the patient's chair.

'Have you had any more panic attacks?' the doctor asked, taking her seat opposite Edie. 'Or episodes like that one in the hospital?'

'Not really,' Edie replied, more measured. 'I've been pretty well.'

'*Pretty* well? Any anxiety at all, then?'

'Well, I guess, yes … some anxiety … I've been in a few stressful situations since I last saw you.'

'A few?'

'Yes, well, maybe one or two. But I did what you told me – taking deep breaths, sitting down, thinking of something relaxing – plus my mum's Three Principles stuff has been helpful. They've been teaching it at school. Allow your thoughts to calm, and your feelings, like my anxiety, will also settle down.'

'That's wonderful! You've clearly learned a lot. I'm so pleased. And what about your detective work: anything interesting going on there?'

'Not so much,' Edie answered instinctively. Uncalled-for invasions of her space were not welcome. Then again, Dr Young did seem to be genuinely on Edie's side.

'Just some pretty boring cases … stolen phones, lost post … missing dogs. Can I ask you a question, Dr Young?'

'Yes, of course, Edie. Shoot.'

'What would you do if you thought something serious might be about to happen – like with one of my cases – but you weren't completely sure yet and could be wrong?'

Dr Young inspected the young girl opposite with curiosity. 'I thought, Edie, you said your cases were all a bit boring?'

'Yes, they are. Mainly.'

'Okay. Well, this kind of thing does happen in general practice when you're not sure if a patient has something significant or not.'

'Like if they have cancer or not?'

'Yes, that kind of thing. In those circumstances, I gather the evidence as quickly as possible – establish the facts, so as to be sure – before saying anything definitive. But I wouldn't wait too long, especially if I'm genuinely concerned. Err on the side of safety.'

'Thank you, Dr Young.' Edie felt reassured and stood to go, but Dr Young motioned for her to sit down again.

'We might as well do your asthma check while you're here.'

That took another ten minutes.

Edie would reflect in bed that night on all the stops and starts that had occurred during the course of the day, especially through the afternoon, which resulted in her arriving much later than planned at Donna's house.

From the surgery, Edie turned left down Crouch Hall Road and hit Crouch End Broadway fifty metres down, right opposite the Clock Tower. A mime artist was performing on the traffic island at the foot of the tower, and Edie stopped for a few minutes to watch.

On the other side of the Broadway, Edie bought bread at Gail's bakery, as requested by Dad when she'd dropped in to say hi after seeing Dr Young. She then carried on to Weston Park, taking the 'back route' home (as Eli called it). Halfway home her phone rang. On noticing the caller's name, Edie sat on the nearest wall to answer.

'Hi, PC Brearley … I mean Jessica.'

'Hello, Edie. I've got some interesting news which I wanted to share, although I'm not quite sure what to make of it yet.'

'Right,' Edie responded, her attention now focused. 'What is it?'

'I looked further into those cases of the missing dogs – the ones you detailed plus one or two others I located. Most of the cases have already been solved: the dogs have been found and returned to their owners. They were genuinely lost. But there are two or three cases, including Mrs Solomon's dog, where something peculiar seems to be going on.'

'What exactly?'

'Well, let me try and explain. Mrs Solomon didn't have her dog, Quincy, from a puppy. She got him when he was older.'

Edie contemplated telling PC Brearley about the dogs in Faws Grove, but for some reason she held back.

'Like a rescue dog?' she posed instead.

'Not exactly, Edie. Quincy was a specially trained police dog, but sadly he got injured on duty – at the airport, apparently, hit by a car. That's why he has a limp. There's a woman who runs a specialist organisation – a sort of dog rescue company – where she takes those dogs from the police and keeps them until suitable owners are found. She's obliged to keep a register because of the dogs' background with the police.'

'Okay, but I don't really understand – what's the problem?'

'Here's the thing. It looks like a couple of the other missing dogs were also on that register … were also specially trained police dogs who'd been similarly retired from the force due to injury. There might even be more dogs that we don't know about.'

PC Brearley paused, allowing Edie to compute.

'Are you saying these dogs, or at least some of these dogs, were deliberately stolen – targeted – because they had been trained by the police?' Edie fiddled subconsciously with the fingernail skin that had finally regrown.

'It looks like that may be so. But I need to find out more. Establish the facts. I'm trying to talk to the woman who runs the register. It's possible she's involved – could even be the perpetrator.'

'Or she's been threatened … or bribed?' Edie suggested.

'Yes, that's also possible. She's not answering her phone or returning my messages, so I might have to go round to her place. Tomorrow, probably.'

'One other thing,' Edie probed. 'What exactly were these dogs trained for?'

'Oh,' said PC Brearley with surprise. 'I thought that was obvious. They're all sniffer dogs, trained to smell out drugs or explosives … or even scents on clothing to help catch criminals.'

Edie was about to end the call as she really needed to get on with the afternoon, but PC Brearley wasn't quite finished. 'Be careful, Edie. Please. You've done well to pick this up, but we don't know what we're dealing with here.'

Edie slid off the wall. She'd turned right up Drylands Road and then zigzagged onto Gladwell Road when her phone rang again. Without an obvious wall for a seat, she stood by the quiet gated entrance to Olivers Row. She smiled on seeing the caller's name.

'Hi, Ethan.'

'Hiya. How are you doing today?'

'I'm fine. What about you?'

'Yeah, okay, though I didn't sleep very well. I can't get the image of that axe out of my mind.'

'And those poor dogs,' Edie added. 'I know you didn't see them, and it may not be our business, but I think I should let the police know.'

'I'm not sure the police will do much about the dogs. But you could call the RSPCA, the charity, although it doesn't sound like the dogs were being mistreated.'

'Yeah, I've sent a message via their online form, but they haven't replied yet.'

'But that's not why I called,' Ethan continued. 'It's about Martin. He found out today – at uni – that they've reversed their decision about the biochemistry exam, that everyone who wrote about the exocrine pancreas has now passed. They're keeping it pretty quiet though. All the people who wrote about the endocrine pancreas have still passed, but he doesn't care about that. He's just delighted not to do a retake and risk being thrown out. Plus, he's happily in love.'

Edie smiled. 'That's great news, I'm really pleased.' She started to walk up the short hill to Cecile Park.

'And Martin wanted to say a big thank you. Whatever you did, it worked. By the way, what did you actua …'

'Ethan,' Edie interrupted as she approached the top of Gladwell Road. 'I've got to be somewhere now. Can we speak later or tomorrow?'

'Sure. No problem. Bye.'

Slightly out of breath, Edie entered the house and went straight up to her bedroom. She grabbed her notebook, papers and rucksack and went into the kitchen for some water. Before she turned on the tap her phone rang again. Four o'clock now, very late for Donna, but she needed to take this call too.

It was an anxious Heath Coranger, and it took a further ten minutes for him to convey that he'd heard nothing from Harry and was considering calling the police.

By the time Edie finally left the house, it was almost a quarter past four.

The surreal sequence of events that followed felt like they happened in slow motion, as if removed from or on top of reality.

As Edie stepped out onto Cecile Park, a surprisingly chilly wind blew strands of hair across her face, so she stopped for a few moments to tie her hair back. There was nobody in sight as

Edie re-embarked on the short journey to Donna's house. Edie was halfway when the first of the bizarre set of events happened.

About fifty metres ahead on Edie's side of the street, out of the gateway from one of the houses, a ball rolled onto the pavement. At first, Edie thought nothing of it. But as the pink ball trickled across the pavement towards the kerb, she realised that it resembled the one that Donna's children had been chasing around the lounge.

Still, Edie thought little of it. She'd pick the ball up when she arrived at Donna's and take it into the house.

That thought, however, was quickly disturbed by a noise emerging from much further down the road. In the mid-distance, a red vehicle was barrelling along at some speed. Initially, Edie couldn't be sure of the velocity, but her concern was justified when the car bounced over one of the speed bumps, momentarily lifting off the tarmac.

At the same time, Edie could hear music, which must have been blaring from the in-car stereo if she could pick it up from where she was standing. And the sound was getting louder by the second.

Edie looked back down to see that the ball had dropped off the kerb into the space between two parked cars and was now wobbling towards the centre of the road. In her head, Edie was rapidly computing various possibilities.

The red car careened over another speed bump, and the volume of the music intensified.

Then, from the pathway to Donna's house, a small child emerged, tottering across the pavement in that awkward manner of toddlers. The pink ball had come to a standstill in the centre of the road, and the child's attention was transfixed on the object she'd pursued so determinedly inside the house.

Olivia. It was definitely Olivia who stepped off the kerb and was making her way between the parked cars.

Edie stopped in her tracks.

With no sign of slowing down, the red car was now worryingly close, seemingly oblivious to both ball and child. The tinted windows meant Edie was unable to see the driver, but she could make out the style of music: hip-hop, played very loud.

Olivia took a few toddler-sized paces from between the cars to reach the middle of the street, where she leant down and picked up the ball. With child-like innocence, she was completely unaware of the impending, life-threatening danger.

Edie imagined the terrible outcome. The driver was oblivious. Within a few seconds the car would hit Olivia full-on. Such a blow would be fatal. Olivia's life over before it had really begun. Even if Olivia saw the car now, there probably wasn't enough time to avert the crash. And Edie was too far off to be able to help.

Frozen to the spot, Edie instinctively screamed as loud as she could.

'OLIVIA! OLIVIA! GET OUT OF THE WAY!'

Waving her arms furiously, Edie repeated: 'OUT OF THE WAY!'

Startled, Olivia turned towards the shouting. On seeing Edie on the pavement, Olivia smiled sweetly, proudly holding up the prized ball.

Having hurdled the final speed bump in its path, the hurtling car was now within metres of the toddler, a collision unavoidable.

Edie closed her eyes involuntarily.

But, as she did so, she caught a momentary glimpse of something – a rapid movement.

Opening her eyes, Edie was astonished by what came into view. From the Womersley Road junction directly opposite where Olivia was rooted, a person had appeared and was haring across the road towards the child. Even so, it still looked like the car would hit Olivia first.

But Edie's mental calculation was wrong.

With incredible athleticism, the sprinting figure, who Edie now realised was a woman, scooped up Olivia in one swift action and dived towards the kerbside and safety. The red car whistled by a millisecond later, clipping the woman's lower leg and knocking her and the child sideways into a parked silver Mini.

Slamming on its brakes, the car screeched to a halt close to where Edie was standing, and she immediately took a photo of the registration number. As the car accelerated away, she raced towards the fallen woman and child.

Flying out from the doorway of her house, Donna almost bumped into Edie as they reached Olivia simultaneously. Upright and clearly unhurt, Olivia was grabbed by her mum and squeezed hard in a hug. The look on Olivia's face suggested she had no idea what all the commotion was about.

Edie focused her attention on the figure on the ground. Now in a seated position, propped up on the wheel of the Mini, the woman's back was facing her.

She turned towards Edie as Donna looked up from her hug to thank the saviour of her daughter's life.

Gobsmacked, Edie and Donna cried the same word at the same time: 'Rachel?'

CHAPTER 15

BE BOLD, BE BRAVE

The rest of the afternoon and early evening tumbled by in a blur.

For two further hours, Edie stayed at Donna's house amidst the atmosphere of utter relief. At first, Edie sat with Donna and Rachel (whom they both agreed to call Rochelle from now on) in the lounge as they talked through the series of events.

Put simply, Rochelle had saved Olivia's life. If she hadn't been coming down the hill to the junction with Cecile Park at that very moment, if she hadn't been alerted to the terrible danger in the road by Edie's shriek, then something unimaginably awful would have happened. Every parent's nightmare. Donna had witnessed it all unfolding in those few moments when time stood still, only for life's course to alter in an instant. Olivia and Max soon disappeared into the TV room to watch *Shrek*, attended by a watchful Christina.

Edie listened as Rochelle – whose leg seemed fine – explained why she was actually on that particular street corner at that very point in time. Rochelle had indeed changed her mind about the crazily serendipitous encounters with Donna, despite her initially adverse reaction to the idea.

The opportunity that life had presented to reconnect with her old friend was too much for Rochelle to squander, so she'd delayed her flight for a few days and chosen to walk over that afternoon on the off-chance that Donna might be at home. Google Maps had selected the route – ten houses from the address on Edie's business card.

To Edie's pleasure and surprise, the two women seemed to revert effortlessly into their old friendship. Edie could see why they'd been so close. They talked, touched, embraced and told the stories of their lives, to the extent that after a while Edie left them alone and joined the children. When Scott arrived home from work, the conversation from the lounge escalated in volume, although Edie wondered how Rochelle would respond to him. The discussion Edie had been planning to have with Donna just wasn't going to happen. Not today at least.

As Edie tried to make a quiet getaway, however, she was met at the front door by her excitable neighbour.

Edie grinned. 'I'm pleased it's working out well with Rochelle, but I need to get home for dinner now. I'll text you that red car's registration number. Can we talk again tomorrow?'

'Yes, of course. And thank you for everything. I'll get the rest of your payment to you, now the case is … well … solved.'

Edie thanked her and was half out the door, but Donna wasn't quite done. 'Edie, just one thing,' she added, her face suddenly incredibly serious. 'Be careful, please. Be very careful.'

Edie wondered why so many people seemed preoccupied with her taking care, but the unfolding mysteries made her acutely aware of the need for caution. 'Don't worry, I am,' she replied, then said goodbye and walked home.

At the end of dinner, Edie decided to run a bath. Her head had been so overactive that soaking amongst the bubbles brought on a pleasant mental stillness. Half an hour later, she clambered out of the tub. She'd heard nothing further from PC Brearley, Heath or Harry Coranger, and after responding to a few messages, she fell asleep on the bed, still sporting her pink-and-white towelling dressing gown.

'Time to get up!' Dad shouted from the hallway.

Edie emerged slowly from her slumber, semi-registered the command and then immediately fell asleep again.

Fifteen minutes later, the same instruction boomed out, this time from inside her room.

'Come on, luv! Time to get up! You don't want to miss the awards.'

'Hmm ...' Edie managed groggily. 'What time is it?' She twisted in bed and pressed the switch to illuminate the light on her bedside table clock. 'It's ten o'clock!' Edie exclaimed. 'Why didn't you get me up earlier, Dad?'

Dad was about to challenge getting the blame, then decided it wasn't worth it.

Edie was out of bed in a flash. 'What time are we leaving?'

'I told you, luv. Eleven, so we can be there for twelve, like they've asked. The ceremony starts at one o'clock.'

Edie ushered Dad out of her room, showered quickly and then dressed in the clothes she'd already selected and put out. Smart (but still cool) for the awards, like something she'd wear to synagogue for a friend's bat mitzvah: long-sleeved white T-shirt, baby-blue hoodie, tartan knee-length skirt, black tights and dark grey Converse boots. Using the mirror on her desk, Edie applied a little foundation, eyeliner and lip gloss, just in case she ended up on TV.

Mum would have been so proud of Edie today – although probably unimpressed, like her daughter, by the sponsors of the awards. Special moments like these (and birthdays) were still the hardest for Edie to get through as her mum's absence was so blatant. Edie let the sadness come and then pass, without indulging it. She kept her tears at bay as her make-up would run.

After some cereal and a wish-me-luck snuggle with Günther, Edie, Eli and Dad headed off for central London. On the W3 to Finsbury Park station, Edie's phone rang.

'Hi, Jessica,' Edie answered. 'I'm just on the bus ... on my way to the British Museum.'

'Oh, yes,' PC Brearley replied. 'Sorry, I forgot. It's the awards today. It won't take long. I just wanted to let you know that I've found out more about those dogs.'

'Right,' Edie said, turning away from Eli and Dad, who were chatting about the Arsenal stadium tour.

'I spoke to Mrs Carpenter eventually ... took ages as she didn't respond to my calls.'

'Mrs Carpenter?'

'Sorry, she's the woman who fosters the dogs who've been retired from the police … who owns the register. I had to go round there, but she was at home, so I interviewed her. You were right. It seems like she was bribed to give up the names and addresses of people who'd bought retired police dogs from her. That's a crime, so we'll be taking it seriously, but … for now … I was more interested in her list – the register – and to whom she'd given it for money.'

'And?' Edie enquired, realising the bus was about to reach the station.

'I've got descriptions of two men but no names – they paid with cash – although one of the descriptions sounds a bit like the man you saw at the Royal Free Hospital … the one who stole Mrs Solomon's phone. But there are other avenues to pursue. Mrs Carpenter noted down a licence plate when her car was scratched during one of their visits. I should have more later today.'

'Thanks,' Edie said as she descended the bus stairs.

The Franklin family walked purposefully into Finsbury Park Tube Station and took a Piccadilly Line train towards central London. Five stops later, they disembarked at Russell Square, took the lift up to street level and walked diagonally across the large pigeon-filled green space after which the station was named. Eli briefly joined some younger kids dodging the jets of water that sprung from a fountain installation.

Following the instructions on the invitation letter, Edie led the way to Montague Place and the rear entrance to the British Museum. Although supposedly quieter than the notoriously hectic main entrance, it was still pretty busy. Parked coaches lined the street, reminding Edie that not all schools shared the same half-term. Uniformed children stood chattering in groups on the pavement or were queuing in an orderly fashion for entry, interspersed with camera-bedecked tourists.

What caught Edie's attention, however, were the dogs and their police handlers. Edie spotted a German shepherd guarding the museum entrance, two springer spaniels monitoring those waiting for their bags to be checked and another German shepherd patrolling the street.

The handlers wore caps identifying themselves as police, but their uniforms – the stab-proof vests in particular – suggested some kind of special unit. Emblazoned on their backs were the letters MDP, which Edie later found out stood for Ministry of Defence Police, out of which a renowned dog training school operated.

The atmosphere created by the heightened security made Edie feel tense.

'The queue's enormous,' Dad declared. 'We won't get in on time.'

Dad led the children towards the museum attendant standing by the entrance doors, above which capitalised gold lettering read 'King Edward the Seventh Galleries'. As he was showing the attendant their letter, Edie was distracted by a scuffling noise from the nearby gazebo-covered area, where bags were being searched. Edie moved away from the main doors towards a huge lion statue, several steps closer to the growing commotion.

Vigorous barking now accompanied the kerfuffle and Edie noticed one of the springer spaniels jumping up at a schoolchild by the bag search desk. The professional handler prevented the dog from doing any harm, but the restraint clearly required considerable effort. An accompanying teacher looked displeased whilst doing her best to protect the pupil. The second springer spaniel then started forcibly weaving between people in the queue, sniffing energetically and breaking up the line.

'What's going on?' came a voice from Edie's side. Eli had joined her.

Before Edie had a chance to reply, from the pavement area by the cycle racks one of the German shepherds became agitated, barking fiercely whilst pulling its handler towards a queuing pair of tourists, sporting matching green parkas with the national flag of Japan on the sleeve.

Edie surveyed the scene. The dogs were scary and people were beginning to panic. Something didn't feel right.

Behind Edie, the German shepherd guarding the front door now also started to bark, leading the police handler away from the doors and towards the lion statue.

'Don't worry, son,' the handler said to Eli, noting the concern on her brother's face. 'This sometimes happens. One of them starts barking, then they all kick off – probably just a sandwich in a lunchbox.'

Edie wasn't convinced. Distraction provided opportunity.

'Come on kids!' Dad beckoned loudly from behind Edie. 'They're letting us in.' He waved the letter in the air.

Edie turned round and made for the entrance, only for her attention to be diverted by some jostling behind Dad. A few people were taking advantage of the momentary loosening of security and were barging their way directly into the museum, keen to avoid the long queue. The single remaining attendant was busy trying to settle the whole situation down and was powerless to stop the onrush.

The profile of one opportunistic individual caused Edie to stop and do a double take. He seemed more measured and prepared than the others. Edie fixed her stare to be sure her initial impression was correct. As the man twisted his way through the throng at the entrance, Edie became more certain, even though she'd only met him properly once – if you didn't count the encounter at the pub in Camden.

Edie was ninety-five percent sure it was Sven. And he was carrying a large black holdall.

Edie pushed past Dad, but the museum attendant was now trying to restore order and obliged her to slow down. Edie protested, but precious seconds were lost.

By the time they were all allowed through the door, Sven – if indeed it was him – seemed to have mysteriously disappeared. In the hallway, Edie checked the small cafe and the visitors mingling around a series of carved Asian gods and goddesses representing the nine planets, but Heath Coranger's friend was nowhere in sight.

Edie started to doubt herself.

'Follow me,' Dad summoned, and he guided the children past the bust of Edward the Seventh, up two flights of stairs, through the Africa gallery and into the Great Court.

Immediately, Edie was astonished by the expansive grandeur of the court, a huge square-shaped area with each side of the square measuring well over 100 metres in length. High above them was a spectacular tessellating glass roof, blue sky and clouds clearly visible despite the zigzagged metal lattice.

Visitors were milling around the vast space: small groups, large groups, smiles and camera clicks. Edie noticed a cafe in the far corner with a line of benches and a large gift shop nearby.

'Over there.' Dad pointed at the diagonally opposite corner of the Great Court. 'That's where the awards are happening.'

Dodging tourists and veering around the gigantic cylindrical construction in the centre of the atrium, Edie crossed the court briskly. A plaque named the cylinder as the Round Reading Room, with the Great Court Restaurant on its upper level.

A whole section of the far corner of the Great Court was cordoned off with stanchions and barrier belt, like Edie remembered from passport control at Heathrow Airport. Inside the barricaded space was a stage with fifteen rows of seats – around 150 chairs in total by Edie's quick calculation. Behind the last row was space for standing as well as tables laid out with sandwiches, salads, canapés, cakes and soft drinks. A bigger table contained numerous bottles of champagne, some already opened in ice coolers. Waiting staff, smartly dressed in black and white, carried trays with pre-filled champagne flutes.

Edie felt nervous. This seemed a much bigger deal than she'd imagined. On both sides of the stage were large rectangular banners, plus an even bigger one raised high above the stage on tall posts. Lettering inscribed in bold across all the banners left nobody in doubt as to the nature of the event: The Annual Brave People Awards. Underneath was the famous Brent Petroleum logo.

'Welcome,' boomed a male voice that startled Edie. 'You must be Edie Franklin.'

Edie turned to face a middle-aged man, formally attired in suit and tie, his expensive clothing matching his posh Oxbridge voice.

'The name's Smithers-Jones – Justin Smithers-Jones – and you must be Edie's family.' He shook Dad's hand with purpose.

'Yes, I'm her father, and this is Edie's brother, Eli.'

'Hello, young man,' said Smithers-Jones without even looking at Eli. 'Well, I'm the CEO of BPUK – that's Brent Petroleum in the UK – and we're delighted to have you all here today.

Nobody said anything.

'And congratulations, Edie,' Smithers-Jones continued, 'for making this shortlist with your extraordinary accomplishments. Quite something, really … In fact,' he added after a pause, 'all the shortlisted candidates have achieved something truly special. The others are already here.' Smithers-Jones pointed to the front row of seats. 'Now, we'll be starting soon, so come on through.' He instructed an official guarding the cordon to allow the Franklin family through.

'I'll be there in a minute. You two go in. I just need to … to check my coat in … won't be long.'

'Ah, coat check is just around the corner, by the main entrance,' Smithers-Jones indicated. 'See you shortly – and I know the TV people are looking for you, when you're back.'

But Edie was off. She already hated one CEO and had taken an instant dislike to this one's smarm. Plus, she needed a moment alone. The awards ceremony area was rapidly filling up and Edie couldn't face talking to people yet – and certainly wouldn't welcome being interviewed by one of several TV crews gathered in the enclosed space.

By the marble statue of a man on horseback, raised high on a gigantic plinth, Edie was surprised by a tap on the shoulder.

'Edie, we wanted so much to support you today,' announced the Highgate Hill head teacher with a smile. 'So, we all decided to come!'

Edie's heart sank, and then sank further as she noticed that Mrs Plunkett was accompanied by Mr Bowling, Miss Watson and even the geography teacher, Ms Dylan. Edie wished she'd never agreed to come to the stupid event.

'Oh, thank you,' Edie replied unconvincingly. 'I'm just putting my coat …' She pointed towards the museum's main entrance.

'Not to worry,' Mrs Plunkett intervened helpfully. 'Best of luck!' Echoes of support were voiced by the other teachers, and Miss Watson touched Edie's arm encouragingly. 'Don't be too long, though,' Mrs Plunkett added with an eye on her watch. 'Only a few minutes until it all starts.'

Edie strode off and turned right before reaching the front entrance, and then followed a sign directing her down a corridor to the coat and bag check facility. Through glass-panelled revolving doors on her left, Edie saw throngs of people outside waiting patiently to get in and more sniffer dogs with handlers circulating around them with interest.

Fifty metres down the corridor, Edie arrived at the cloakroom. After standing in line at the counter for a minute or so, Edie handed over her coat to a girl who didn't seem much older than herself. On the counter surface Edie noticed a bowl labelled 'tips' with nothing inside.

As she waited to be given a ticket, Edie peered inside the cloakroom area. Hundreds of coats were hanging on pegs and almost as many bags. What a repetitive job, Edie thought, putting items on pegs then removing them later. Over and over.

As the cloakroom attendant held out a hand, Edie caught sight of a male figure deep inside, half-hidden in the shadows, organising bags and moving hangers around. Edie stared closer. Despite the dim light, the figure resembled Jarrah.

'Your ticket, Miss,' the cloakroom girl announced, accustomed to vocalising the obvious.

Edie squinted to try and bring the image into focus.

'Your ticket, Miss,' the girl repeated more insistently, before turning to see what Edie was gazing at.

'Oh, he's new. Only been here a few days. Doesn't say much.'

Edie was about to ask his name, but the girl was already on to the next customer. Edie was unaware of the queue that had rapidly built up behind her.

Unsettled, Edie meandered back. She'd been paying attention to being observant and felt there was a good chance that she'd seen Sven and Jarrah. Then again, it was completely possible that Edie was overthinking things; that she'd imagined seeing the men simply because they were on her mind. Or perhaps there was a completely innocent explanation: that it was indeed Jarrah but he worked at the British Museum. This was merely his job, albeit a new one, and Sven was visiting him.

No, that didn't feel right. Edie stopped for a moment at a dramatic twelve-metre-high totem pole in the Great Court. The cedar wood post contained sculpted birds and fish and, according to the plaque, told the story of the indigenous Haida people of British Colombia in Canada. There must be a lot of knowledge embodied in the pole, Edie thought. No, not knowledge, wisdom. Tribal wisdom. Wisdom of the elders.

Trust your wisdom, Mum said. Your deeper knowing. And Edie's deeper knowing was telling her that these encounters were not coincidence. They were not just a matter of chance.

At the awards space, Edie was ushered through quickly and was amazed to see how full the area had become in the few minutes she'd been away. Many of the seats were taken, whilst some people stood at the back chatting. Food and drink were being readily consumed, the waiting staff ensuring that champagne glasses were soon refilled. Smithers-Jones got up onto the stage and announced through a microphone that the awards ceremony would begin in five minutes.

'Where have you been?' came a slightly irritated voice to Edie's left. 'Come on,' Dad added more softly, 'we've got front-row seats. I thought you were going to miss it.'

As Dad led his daughter down the aisle, a chorus of female voices shouted Edie's name in unison from the fifth row. Lizzie, Yasmina and Charlie had all come and were waving their arms frenetically. Edie had been given extra invites, but she wasn't sure whether Lizzie would come, so she was especially pleased to see her best friend. She smiled back at the girls as Dad hurried her along.

Once ensconced safely in their seats, Dad let go of Edie's hand and exhaled.

'I got on TV!' Eli proclaimed excitedly and pointed. 'That camera over there!'

Over her shoulder Edie saw the camera, as well as the other contestants and their families nearby in the first and second rows. But there was no sign of Harry, the only other school friend Edie wished was there. She was worried for him.

Smithers-Jones was up on the stage again. He tapped the microphone annoyingly to obtain silence, which made visitors further off look over to find out what was going on. After introducing himself and describing his role, Smithers-Jones talked about the values behind Brent Petroleum, and why they were so proud to be sponsoring this important event. He cited the company's corporate sustainability plan as evidence of their environmental priorities, which Edie found dishonest and repugnant, given their role in oil and gas production.

In due course, Smithers-Jones got back to the awards and invited the five finalists to join him on the stage. Assistants in Brent Petroleum T-shirts brought five chairs on stage and arranged them in a semicircle behind the CEO. Nobody had told Edie this was going to happen.

With Edie showing no signs of movement, Dad nudged her in the ribs as the other four contestants emerged from their rows. Reluctantly she stood up, climbed the few steps onto the podium and took the last remaining seat at the end of the semicircle. Applause accompanied her completing the line of finalists. Edie blushed, wishing she was at home cuddling Günther.

For the next twenty minutes, Smithers-Jones told the stories of the various heroic exploits: a middle-aged woman who dived off a pier to rescue a child from icy water in the Lake District; an elderly man who beat off three young assailants during a home burglary in Birmingham; a student who fought off a crocodile attack whilst white-water rafting in the Zambezi river, saving the life of her closest friend; and a refugee from Kurdistan who managed to keep his family and several others safe when their dingy capsized whilst crossing the Channel from France to England.

Edie was the only young person of the five. When Smithers-Jones summarised her valiant exploits, she became sad (as well as embarrassed). Mum would have been so delighted, but she wasn't here to witness her daughter's achievements. And Edie realised, perhaps for the first time, that Mum wouldn't be around for future memorable activities: the bat mitzvah, Edie's eighteenth birthday, university graduation or Edie becoming a mum herself one day.

To avoid becoming morose, Edie looked past the heads of the gathered crowd into the vast space of the Great Court. Some people were continuing with their visit, inspecting various artefacts, whilst others had stopped to watch the event. A large group of tourists were gathered in an enclosed space adjacent to the court, close to the west stairs, where Edie had noticed a sign up to the Members' Room.

Edie's eyes were drawn to a second totem pole, near to the one she'd admired earlier. A bolt of adrenaline coursed through her body.

'Once again, congratulations to all our finalists,' Smithers-Jones bleated on in the background, Edie barely noticing. 'In third place, for incredible outnumbered bravery during a home invasion …'

A lone figure stood next to the totem pole. He was coughing into a tissue, but in-between bouts he was staring in Edie's direction. Applause rang out as the elderly contestant, three seats from Edie, stood up and collected his envelope.

'In second place,' Smithers-Jones continued, 'for outstanding courage in treacherous seas and saving lives before the RNLI rescue was possible …'

Why on earth was Heath Coranger at the awards? Edie wondered. Was there some news on Harry? Hopefully only good news, Edie fretted internally.

A man in his thirties collected his prize, and then returned to his seat on the other side of the semicircle to Edie.

Or was there a more nefarious explanation – a connection with her possible sightings of Sven and Jarrah? Or, quite possibly, a completely different reason for Heath's presence at the museum? He seemed a genuinely good person at heart.

'And the winner of this year's Brent Petroleum Brave People's Awards …' Smithers-Jones' voice rose to a crescendo of excitement.

Edie observed Heath stagger slightly as he stepped away from the pole towards her, their eyes meeting despite the distance. Watching his delicate gait, Edie experienced a feeling of loving concern for Harry; it would be so tough for him to lose his father. At least Edie still had one parent to look after her.

'… for outstanding gallantry in the face of murder, corporate crime and significant risk to the public's health … is … EDIE FRANKLIN!'

Whoops and jeers erupted from the crowd, many of whom stood up and clapped unreservedly. In slow motion, Edie's mind linked the announcement of her name with the cheering. She was jarred into the present moment by Dad's familiar wolf whistle. Bemused, she looked around and took in Heath making a thumbs-up sign.

'Come on up, Edie,' Smithers-Jones summoned. 'Come and collect your £50,000 prize!'

Gingerly, Edie made her way over to Smithers-Jones, who shook her hand, handed her an envelope and indicated to her to make a speech.

Edie stood by the microphone stand, which Smithers-Jones lowered to her height. The audience sat back down and Edie spotted Dad and Eli beaming in the front row. Slowly, Edie reached into her pocket for her emergency, semi-prepared speech – what she'd use if she was really stuck. Her hand felt the paper, but she didn't pull it out.

Instead, Edie just stood and waited. To the onlookers, it seemed as if nothing was happening and they became uncomfortable as the seconds passed. But inside Edie something was happening. In the here and now, Edie had an insight. Touched by her inner wisdom, Edie felt connected to a deeper sense of self and she knew exactly what she had to do.

'My mum is the one who really deserves this award, not me, for all her amazing human rights work,' she began. 'Mum – and my wonderful dad – are the reason why I've been able to do what I've done. But Mum wouldn't have accepted the award ...'

Edie picked up on some twitchiness in the audience, the shuffling of bums on seats. This wasn't what people were expecting. But Edie felt nerveless and pressed on.

'She wouldn't have accepted the award because of the sponsors, Brent Petroleum, and their role in oil production, environmental degradation and climate change.'

People in suits started muttering and Smithers-Jones began to sweat. This wasn't what was supposed to happen, especially not in front of TV cameras.

'For the same reason, I cannot accept this prize ... for me ... not for me ... But I *can* accept the money to pay for a friend to get life-saving medical treatment for their blood cancer. To save his life.'

At the entrance to the awards area, Heath stopped on the spot. He smiled kindly at Edie, who remained at the microphone with nothing else to stay and unsure what to do next.

The awkward silence only lasted for a few seconds, as it was interrupted by a high-pitched shriek from across the Great Court that everyone present would remember for as long as they lived.

'BOMB!' a male voice boomed.

People looked over, initially with surprise and then confusion.

'BOMB! THERE'S A BOMB! RUN!'

And then the blind panic began.

Screams came from some, whilst others yelled out to locate loved ones. British Museum officials shouted for everybody to evacuate the building, their voices soon drowned out by a deafening alarm.

On the stage, Edie at first watched on in astonishment, her legs immobilised, until Dad jumped up and dragged her off. In his other hand he held Eli firmly.

It was mayhem in the awards ceremony area. Chairs flew and drinks trays crashed to the floor, which became slippery and littered with broken champagne flutes. Brent Petroleum staff were the first to scarper, disregarding their guests. Edie slipped and was pulled to her feet again by Dad. She glimpsed Yasmina, Charlie and Mrs Plunkett, but only briefly as it was every person for themselves. The *Titanic* was sinking and selfish desperation abounded.

The siren continued to blare and Edie felt like she was in a disaster movie.

The mob in the Great Court swelled in size as it was the main route to the exits. People collided and Edie lost Dad's hand twice.

'Let's get out the way we came in,' Dad yelled. 'Montague Place – the main entrance looks impossible.'

'I'll follow you,' Edie shouted back, waving his hand away as it was slowing them all down.

A woman holding a baby whacked into Eli sending him tumbling, but Dad yanked him up and they pushed on past the totem poles. A young girl lost her footing on the spiral stairwell of the Round Reading Room and tumbled down the final flight of steps, only to be inadvertently trampled on at the bottom by an elderly woman. Edie pushed her way over and helped the distressed girl to her feet, who was reunited within seconds with her distraught mother.

Dad. Where was Dad? Diverted, Edie had lost track of him and Eli. The Great Court was clearing fast, but Edie's family were nowhere to be seen.

Edie stopped in the zone next to the west stairs. The Africa room was to her right, where Dad had been heading. Once through there, she'd be close to the rear entrance and to safety.

To her left, Edie's attention was drawn to a man standing by a large granite Hindu statue of Nandi, the humped bull. Unmoving, he was making no attempt whatsoever to escape.

'Get out! Now!' bellowed a bearded museum official in Edie's direction. 'Last chance!' he emphasised even louder, indicating wildly towards the Africa room before racing off. For a split second Edie questioned internally what exactly he meant, before turning back to the stationary man.

Edie took a step towards him, and therefore away from the exit. By now, the Great Court was virtually empty, but a handful of scared-looking people, mainly older, were still descending the west stairs from the Members' Room and hurrying right past Edie – as fast as they were able.

Edie continued past the strange bronze exhibit of a snake in a cage, whilst the man began to approach her. They met next to a beautiful modern iron sculpture that looked like a giant hieroglyphic. Later, Edie would learn that this was a Sufi-inspired object relating, relevantly, to a person's journey of transcendence.

'This is all my fault,' Heath explained. 'All my fault …'

'We've got to get out of here now. Right now!' Edie pleaded.

Heath shook his head. 'I'm not leaving. I've got to try and do something.'

'No! We've got to get out,' Edie implored. 'Please, come with me. You're no good to Harry if you're dead.'

'I'm dying, anyway,' Heath said tearfully.

'You'll get treatment. With the money. You'll get better. Harry adores you and … he needs you. Trust me, I know how much a child needs a parent they love.'

Heath looked down at his feet, averting his gaze from that of the brave young girl. A sudden clunk and a ding behind him made Edie jump, but it was the lift bringing down the last few stragglers. A terrified-looking mother emerged holding the hand of a small child and wheeling a pram containing a sleeping baby.

'I've dragged the bomb into this area, away from the main court,' Heath uttered calmly. He pointed a few metres away to a large black holdall in a nearby corner of the semi-enclosed zone. 'There's seven minutes left on the timer ... probably five now ... You should get out, Edie - there's still time. I'm going to see what I can do.'

'I'm not going anywhere without you,' Edie replied, grabbing Heath's hand. 'Now come!'

Heath yanked his arm away and turned towards the holdall on the ground. Edie was about to shout at him when three loud beeps rang out. For a second, Edie feared the worst, then realised they weren't coming from the bomb bag. A moment later, a whooshing sound accompanied heavy metal shutters falling rapidly from the ceiling, sealing off the zone in which they were standing.

As the shutters hit the floor, Edie realised she was now confined to this zone, unable to escape through the archway to the Great Court, through the Africa room or via the west stairs. Presumably, the grilles were to prevent a fire or bomb blast spreading outwards. However, those left inside were now inadvertently trapped. Edie was imprisoned, together with Heath, the woman with the children and an older couple.

Panic coursed through Edie's body and her throat tightened.

Calm. You've got to stay calm, Edie told herself. Despite the emergency, Edie closed her eyes, thought of Mum and took three slow, deep breaths. It'll be okay, she told herself. What you need will come to you. Even in a crisis.

Opening her eyes, Edie made her way over to the holdall, which was partially unzipped. The young mother shrieked when she caught a glimpse of what was inside, whilst the older couple watched with grave concern.

'All of you,' Edie commanded, 'go over to the other side of this area … behind the statue … a plinth … as far away as you can get.'

Edie and Heath exchanged a look, a shared knowing of the seriousness of the situation. Heath reached down towards the zip.

'No, let me,' Edie insisted, carefully moving aside Heath's shaking hand.

Before Heath could say anything, Edie leant over the bag, pushed away the grey handles and gently drew apart the full-length zip, now wholly revealing what lay inside.

Edie gasped. A central package, about the size of a medium-sized cardboard box and wrapped in thick cellophane, sat in the middle of the holdall. Inside the package were about twenty clear zip-lock bags, each packed with a white material, which Edie assumed must be the explosive.

The holdall was stuffed with nails, screws and pieces of coloured glass and pottery. On top of the main package was a black box, with a mobile phone firmly attached with brown packaging tape. Various wires extended between the phone, the black box and the explosive package.

A timer on the phone blinked steadily in countdown mode.

There were four minutes and forty-eight seconds to go.

4:48 … 4:47 … 4:46 …

'We shouldn't move the bomb.' Edie stated the obvious. She looked up from the timer directly at Heath and asked urgently: 'Do you know how to disarm it? I mean, if you were involved …'

'I told them not to do it,' Heath insisted. 'I told them not to … but they wouldn't listen.'

4:23 … 4:22 …

'That doesn't matter now!' Edie interrupted fiercely. 'Do you know how to defuse the bomb or not?'

'No,' Heath replied meekly, almost lost in thought. 'Jarrah made the bombs … and Sven helped. I've got no idea.'

Edie was going to have to do this herself. 'Don't touch it,' she instructed Heath, then stood up and looked around the zone, noting the cowering group on the far side. There was no obvious CCTV in the area so they were unobserved.

Close to Edie was a seat for the museum official who marshalled visitors through the entrance to special exhibitions. That entry point was now barred by a metal bomb-blast shutter, but next to the seat was a wooden lectern.

Edie sped the few steps over to the lectern, which had two shelves at the rear. On the top shelf were stationery and other office materials: badges, string, sticky tape, scissors and lanyards. Underneath sat a corded landline phone, which sparked an idea. Assistance from somebody who knew about bombs was what Edie desperately needed.

Edie got out her own phone, scrolled through her contacts and pressed 'Call' when she found Donna Redmond's details.

3:34 … 3:33 …

The call didn't go through, and Edie swore out loud.

'The police are probably blocking mobile signals,' Heath advised, 'to avoid somebody detonating the bomb by phone.'

Edie wasn't listening. She grabbed the handset from the lower shelf of the lectern. Pulling the long cord, Edie was able to make her way back to the bomb, where she placed the phone on the ground. On her phone, Edie quickly scrolled through contacts again until she found the name and number she needed.

Please, please, please let this work, Edie prayed. Holding the handset to her right ear, Edie pressed the zero button on the phone unit. An exhalation of relief: she heard the ringtone of an outside line meaning she could make an external call.

Fingers shaking, Edie hastily pressed the buttons to dial the number displayed on her phone. It rang and Edie waited.

Please, please, please, not an answerphone.

3:08 … 3:07 …

'Hello, this is …'

'Hi, Mrs … Donna,' Edie interrupted urgently. 'This is an emergency. I don't have long.'

'What exactly is the prob …'

'I'm in the British Museum … Brave People Awards … and there's a bomb …'

'What?'

'A BOMB!' Edie shrieked. 'I'm next to a bomb! Trapped inside an area where security shutters have come down from the ceiling.'

'Christ!' Donna exclaimed. 'I heard about the incident through work … but I forgot you'd be there.'

'Tell me what to do,' Edie pleaded.

Donna's voice suddenly went into professional authoritative mode, as if she'd encountered this kind of problem before. 'Okay, Edie. Listen to me. I'm going to talk you through this. Understand?'

Relieved, Edie sighed. 'Yes. Understood.'

'Now, how many people are in there with you?

'Six,' Edie answered instantly. Heath was right next to her, now helpfully holding the phone to Edie's ear. 'Two are kids … a baby.'

'Right. Get them as far away as possible, behind whatever protection there is.'

'Already done. But there's hardly any time and we can't get out.'

'What do you mean "hardly any time"?'

'The TIMER!' Edie howled. 'It says two minutes and thirty-six seconds, thirty-five …'

'Alright.' Donna spoke steadily. 'That's enough time. Stay calm and tell me exactly what you can see.'

Edie cautiously parted the folds of the holdall back even further so she could see what was inside. 'It's a large bag … like a sports bag … a long zip on the top which I've spread open.'

'Okay, and what's inside?'

'Inside there's … like … twenty parcels of white stuff, each the size of a bag of sugar … all bundled together tight with sort of cling-film.'

2:15 … 2:14 …

'You're doing well,' Edie heard Heath whisper.

'What else?' Donna pressed.

'Hmm … around the whole package … filling the bag … are loads of loose nails, screws, glass. Shall I scoop them out?'

'No. No,' Donna instructed firmly. 'What else do you see, Edie? Electrics?'

Her heart thumping, Edie wiped away a bead of sweat from her forehead with her sleeve. 'Yes … sorry … of course. There's … like … a black plastic box on top of the package.'

'How big? Quickly.'

'Hmm … maybe twenty centimetres by fifteen.'

'The detonator,' said Donna. 'That's the detonator. Possibly also a booster. What else, Edie? Be precise. Details.'

'I'm trying!' Edie explained, choking up. 'I'm doing my best …'

'You're doing fantastically,' Donna reassured her. 'Now just tell me what else you see.'

Locked into the mental zone of what was directly in front of her, Edie was completely unaware of her surroundings. The crying of the baby didn't register, nor did the older man standing up to help only to be screamed at by his wife to get back down. Even the trembling of the phone held close to her ear went unnoticed. Edie was immersed in the present moment like she'd never been before. Each second precious.

'A mobile phone … Samsung … is strapped to the black box with tape. It's a basic kind … simple … and the timer is counting down. One fifty-three now, fifty-two …'

'Ignore the clock, Edie,' Donna commanded. 'Listen to me. Wires. Tell me about the wires.'

Bending down, Edie got a close look then leant around to see from behind. 'Okay, there are grey wires … two at the front, two at the back … going from the box … from the detonator … into different points in the main package.'

'Excellent. Other wires?'

'Yes, there's a red wire and a black wire going from the phone to the detonator, and another red wire … and another black … from the detonator to the package.'

1:29 … 1:28 …

Edie took a deep breath in and out.

'Good. Now listen, Edie. Do you have anything to cut the wires with?'

'No,' she responded immediately, and turned to Heath. 'Do you have a knife … something to cut with?'

Padding down his jacket quickly to check, Heath shook his head, the handset slipping momentarily from his grip.

Suddenly, Edie remembered what she'd seen earlier and made for the lectern where she grabbed a small pair of scissors lodged on a shelf behind some lanyards.

'I've got scissors!' Edie yelled.

0:56 … 0:55 …

'That's great, Edie. Well done. Now, first I want you to cut the red wire that leads from the detonator to the package of explosive. The *red* wire. Double-check first that it does go from the detonator – the black box – to the package.'

'Can't I just pull it out?'

'NO, Edie! No pulling. Don't touch anything. Just check visibly.'

Edie made sure, or as sure as she could be. 'Yes, it goes from the box to the package. What happens if this is wrong?'

0:38 … 0:37 …

'Don't think about that. It's not wrong. Just cut the red wire.'

Hand shaking, Edie leant in and placed the blades of the scissors around the red wire. Her heart was pounding at breakneck speed. She closed her eyes.

SNIP.

No explosion.

'It worked! But there's only half a minute left!'

'Now, Edie, cut the RED wire that goes from the phone to the detonator. The RED wire. Now!'

Edie moved her hand across, but her fingers were so slippery with sweat that the scissors slithered from her grasp, landing on the bomb phone and then sliding down the side of the bag.

'Shit!'

'What is it?'

'I dropped the scissors.' Edie reached down and grabbed them from the bed of nails.

'The RED wire, Edie. Cut it now!'

Edie placed the scissor blades around the red wire, ready to cut.

0:20 … 0:19 …

A thought suddenly flashed across Edie's mind. How could she be sure Donna was on her side? The neighbour had a strange manner and was caught up in all kinds of unusual happenings. Fate … destiny … here they were together now.

Donna could easily be one of the terrorists, deliberately telling her to cut the wrong wire. Maybe she was the woman from the pub?

Edie moved her hand to the black wire.

0:14 … 0:13

My age, Edie observed randomly.

'Cut the RED wire, now!' Donna screamed.

Edie moved the scissors back to the red wire where her hand hovered, overcome by a feeling of paralysis.

Shutting her eyes once more, Edie gathered a mental picture of Dad and Eli. And Mum, of course.

Edie began closing her fingers to cut, and could almost feel the resistance of the wire bite, when she felt a firm hand on her shoulder. Another hand was now strongly supporting her own arm.

'We'll take it from here, Miss,' a male voice declared calmly.

Edie opened her eyes to see the scissors being removed gently from her hand.

A man's finger then reached down to press the 'stop' button on the phone timer.

0:07.

Edie looked up to find a man wearing a helmet and thickly padded protective clothing, the words 'Explosive Ordinance Disposal' emblazoned on the front. Behind him were two other explosives officers from the same police unit, similarly attired.

One of the security shutters was now open, but Edie had been too preoccupied to hear it happen. The woman, children and older couple were being ushered out. Over her shoulder, the mother mouthed 'Thank you' in Edie's direction.

Down the museum phone handset, now lying on the floor as Heath was escorted away, Donna was saying something complimentary.

But Edie couldn't hear as she gradually became aware of the wailing sirens.

Shell-shocked, Edie was brought to her feet by a police officer who gently led her away.

Outside the British Museum, a mass of police cars, ambulances and fire engines were gathered, along with army personnel and more explosives officers. Excitable sniffer dogs and their handlers milled around.

Some visitors were being given attention by the emergency services, although Edie wondered if they were being simultaneously vetted as possible perpetrators. Red and blue lights flashed incessantly.

'They're just searching the premises for other bombs,' the police officer advised Edie before handing the young girl over to an ambulance crew.

Edie was wrapped in a blanket, even though she wasn't feeling cold. Gently, the paramedic checked her over, interrupted near the end of the process by Edie leaping to her feet.

'Dad!' Edie shouted on sighting her father and brother approaching from the crowd.

Edie wrapped her arms around Dad and then gave Eli an equally strong embrace. They talked for ten minutes about what had happened with Edie and the bomb, Dad looking on disbelievingly as he learned of his daughter's latest heroics.

'They'll give you another Brave People Award next year,' he remarked.

'I won't accept it,' Edie replied. 'I only did this time so Harry's dad can get treatment for his blood cancer in the United States.'

By the expression on his face Edie could tell that Dad was impressed, but her own thoughts were elsewhere. Edie didn't have time to explain the complicated backstory as she needed to locate Heath Coranger, to check he wasn't in trouble and to thank him – and also to find out if there was news on Harry.

'I've just got to find somebody,' Edie announced, standing up from the back of the ambulance. Dad's expression turned to flabbergasted.

'I'll just be a minute, Dad.' She touched his hand softly. 'I promise. I do have to do something, though.' Dad wasn't convinced, so Edie tried harder. 'Look, keep my bag here with you – I'll only take my phone. Just stay here, I won't be long.'

Knowing his protests would be futile, Dad simply told her to be careful – and Edie was off. Wandering between the various emergency services vehicles and police cars, Edie noticed a number of visitors she'd seen inside the museum. Smithers-Jones, who failed to respond to Edie's greeting, sat on a chair lost in a stupor.

Much calmer were Mrs Plunkett and Mr Jones, to whom Edie said a quick hello in passing. Mrs Plunkett murmured something indecipherable back. No sign of Yasmina or Charlie, but Edie was overjoyed to bump into Lizzie, leaning against a fire engine and drinking hot tea.

They embraced wildly and both cried. They were alive, they had survived the ordeal and all else seemed unimportant and forgiven. Edie felt relieved as they perched on the rear step of the vehicle talking. After the tears had subsided, Edie was about to run Lizzie through what had happened when her phone pinged. She grabbed it from her pocket and looked down, expecting to see a message from Dad.

But it was something else. Something sinister.

Accompanied once again by foreboding music, the skull-and-crossbones symbol was back. As the image slowly enlarged to fill the screen, some words appeared across the middle:

> You didn't let it go but we planned a back-up.
> Now your name will be remembered – for all
> the wrong reasons.

The sentences flashed twice in quick succession, and then the whole image blew up into tiny fragments. Once the pieces had faded away, the whole sequence started again. This time, Edie took a screenshot of the message.

Lizzie stared in bemusement. 'What's that about? It's horrible. Who sent it? And what do they mean by "You didn't let it go"?'

Edie's heart sank, but she was focused on the second half of the message. Jarrah and Sven had escaped, and there was clearly more to their destructive plans. 'I know who it's from,' Edie answered blankly. 'They were in the museum and must've planted the bomb. But it means there's more … probably another bomb … somewhere … and now. Right now. They wouldn't wait as they know they'll be caught soon.'

'What on earth are you on about, Edie?' posed a bewildered Lizzie.

'The bombers,' Edie asserted, 'I know who they are. I've been investigating a few cases – my neighbour … Harry's dad … the missing dogs – and everything's linked. I can't explain now … there's no time.' Edie paused; she'd been speaking almost breathlessly. 'But you have to believe me. There must be another bomb … and I've got to do something!'

'So, tell the police,' Lizzie advised. 'That's what people normally do if they suspect a bomb! And if you won't, I will!'

'There's no time. It'll be too late. And this is personal. Look at what they say about me being remembered for the wrong reasons. They're angry and warning me, but they've given something away … There's a clue – not intentional but still a clue – to the location of the next bomb.'

Two pairs of eyes ran over the message repeatedly, the girls' brains whirring as they sat together on a fire engine in the midst of the frenzied activity.

'It must be something to do with you as a person,' Lizzie said eventually. 'Where you live … your age … what you look like … maybe your family? Your mum, perhaps, and her human rights work?'

Silence for a few seconds.

'Or my name?' Edie queried. 'Just my name?'

'What, "Edie"?' Lizzie answered, looking perplexed. 'What place in London – if it even is London – has something to do with the word "Edie"?'

More silence.

A firefighter checked they were both okay.

'No, not my first name. My surname,' Edie ventured. 'Franklin. The answer must have something to do with Franklin.'

Lizzie quickly googled the surname and found a Franklin Hotel in Knightsbridge, Franklin House near Heathrow and Benjamin Franklin House in Covent Garden.

'Maybe this one,' Lizzie suggested, pointing to the museum dedicated to the former US president.

'Could be,' Edie agreed. 'The United States is the second biggest contributor to climate change, so that could make sense as a target. But ... I don't know ... it doesn't seem like a big enough statement. A significant enough landmark. They've already gone for the British Museum ... and Brent Petroleum.'

A few more seconds of quiet thought.

'Maybe it's not Franklin,' Lizzie proposed.

'What then?'

'Marble. Perhaps they mean your mum's last name – and what you've adopted as a detective.'

'That's possible,' Edie granted. She'd read that the famous Elgin Marbles were kept at the British Museum, but that wasn't even her name and was probably incidental.

All of a sudden, the penny dropped. They knew exactly where the next bomb would be and said the location in tandem.

'Let's go!' Edie exclaimed. 'Look, Google Maps says it's only 1.7 miles from here. We can run.'

'No, let's tell the police.'

'No time,' Edie insisted, jumping up. 'It'll be too late. Are you coming?'

Lizzie's hesitancy was all Edie needed to know. She touched her friend's arm, told her not to worry and set off at pace.

Following the maps app on her phone, Edie weaved hastily between the gathered throng and made her way through the museum courtyard, out the main gates, down Great Russell Street and over to Tottenham Court Road. By the Dominion Theatre, she crossed over to Oxford Street and charged down the busy thoroughfare.

Past McDonalds, Primark and Matalan, one shopper after another repeatedly got in Edie's way, and after numerous bumps she was eventually knocked over outside Urban Outfitters by a middle-aged woman with more store bags than awareness. Helped to her feet, Edie realised she was completely out of breath, wheezing slightly and unable to run any further. Her asthma inhaler was in the bag she'd left with Dad.

The traffic was virtually at a standstill, so a bus or taxi would be useless. Using her iPhone to pay, she could get the Tube, but a glance at nearby Oxford Circus Underground Station suggested it might be closed because of the bomb incident.

What to do? And then, as seemed to happen increasingly, the solution came to Edie. In this case, quite literally. At the kerbside next to Edie, a cycle rickshaw pulled up, the newly popular transport option for tourists in central London. On the saddle of the multicoloured bicycle sat a boy of Ethan's age.

'You alright?' he asked.

'Yes, I'm fine,' Edie replied, clambering into the two-seater carriage. 'But I need to get to Marble Arch. Fast!'

'Ten pounds. You got money?' the boy asked unhurriedly.

'Yes! Apple Pay,' Edie barked. 'Now go!'

'Sorry. Cash only,' the boy insisted serenely.

'Ahhhh!' Edie yelped, but her despair was interrupted by somebody barging their way into the seat next to her.

'I've got cash,' Lizzie puffed.

Edie smiled and grabbed her best friend's hand. 'Thank you.'

The cyclist navigated the traffic skilfully, whilst Edie managed to call both Dad and PC Brearley to alert them of the turn of events. Seven minutes later, Edie and Lizzie were deposited between Foot Locker and Marble Arch Underground Station, directly opposite the famous London landmark.

Originally intended to be part of Buckingham Palace, the monument – actually comprising three archways – was relocated in 1851 to where it stood today. The girls negotiated the busy pedestrian crossings over Oxford Street and Park Lane, the exhaust fumes exacerbating Edie's laboured breathing. Edie imagined this spot had been targeted by the eco-terrorists due to its location in one of the most polluted parts of London, rather than because of her name, but she wasn't sure. The marble was more of a grey-black colour than its original white.

As Lizzie and Edie approached the large monument, at first everything seemed completely normal. The space in which the arch was situated was a sort of giant traffic island, pedestrian-only with areas of trees and grass that were part of Hyde Park. A handful of visitors were exploring and taking photos. Nothing untoward to see.

Edie was disappointed and wondered if they'd failed to solve the clue correctly, when her eye was caught by a dustcart on the pavement next to the smaller of the three archways, closest to Park Lane. Metal wheeled carts of this kind were a common sight across the city, part of the council's street cleaning services. The brooms and shovels lodged on either side of the cart leant further credibility.

Intelligence, though, was central to detective work. Nowhere to be seen was the high-vis jacketed road sweeper. And that just didn't seem right.

Edie strode over, Lizzie following cautiously. First, Edie scrutinised the cart close-up. No giveaways, so Edie deftly lifted the metal lid.

Inside, immediately visible, was another sizable bomb, complete with a similar-looking detonator and timer.

3:23 … 3:22 … 3:21

Lizzie gasped audibly, but Edie stayed calm.

'I've got this,' Edie told Lizzie. 'You go right over there.' She pointed past her friend to some benches way off on the lawn of the park. Lizzie meekly beckoned Edie to come with her, but by now she knew better and followed the instruction.

Edie hollered as loud as she could to be heard over the din of the traffic: 'BOMB. EVERYBODY CLEAR AWAY. THERE'S A BOMB!'

It took a few seconds, but orderly panic spread amongst those in the vicinity, who started running in different directions away from Marble Arch. Infectious terror led others to follow suit and flee.

'See one, do one' was a mantra they were often reminded of at school. Well, Edie thought, I've seen one of these before, I learned how to defuse it, so I should be able to have a go myself. For the second time in an hour, Edie's hand hovered over a phone timer. She was about to press 'STOP', then recalled that previously she'd cut a wire first. Should she do the same again? Maybe this bomb was designed differently.

Sirens wailed as multiple police cars bore down from Edgware Road, Park Lane and Oxford Street, rapidly bringing all the traffic to a stop and creating a barricade around the whole Marble Arch area.

As Edie paused, she looked up from the dust cart and saw, moving against the tide of people running away, two men and a woman closing in on her and the cart. They must have stayed nearby to ensure that this bomb was a success.

Edie reached down again, but she was now too nervous to press the button.

'Leave it alone!' Sven screamed at her.

'Get away!' Jarrah yelled aggressively.

Edie's eyes were locked on the woman, though, who was now only a few metres away. Edie couldn't quite believe what she was seeing. 'You!' she screeched. 'How could you?'

'It's the only way.' Ms Dylan, the geography teacher, defended herself vigorously. 'The *only way*. Humans are wrecking the planet ... destroying ecosystems ... poisoning the oceans and sea life ... bringing about mass extinction ... and the havoc caused by climate change. And nobody is doing anything. *Nobody!* The politicians don't care, don't want to hear. People don't want to change their self-interested lives. And it's almost too late. Maybe it already is too late.'

'We have to make a *louder* noise,' Sven growled. 'Grab people's attention. Shake them up. Make them listen!'

'It's the only way to save the planet,' Jarrah echoed with a steady ferocity. 'People don't matter ... they're the cause of the problem ... but we must preserve the beauty of life on earth.'

The three were upon Edie now, but she had shifted position and was holding her ground between them and the dust cart. Looking down over her shoulder, the timer wasn't waiting for anything.

2:08 ... 2:07 ... 2:06

'This isn't the way to go about it,' Edie retorted. 'It can't be. I agree with what you said about climate change and saving the planet, but this is *not* right! What sense is there in killing people at the museum? Or here. Causing all that sadness for families. Blowing up monuments. And it might not make any difference!'

'Eco-terrorism!' Jarrah shouted loudly and suddenly, the shock jolting Edie. 'The last resort!' As Jarrah spoke, he stepped forward and grabbed Edie, wrapping his arms firmly around her and immobilising her arms.

Edie cried out and grappled momentarily to free herself, then paused. Behind the three eco-terrorists, she saw police approaching from all directions and specialist firearms officers lying flat in the grass nearby, long-barrelled rifles pointed in her direction. Lizzie watched on from afar.

Glancing down, Edie checked the timer.

1:23 … 1:22 … 1:21 …

Jarrah's arms were encircling Edie from behind, but she knew exactly what to do, just as she'd practised with Sensei Dominic. Instead of trying to pull herself away, Edie pushed her right hip firmly into Jarrah's waist whilst raising his right arm to the level of her ear. Koshi Guruma. Edie leant over forwards to almost ninety degrees, pushing her bum further into Jarrah's waist, then yanked hard on his right arm. Just as she'd done successfully in judo class, her assailant tumbled over her head first, landing on his back on the ground with a thump.

Edie ran towards the police, hearing several quiet clacks and feeling a whoosh of wind zip past her. She turned briefly to see bullets hit the shoulders of all three eco-terrorists, who slumped to the ground. Rapidly arriving police officers ensured they were fully incapacitated.

Out of nowhere, explosives officers reappeared and applied their skills for the second time that day.

Swathed in yet another emergency blanket, Edie was whisked away from the scene.

CHAPTER 16

AFTERMATH

All through the following day, Dad patrolled the front door as if on guard duty at Pentonville prison – even though an actual police officer was stationed outside the house the whole time.

Those excluded from entry included the press. Vans, cameras and reporters from national and international TV and radio news broadcasters, including Sky and the BBC, gathered outside the Franklins' home. It was extraordinary how quickly they'd worked out where Edie lived; the quiet street in Crouch End had never seen such a frenzy of activity. The street was as far as they got, however, as Edie had learned about the stresses of media interviews three months earlier and had no intention of repeating the same mistakes. The only exception was a short telephone discussion for a feature article in *The Observer* newspaper, through which Dad had been present throughout.

Others barred from seeing Edie on Friday included school friends and teachers, although Dad made an exception for Lizzie. For the permitted hour, Edie and her best friend talked incessantly. Edie explained the whole incredible story, filling in the bits she'd left out previously and leaving Lizzie open-mouthed in astonishment. Despite Edie's reticence about the press, Lizzie had enjoyed her own moments in the spotlight, doing two TV interviews in which she described the rickshaw speed-trip down Oxford Street and the events at Marble Arch.

'Mum and Dad have bought the flight tickets for Washington,' Lizzie shared anxiously towards the end of their time together. The summer move to the United States was definitely on.

'Gosh. That makes it concrete, I guess.'

'Yes, it's really happening.' Lizzie started to tear up. 'I'm going to miss you a lot.'

'I'm going to miss you too,' Edie replied, starting to cry. 'Sooo much. And I'm sorry about how I behaved – it was selfish to ask you to come to Swinbrook with the stuff going on with your parents. I'm gonna try to do better.'

'It's okay. And thank you.'

Edie reached out and the hug was filled with affection. It felt wonderful to have the closeness back with her best friend.

Suddenly, Edie had a thought. 'Maybe I can visit?' she suggested as they embraced.

'That would be amazing, if you can.'

Edie spent much of the rest of the day in her room. Dad was allowing her to take video and voice calls. Mrs Plunkett chose voice. 'On behalf of the school, Edie,' she said very formally, 'I want to congratulate you profusely on your immeasurable courage. And, just so you know, Ms Dylan has been dismissed from the school.'

Yasmina and Charlie arranged a three-way WhatsApp video chat and had a lot of questions. 'How come all the cases were connected?' Yasmina enquired bemusedly. 'What did it feel like to defuse a bomb – to be seconds from death?' Charlie wondered. They were sweet and meant well, but answering was exhausting work.

Other people from school and the synagogue made contact, but Edie restricted her responses to messages or to nothing at all. Dad said it was Edie's right not to reply if she didn't feel like it, and he suggested that some callers were more motivated by being part of the action than genuine concern for Edie.

Martin and Ethan both sent text messages:

Martin: You did brilliantly, Edie. And thanks again for the exam stuff!

Ethan: You're a star. A real star.

Edie opted to answer a call from Rabbi Abby. 'My, what *has* been going on, Edie?' she asked. 'You're a national celebrity – again!' Edie expanded on what she'd shared previously about two people appearing destined to meet, and probed Rabbi Abby about whether she thought everything that had happened was predetermined and meant to be. But Rabbi Abby was disappointingly non-committal in her response. 'Don't worry too much about all of that, Edie. You did something amazing, of which your mum would be proud. Now just rest up.'

Edie wondered if the rabbi was more comfortable with philosophical theorising on a piece of paper than accepting the ideas in real life.

Edie slept through a fair part of the afternoon, mind and body shattered. Mama and Papa joined for dinner, and Edie was delighted to be treated to Mama's cooking again: kreplach (home-made dumplings in chicken soup) followed by chicken meat loaf, which only came out on special occasions because of the fiddly, time-consuming preparation. Emmeline Watson asked for second helpings of both.

By the end of dinner Edie was, to her own surprise, tired again. Knowing the next day would be busy, she went back upstairs to bed.

Edie should have been able to get straight back to sleep, but there had been no word all day from either Heath or Harry.

The doorbell rang at ten o'clock sharp on Saturday morning. Dad answered, and in walked the familiar faces of Chief Inspector Penrose, PCs Wiltshire and Wilkins and, to Edie's joy, PC Jessica Brearley. Wiltshire promptly relieved the policeman standing outside the house, although the media had by now dispersed. Dad led the way into the kitchen, whilst Edie hugged PC Brearley.

Penrose removed the police cap from under his arm and placed it on a side unit by the fridge. Wilkins stood by the back door, overlooking the garden, whilst the rest took seats at the kitchen table. Emmeline, whom Edie realised discomfortingly had stayed overnight, made teas and coffees.

Eli made his way in from the playroom and sat on a stool away from the table.

'Well, here we are again,' Penrose began with a wry smile. 'And quite a story, once again.'

Dad beamed and Edie blushed.

'We've been working on all of this solidly since Thursday,' Penrose continued, 'and I'd like to share what we've found out so far – that is, what I'm able to share with you as some of it is classified as top secret. A matter of national security.'

'We understand,' Dad said unnecessarily.

Penrose took a sip of coffee. 'First and foremost, hats off – if that's the right phrase – to you, Edie, for a formidable piece of detective work, and for your sheer bravery in the face of extreme danger. As I've said before – and imagine I may say again in the future – you are a remarkable young woman, and the country is in your debt.'

Edie blushed again, this time more deeply. Edie noticed that Dad was holding Emmeline's hand, and he squeezed it lightly on hearing the compliment.

'Okay,' Penrose began, 'we have all the eco-terrorists in custody, and we believe the three of them were working alone. There are no other suspects at present.' Edie was about to ask about Heath Coranger but thought better of it.

'The bombs were home-made and were both significant in nature. The one in the British Museum would have caused significant loss of life and extensive damage to priceless artefacts. Luckily, there were no booby traps in the wiring – we don't believe they were sophisticated enough bomb-makers for that – and the detonation device and timer were fairly standard. You did unbelievably well, Edie, keeping cool in a nerve-wracking situation.'

Edie posed a question that had been very much on her mind: 'What would have happened if I'd cut the red wire at the end?'

'That would have been alright too … but it was easier to stop the timer,' Penrose explained reassuringly. 'Donna Redmond did an excellent job on the other end of the phone: she's experienced in that aspect of the security world. Very smart of you, by the way, to use the landline for the call. We had electronic countermeasures blocking mobile phone signals in and out of the whole museum area to avoid remote detonation.'

'What about the other bomb?' Dad enquired. 'At Marble Arch.'

'Hmm,' Penrose muttered. 'The back-up bomb, which they weren't intending to detonate unless the British Museum plan failed. The word "Marble", by the way, was coincidental, although it worked against them ultimately.' Edie grinned as Penrose continued.

'It was an even bigger bomb, and they were all present to make sure it happened. They used Semtex – plastic explosive – and there was enough in that dust cart to destroy Marble Arch and cause major disruption.'

'How did they get the Semtex?' Eli chipped in from the side.

'We don't know yet, young man. It's usually owned by the military, but we'll find out in due course, I'm sure.'

Everybody paused for breath. There was a lot to take in.

'And what about the dogs?' Edie asked. 'The sniffer dogs at the museum?'

'That's very interesting, Edie,' Penrose answered. 'One of the terrorists, Sven Olsen, created a diversion outside the museum, as I believe you witnessed, creating an opportunity to bring the explosive materials inside. They smuggled in the other bomb parts in the bags of a school party, orchestrated somehow by Ms Dylan. We're still checking exactly how. Then Jarrah Guyula – who you encountered working at the bag check counter – joined everything together on the day. He got the job at the museum as cover.'

'Right,' Edie interjected. 'What I really meant was about the training the terrorists … the eco-terrorists … did to escape the sniffer dogs. You know, with the stolen dogs in the Cotswolds.'

'Eco-terrorists are still terrorists,' Penrose corrected, raising his eyebrows. 'It doesn't matter what the reason is behind the terror.' Penrose nodded in the direction of Edie's police officer friend, passing the latest question over to her.

'Yes, sir.' PC Brearley took the hint. 'I can fill in this part. It looks very much like two of the terrorists, Olsen and Guyula, were responsible for abducting dogs over recent weeks from parkland in north London, including Hampstead Heath.'

'And Quincy was one of those?' Edie queried.

'Yes. They somehow got hold of Mrs Carpenter's details. She's the woman who runs the adoption service for dogs retired from the police force and the army, and they bribed her to share the list of new owners. It seems Mrs Carpenter has a gambling problem and considerable debts. She'll be charged with a breach of data protection law – although, to be fair on her, she hadn't a clue about the terrorist plots.'

'What did they do with the stolen dogs?' Eli asked innocently.

'Well,' PC Brearley continued. 'It appears they used those dogs, who'd been specially trained to sniff out bombs ... explosives ... to work out what they could conceal in a holdall. And how best to wrap up the materials in the bag to avoid being detected by the sniffer dogs outside the museum. I'm not sure how well all that worked, to be honest, which may be why they also needed the diversion, but those were their intentions. And we're still questioning them, of course.'

'What about Quincy?' Edie was desperate to know.

'Quincy seems alright,' PC Brearley answered. 'Thin, and a bit shaken, but he's alright. And I understand his owner, Mrs Solomon, is doing much better.'

Penrose finished his coffee, looked directly at Edie and took up the story. 'We rescued the lad – your friend Harry Coranger – yesterday from the house in Swinbrook to which you alerted us. Great detective work again, by the way, with the mobile phone strapped underneath his dad's car.'

Edie grinned: she was proud of that touch. Dad and Emmeline gazed on in disbelief.

'From our interrogation, it appears the terrorists located the deserted building in Swinbrook weeks back. It was ideally placed – away from everyone – and they used the house for the bomb-making. Materials were often bought in

London, stored secretly for a while and then transported to the Cotswolds. And the stolen dogs were kept in that strange hut in the woods, apparently to keep them separate from the house so they wouldn't be heard. Peculiar, I know, but they kept the animals in reasonable conditions.' Penrose shrugged his shoulders. 'I guess they are environmentalists, supposedly.'

'What about Harry?' Edie pressed.

'Oh, sorry. Brave fella – in your own mould, Edie.' The police chief grinned. 'It seems Harry made his own way over to Swinbrook on Wednesday by train and bicycle – he was concerned about the imprisonment of those dogs – but he was captured by Guyula in the woods. Faws Grove. Then he was locked up in a room in that house … given food and water but no way of getting out. Guyula took his phone. Harry's perfectly fine now. Another charge there for Guyula – kidnapping – plus harassment and assault for that stunt with the motorbike and the axe.'

As Edie suspected, Helmet Head was indeed Jarrah.

Once again Dad looked staggered, this time at the mention of an axe.

Emmeline's mind was elsewhere, though: 'And what about the nasty messages Edie was sent?'

'Oh, yes,' Penrose replied. 'Glad you brought that up. It seems the terrorists were aware that Edie might be on to them, but they didn't know exactly how much she knew. Something about catching sight of Edie at the pub in Camden.'

Penrose glanced over at Edie, but she remained stony-faced.

'Anyway, they decided to bug Edie's mobile phone. Ms Dylan was tasked with doing that after school – I think there may have been an opportunity around a late finish day after some sort of resilience training – but Olsen wanted more definitive action. He felt that Edie was a risk to the whole plot. So, Ms Dylan got hold of Edie's personal Gmail address through the school office and sent the threatening email there as well as to her detective account.'

'So, did they bug my phone?'

'I believe so, Edie,' Penrose responded. 'That's why you were sent those horrible skull-and-crossbones images – which, ironically, led to the terrorists' own downfall.' Penrose paused and then added: 'We'll get your phone fully checked, Edie, but it should be fine.'

Eli had a question which they were all interested to have answered: 'How long will they go to prison for?'

'Well, that's for the courts and the judge to decide. But there are multiple very serious charges … terrorism, assault and battery, kidnapping, arson, cruelty to animals … and probably more.'

'What about Ms Dylan?' Emmeline asked.

'Each person may get a different sentence – Ms Dylan possibly less than the others. But they will all still be going to prison for a long time.'

Edie was intrigued. Penrose hadn't mentioned one particular person about whom she was anxious to know more. 'What about Heath Coranger? Harry's dad?'

'Yes, the lad's father. Well, as far as we can ascertain, he tried to stop the British Museum bombing and didn't know anything about Marble Arch … and he wasn't involved in any of the other nasty stuff. The three others don't seem to be disputing that – they'd ostracised him from the gang – but he could still be charged with failing to notify the police of a possible terrorist attack.'

'Will he go to prison?'

'I don't believe so, and I will certainly be doing my best – in terms of police evidence – to avoid that happening. And his health condition will be taken into consideration. We've been interviewing him, but he's at home now and hasn't been charged with anything yet.'

Edie breathed a huge sigh of relief at the very moment the doorbell rang again.

'Ah, dead on time,' said Penrose. Edie observed that the microwave clock read precisely 11:00.

Edie jumped up and raced to the hallway. When she opened the front door, however, the person wasn't whom she'd been anticipating.

'Good morning, Edie,' Donna Redmond greeted.

'Oh, hi, Mrs Redm … I mean Donna.'

'You seem disappointed,' the neighbour intuited.

'No. Not all. It's lovely to see you. I just thought it might be … doesn't matter. Come in.'

In the hallway, Donna leant over, a little awkwardly, to embrace Edie. 'You were amazing, Edie. Quite the hero … heroine. Truly incredible. Well done.'

'Thank *you*,' Edie rejoined. 'You were amazing too. I couldn't have done it without you.'

'That's just my training, Edie. Doing my job. But thank

you, anyway. Now, just come in here with me for a second.' She beckoned Edie into the lounge.

Edie took a few steps into the lounge. Before Donna could speak further, Edie asked: 'How's Rochelle?'

'Oh, that's sort of what I wanted to talk about.' Donna dropped her voice down a notch and said softly: 'Rochelle is doing very well, thank you. She's back in Canada now, but we spent ages together – and it's amazing to have my best friend back. Truly amazing, like we've never been apart. And I think she's okay with Scott. We'll be tracing the car that hit her, thanks to you getting the number plate. Rochelle's going to send you and me a copy of her book when it comes out. Thank you, Edie, so much for bringing us back together again.'

Edie smiled. 'That's good, I'm pleased.'

Donna's voice then quietened almost to a whisper. 'By the way, here's the remainder of the payment for your work.' Donna handed over an envelope. 'Put that in your room, please and … how do I say this … there's really no need to mention to the police our financial arrangement or anything about the encounters with my friend and fate. It'll make me sound a bit crazy.'

'Don't worry. I haven't said a word.'

Donna smiled and touched Edie on the shoulder in gratitude before they made their way into the kitchen.

'Ah, MI5 has arrived!' Penrose joked whilst standing up. 'Now we're all safe!' The manner of his friendly handshake with Donna suggested they knew each other professionally. 'I asked Donna Redmond to join us, just to help fill in any gaps. To the degree that she's allowed, of course. National security and all that.'

Edie slept for another twelve hours that night and awoke just after nine.

The first thing she observed was the even manner in which the morning sunlight shone through the window and entered her bedroom. The blind had been fixed. Edie didn't know when or how, but Dad had repaired it. She beamed adoringly. He really was a very, very good dad.

On her iPhone, Insta, Snapchat and WhatsApp showed the usual range of messages and images, but Edie had received one email from an unexpected source. It was an old-school letter in PDF format from the head of CAPE. In the letter, the head thanked Edie for helping to bring environmental activism and climate change even further into the public consciousness. Violence and terrorism weren't acceptable, the head agreed, but the attention the issue had received – of which Edie's efforts were an essential part – had sent membership of CAPE rocketing, alongside a dramatic rise in public interest in renewable energy suppliers. The head offered Edie lifetime honorary membership of the organisation.

An hour later the doorbell rang, and this time Edie raced to the front door before Dad could get there. Her heart thumping, Edie pulled open the door.

'Hiya,' said a young male voice.

Before he'd received a greeting back, Edie wrapped her arms around Harry. 'It's so good to see you,' she declared, eyes closed and not loosening her grip. 'I'm so pleased you're okay.'

'It's good to see you too,' Harry managed to squeeze out from his lungs.

'You've been quite the hero,' Edie eventually proclaimed. 'Going back to Swinbrook to rescue the dogs.'

'No! *You're* the hero ... heroine, Edie. I just got bored being locked up in a house. If I can put up with being mixed race at our school, I can put up with that! You, on the other hand, defused bombs and brought down a terrorist ring!'

'Eco-terrorists,' Edie responded, grinning. 'By the way, how's your dad?'

Edie ushered Harry into the hallway where he leant his bike against the mahogany console with extra care. 'I'll make sure I don't scratch it,' he teased.

Edie smiled again. He could get away with that one.

'My dad's good. And – thanks to you for amazingly giving us that money – he'll be getting a new treatment for his myeloma in the United States soon. He's already been speaking to the consultant, and the police have said it's fine for him to leave the country.'

'That's brilliant. And will he be meeting us at the hospital later?'

'Yes,' Harry confirmed. 'I told you yesterday.'

'I know. Just wanted to check. And he'll be bringing ...'

'Yes! He will!'

For a further hour, Edie and Harry chatted in her

bedroom about everything that had happened. They were even able to share a joke about the terrifying Helmet Head episode. Harry seemed to have forgiven Edie completely for withholding information.

Dad then drove them both over to the Royal Free Hospital in Hampstead, reminding Edie along the way about her three o'clock appointment later in the afternoon, and double-checking that she was still up for it, which she was.

Outside the hospital, Heath Coranger was waiting by the main entrance as Dad deposited the children. 'Hope it goes well and see you back home.' Dad kissed Edie on the cheek then headed off.

Once Dad's car had disappeared, Heath hugged Edie fondly, handed over the package and said he'd wait for them in the ground floor cafeteria.

In the lift to the sixth floor, Edie told Harry that she'd spoken to Dr Babinski at the National Hospital for Neurology and Neurosurgery at Queen Square, who'd explained that Mrs Solomon had woken up from her coma, thankfully had no brain damage and was now recuperating back at the Royal Free.

As they entered the corridor to Ward 6 East, Edie had a discomforting flashback. At the central nurses' station, Sister Gemma's affectionate greeting was a welcome distraction. 'Lovely to see you again, Edie. I know Mrs Solomon will be thrilled you've come, and I'm so glad the police have captured the man who assaulted her and stole her phone.' Sister Gemma looked behind Edie and winked: 'Not really allowed. But on this occasion ...'

A sign on the door of the same single room once again read 'Violet Solomon, age 78'. Edie knocked and a croaky voice from inside told her to come in.

'Hello, Mrs Solomon. I'm not sure if you remember me but …'

'Of course I remember you, my dear!' Mrs Solomon stated delightedly. 'I may be old – and had a brain haemorrhage – but I'm not stupid! And I've been reading the papers … I saw a picture of you on the news too … My, that was quite something. Now, how are you?'

'I'm absolutely fine,' Edie replied. She took a few steps towards the bed to grasp the hand held out by Mrs Solomon. Apart from some shaved hair, presumably where they'd done an operation, Edie thought she looked remarkably good. In fact, better than last time as the bruises from the assault on Hampstead Heath had largely faded. And her demeanour seemed more sprightly.

'You're so pretty,' Mrs Solomon admired. 'And so smart. Solving all those crimes.'

'Thank you.' Edie reddened. 'How long will they keep you in here?'

'Not too long, I pray. A week, maybe two. Depends on how the recuperation goes, but I'm walking again now. I can't wait to get out of here.'

'Well.' Edie had been looking forward to this moment. 'I've got a bit of a surprise for you.'

Mrs Solomon looked genuinely perplexed. 'A surprise? How nice. Whatever might that be?'

'Harry,' Edie shouted towards the door. 'You can come in now.'

The door opened and in walked Harry, lead in hand. Immediately, the dog started barking excitedly, presumably from the familiar smell. The dog looked at Harry, then at Edie, unsure what was going on and what to do.

'Quincy!' Mrs Solomon yelped. 'Oh Quincy! Come here!'

On hearing her voice, Quincy bounded onto the bed and into his owner's arms, breaking all hospital protocols.

Over and over, Quincy licked Mrs Solomon's face, whilst she held him with all the love in the world, tears streaming down her face.

For the second time in a few months, Edie found herself visiting the Emirates Stadium. Not for an Arsenal match on this occasion, but for the Stadium Tour that Dad had booked weeks back, before becoming aware of Edie's latest adventures.

Edie wasn't sure whether she wanted to go and wasn't overly interested, but she was conscious of how much the tour meant to Eli. Plus, he'd been a real asset again in her investigations, as well as a great brother.

Edie had got back in good time from the visit to the emotionally overwhelmed Mrs Solomon – to whom she'd explained that Harry and his dad were taking care of Quincy until she was safely back home and able to take over. Mrs Solomon had found it hard to convey the immensity of her gratitude.

After a scrambled eggs lunch with Dad and Eli, the Franklins took the W3 to Finsbury Park and then walked for fifteen minutes through the back streets to the stadium. No red-and-white face painting this time. At the meeting point in The Armoury gift shop, Edie and her family, along with about ten others on the tour, were greeted by the guide. He explained that the tour was largely self-guided within confined spaces, with stewards patrolling regularly to ensure compliance.

Cheap red headphones were handed out and Edie copied Eli in choosing Lee Dixon – ex-Arsenal full-back and now TV pundit – as their voice guide. First, they were shown the players' entrance to the stadium, hidden deep in the underground car park, then directed to the stands, where they saw the Diamond Club and the Directors' Box. But Eli wasn't particularly interested in fancy seating and hospitality facilities he'd never be able to enjoy.

Next, they were led back down to ground level where the fun really began. Eli loved seeing the Arsenal dressing room, with named bench areas signalling the changing space for each of his first-team heroes. The away team dressing room was noticeably, and amusingly, smaller.

Even better was the players' tunnel, where the gladiators lined up before making their way into the arena, and the dugout where the manager and supporting staff were stationed. Very best, without a doubt, was the pitch itself, a pancake-flat playing surface which they were told actually contained a small amount of artificial grass. Cheekily, Eli grabbed a ball from pitch-side and dribbled with it all the way to the goal in front of the North Bank stand.

Around the penalty spot, Eli walloped the ball into the back of the net, raising his hands aloft amidst an imagined cacophony of cheers, his Roy-of-the-Rovers moment scoring the winning goal in front of an adoring crowd. When he returned back to pitch-side, Edie and Dad jumped all over him in mock player celebrations.

Eli, however, was instantly distracted. 'That's Ian Wright,' he shrieked, pointing at the Arsenal legend and TV celebrity, who was chatting to Arsenal officials near the corner flag. As Eli raced off towards the action, with Dad in hot pursuit, Edie's phone pinged.

Automatically, Edie pulled the phone from her pocket and saw she had a new email. Oddly, it was to her ediemarblesupersleuth@gmail.com account, which was hardly ever used. She opened the message:

> Dear Edie,
>
> I'm not very good with all this electronic communication, and I hope I've sent this message to the right place.
>
> I know we don't speak very often, but I read about what you did in London, with the bombs and your detective work. It was quite brilliant.
>
> Here's the thing. I've got a bit of a problem of my own and could do with your help. Your Dad doesn't know about it, so please don't say anything.

I look forward to hearing from you.

All good wishes,
Grandfather David

Edie grinned. Only yesterday, she'd closed all existing detective cases in anticipation of a well-earned break. Too soon, it seemed.

A new file would need to be opened.

THE END

ACKNOWLEDGEMENTS

This book has taken considerably less time to create than the first in the series, but the debt to others is no less significant.

Many of the acknowledgements listed at the back of *The Five Clues* hold this time around too, but in lieu of repeating those, I wish to focus on a few of particular significance to *Outside Chance*. In the medical professional world, I am grateful to my friends at Cavendish Health – Akbar de' Medici, Colin Gerstein, Mike Patterson, Trupti Patel and Hugh Montgomery – for their encouragement and entertaining company. Collectively, we've managed to advise and steer the UK film and TV industry through COVID-19, whilst Hugh came up with the clever BP pun over a beer and chat together.

With wisdom and kindness, Dicken Bettinger has inspired and guided me through challenging times, and my immersion in the literary world has fostered valuable new friendships, including the wonderful Nina Tara (artist of the fabulous book covers) and the astonishing writer, Sita Brahmachari. A special mention is again merited for my gifted and utterly supportive editor-in-chief, Jon Appleton, and for the fantastic ongoing care, enthusiasm and artistic energy from the team at Crown House: David Bowman, Amy Heighton, Rosalie Williams, Beverley Randall, Tom Fitton, Tabitha Palmer, Louise Penny, Emma Tuck and Lucy

Delbridge. Plus, of course, the indefatigable and excellent Dannie Price. A big thank you to the awesome mental health charity, iheart, for kindly allowing adaptation of images used in their inspiring programmes for children and young adults.

As a writer, my ideas and stories often draw on personal experiences. Along this latest book's journey, conversations with others have sometimes ignited creative directions of travel or led to more specific possibilities. In this regard, some special thanks: to my daughter Leone, for always being game for an artistic discussion or plot line analysis; to Elizabeth for the idea of long-lost friends destined to meet; and to Michael Marmur for the London landmark connection. I studied philosophy as a postgraduate after medicine, but I am grateful to Adrian Viens for his astute academic insights around the philosophical dimensions of determinism and fate, and the time taken to talk these through. John Coggon also kindly contributed to those reflections. For all matters military – including advice on bombs, security measures and counter-measures, and sniffer dogs – a big thank you to Matt Hellyer.

On a personal note, this book would again not have been possible without the love and support of many: my mum and dad for their enduring presence; Karen and Jo, whom I am blessed to have as my sisters; my uncle Bernard's bond and ever-present passion for the project; Jane Slater for her attentiveness and generosity of spirit; David Rowles for his kindness and closeness; Tonia Briffa, Christine Griffin and Ralph Massey for their special since-university friendships; lovely Shula Sarner for the joy she has brought to my life; the amazing Leone; and to Ethan for being, well, just a really great guy.

Finally, I have taken considerable time over creating Spotify playlists for both books in the series. The songs selected have particular relevance to each book and to Edie's journey within the stories. I hope you enjoy them.

The *Outside Chance* playlist can be found here: https://open.spotify.com/playlist/0KNVd8jb0ox7SCsw6uRDOw?si= ndSvOtbzQVWrdooggSF5rw.

The Edie Marble playlist for *The Five Clues* can be found here: https://open.spotify.com/playlist/67OWal3EqGnxFVtfORW 9Ou?si=410e6717dac14586.

More information on the Three Principles understanding of how the mind works, and some educational programmes that draw on this approach, can be found here: https://akessel.medium.com/the-three-principles-understanding-of-how-the-mind-works-an-overview-55c03a255296.